Other Books

Dear Mother

The Forgotten Woman

If Only

Angela
MARSONS
DEADLY FATE

Bookouture

Published by Bookouture in 2023

An imprint of Storyfire Ltd.
Carmelite House
50 Victoria Embankment
London EC4Y 0DZ

www.bookouture.com

ISBN: 978-1-83790-399-3
eBook ISBN: 978-1-83790-398-6

This book is dedicated to my mum, Gillian Marsons, who sadly passed away on 8 January 2023.
Of the many things I hope to have inherited from her, I would most want the determination and spirit that drove her to conquer any obstacle that was put in her way. She will always be with me.

PROLOGUE

Sandra Deakin allowed herself a low groan as she entered the graveyard. The usual group of men were late going into the church tonight and at least two of them looked her way. Normally, she timed it so that she didn't have to see them.

Father George's gaze swept over her. It was fleeting but full of disgust. She stuck her chin out, even though her heart rate increased as she remembered the force of his hands on her body. His actions had left her in no doubt as to how he felt about her. But he couldn't stop her coming to the graveyard to walk her dog. Her hand involuntarily tightened on the lead in her hand. Pickles was a typical Labrador who would sell her out for a handful of treats, but they didn't need to know that.

Terence Birch was last to enter the church, and he stared at her for a good minute after the others disappeared from view. She held his gaze and allowed her true feelings for the creep to show on her face. She knew all about his despicable antics as well.

Despite her bravado, she still breathed easier once they'd both entered the church. As strange as it seemed, this was her place to refresh, to clear her head; and after the last few days, she needed it.

Only hours ago she'd received another one of those poisonous emails. She'd read it and filed it away, telling herself that it was just another nutter who didn't like the job she did. There were plenty of them. She ignored the fact that this particular hater had been contacting her for years. Perversely, she used that same fact to reassure herself that he'd never acted on his threats, but she also had to admit that the messages were becoming more aggressive, more vocal. She had recently considered telling her husband, but she knew he'd make a fuss and insist she involve the police.

She moved slowly among the headstones, reflecting on the week. It hadn't been a good one. A disastrous dinner party and two meetings that had got her nowhere.

She still cringed as she remembered the dinner party from hell a few nights earlier. A fun evening of light entertainment, they'd said. That wasn't what she'd got. Instead she'd been faced with a group of women who had wanted much more from the evening than any of them had let on. Not one of those ladies had been happy with what had come out of her mouth. Add in the incident with a hostile and aggressive husband and the evening had been both ugly and unsettling.

And then there were the meetings. It was because of the first one that she'd been forced to subject herself to being the after-dinner entertainment of frivolous women who couldn't handle the truth. If only he had seen things her way and agreed to hold off on his plans. She wouldn't now be scratting around for work and accepting every engagement that came her way, to pay the bills.

The two of them didn't even operate in the same circles, but he wanted to silence her anyway. It made no sense for him to be trying to put her out of business. She could only imagine he was motivated by some kind of professional jealousy. Her body gave an involuntary shudder when she remembered his last words to her. Jealousy in the hands of a narcissist was not something to be taken lightly.

She paused at a crypt in the middle of the graveyard and placed her palm on the stone. Her issues with that insufferable man weren't going to be resolved with one evening dog walk. Maybe she'd talk to her husband, Will, about that too.

She resumed walking as Pickles got the scent of something ahead.

And the other meeting, well...

The snap of a twig sounded behind her, cutting short her thoughts.

She turned.

Instant heat filled her as confusion shaped her face. The moisture dried up in her mouth as she tried to make sense of the chilling sight before her.

'You,' she whispered as the dog lead fell from her hand.

ONE

Unlike most people, Kim didn't hate the last few hours of Sunday. For many it was a time of forced acceptance that another weekend had flown by and that the beginning of another long working week was inevitable, but for Kim it was a time to reset, to refresh and prepare for whatever challenges lay ahead.

For once she'd had the pleasure of a whole weekend without incident. She and the rest of the team had left work at a reasonable time on Friday, and although she'd been on call for major incidents, the criminal fraternity of the Black Country had seen fit to allow her a whole two days to herself.

With as much time spent on housework as she was prepared to commit, and Barney exercised in the garden before his late-night walk, Kim had ring-fenced these last few hours to devote to the other great love of her life: the Vincent Black Shadow.

This particular bike had always been her dream project. Her foster father, Keith, had shown her pictures when she was twelve years old of the motorcycle produced by Vincent HRD in Hertfordshire from 1948 to 1955. She had waited months for an authentic frame to become available, and it had been over a year since she'd taken possession of it. Since then she'd painstakingly combed the internet tracking down genuine parts for the machine. Some components would need to be fabricated to specification, but she had enough to make a start.

Every single time she'd earmarked a day to get started on the project, something had diverted her attention: a new case, late nights, a near-death experience with a psychopath from her past.

But not this time. The coffee pot was full, her iPod was charged and the Sunday night lull had fallen outside.

'Okay, boy, come on – you know where we're going,' she said to Barney, grabbing her mug of Colombian Gold and opening the door that led into the garage.

Instantly her spirits rose at the sight that greeted her.

It had been a couple of weeks since Bryant had helped her revert the space from the temporary gym she'd used to regain her strength after being almost beaten to death.

Yes, she could have used a spare bedroom for the exercise equipment. She could have left her bike restoration area as it was. But she now realised that clearing away all her stuff had been her way of saying that she didn't have the mental capacity to be herself for a while. She had to push the pause button, put herself on hold while she had single-mindedly focussed on getting back her strength.

But she was ready now, she thought, placing her mug next to the iPod.

She switched it on and the sound of Mozart's 'Requiem' filled the garage.

A feeling of contentment stole over her. This was her happy place. Amongst her tools, inhaling the aroma of grease and oil, good coffee, Barney by her side and twelve hours between now and the beginning of her next shift. She could feel total immersion heading towards her.

She rubbed Barney's head as he waited by her side for direction.

She lowered herself onto the dust sheet that held all the parts she'd sourced for the Vincent Black Shadow. Barney hesitated in coming to join her and remained in the doorway.

'I know it's been a while, buddy, but we've got all night to—'

She stopped speaking as the ringing of her phone rudely interrupted her.

'You have got to be bloody kidding me,' she said, seeing the caller's name.

She pressed the answer button.

'I'm sorry but the person you're calling is currently—'

'Annoying as hell,' Keats finished for her.

'You'd better be calling to congratulate me on an uneventful weekend,' she warned.

'Of course I am, but I'd much prefer to do it in person. How about you meet me at St John the Baptist in say ooh, right now, and feel free to bring a friend.'

The line went dead in her ear as her stomach dropped. This was either Keats's shit idea for a date or he had something he needed her to see.

'Damn it,' she growled. She'd almost had an ordinary weekend like normal people.

She quickly donned her boots, threw on her black leather jacket and grabbed her keys and helmet.

Two minutes ago she'd been set for a few hours of Mozart and relaxation. Now she was heading to see her favourite pathologist at eight o'clock on a Sunday night, at a church in Halesowen town centre.

Something told her the Vincent Black Shadow was going to have to wait.

TWO

Kim turned into Halesowen High Street and stopped at a wall of flashing blue lights, and an external cordon where groups were beginning to congregate.

Recognising the Kawasaki Ninja, one of the officers pulled the end cone across so she could pass. She nodded her thanks and parked up between the two squad cars to the right of the ambulance.

She placed her gloves into her helmet and hung it from the handlebars, then approached the second cordon at the black metal gates that led into the grounds of St John's and held up her ID. 'Where am I going?'

'Round the back. Graveyard, marm.'

Great. This was getting better by the minute, and Keats's idea of a date was truly shite.

As far as she knew, St John's was a town centre church with a thousand-year history. There had been many late nights when she'd been working at the station on the other side of the town and had heard the bells pealing out. The length of the building faced the main road, protected by wrought-iron fencing, and the graveyard wrapped from the east side around to the rear.

She hurried along the pathway that she'd used many times as a constable in her days of searching the overgrown shrubbery of the graveyard, a place for the local criminals to stash stolen goods, drugs and weapons.

A couple of years ago, a community project had been set up with the neighbourhood team and ex-offenders to tidy the whole area up. Contrary to her scepticism, the project had worked and the site appeared to have been kept in order ever since.

Tidy or not, there was still something eerie about being in a graveyard at night, despite the collection of high-vis vests and torches close to the northern edge of the grounds.

Two constables were further along the side of the church with a group of men, all gathered around another man dressed in light jeans and a grey sweatshirt.

'Don't let anyone leave yet,' Kim said to the first constable she met.

She instantly regretted not calling Bryant out to attend with her, but she'd figured one of them could get a full weekend. Normally he would have gathered all the details while she took care of the victim.

'Ah, Inspector, sorry for calling you out at the weekend,' Keats offered, breaking away from the group.

'Liar. You're not sorry at all, but I am consoled by the fact that your own weekend has been ruined too.'

'Already done,' Keats said. 'Been at the morgue since this morning in the company of a homeless John Doe.'

'Suspicious?' she asked.

He shook his head. 'Just unidentified.'

Kim felt a shiver run through her. She hated unidentified corpses. The man had a name, a life before vagrancy, possibly family. She shook the thoughts away. It was a pet hate that had followed her through a childhood spent in the anonymity of the care system.

'Okay, move out of the way,' she said, looking around the pathologist.

'Look, I just want to warn you—'

'Keats, I'm a big girl – I can take it.'

He stood aside and allowed her to take his place in the huddle of people.

'Jesus Christ,' she exclaimed.

'Err... Stone,' Keats said, indicating their surroundings.

'Trust me, I've got worse,' she said, taking a step closer. 'Shit, Keats, you could have warned me.'

At first glance, one could have been forgiven for thinking the female victim on the ground was wearing a red sweatshirt, but splashes of white on the cuffs and collar said otherwise. There were multiple stab wounds, but Kim's gaze was instantly drawn upwards to the trauma above the neck. The woman's mouth had been slashed right across her face. Kim's insides recoiled at the disfigurement that gave her a clown-like expression. The flesh was jagged where it had been brutally ripped. The lower lip hung loose, sagging, exposing all the lower teeth.

For some reason, Kim's first thought was of the family member that would make the formal identification. As if the process wasn't painful enough. Would this be the final and lasting picture they'd keep in their mind? Kim knew that Keats would do everything in his power to minimise the trauma. The identification would take place through glass, to avoid any cross contamination, and she could picture the pathologist placing the body with the worst affected side furthest away. She'd seen bodies where a sheet or a wound covering had been used to reduce the brutality that had been inflicted.

'Post-mortem,' Keats said, following her gaze to the wound across the mouth.

Kim did a quick count of the slash marks in the fabric. 'Ten?'

'Eleven,' Keats said. 'There's one more on the side seam of her jumper.'

So, eleven stab wounds and death hadn't been enough? The killer had still needed to make his feelings clear or send some kind of message after the life had left the body.

Kim started walking around the body as the horror of the scene settled in her consciousness and her memory.

She guessed the woman to be late thirties, early forties. Straw-blonde hair rested on the shoulders. A few strands were stuck to her face by drops of dried blood. Red pools had gathered either side of her. Her palms were covered in blood, where she'd clearly tried to stop her own bleeding, but the attack had been vicious and brutal. Two fingernails on the right hand and one on the left had been broken. She hadn't gone quietly.

Further down the body, red lines and droplets were visible on the light-coloured jeans and the trainers, indicating that the deeper stab wounds had come later and that part of the confrontation had taken place standing up.

Small areas of reddened earth showed there'd been some dodging and staggering. This had not been a quick death.

Kim walked around again, taking in the finer details as Keats gave the nod for the photographer to begin.

A satchel had been cut away from her body during the attack and now lay at her feet. The magnetic catches didn't appear to have been tampered with, but something green peeped out the top.

Kim looked around. 'Where's the dog?'

Keats shook his head. 'No dog.' He looked around too. 'No lead either.'

'The lead will still be attached to its collar. She'd have dropped it and the dog would have run.'

Keats eyed her doubtfully.

'Those are biodegradable poo bags. I have the same ones.

Pretty sure she wouldn't be carrying them around to fill up her handbag.'

She turned to a constable. 'Call it in to the cordons and go find the dog.'

Poor thing was probably terrified.

'Nobody opened the bag for ID yet?' she asked, turning back to the victim.

'We were waiting for—'

'Sorry I'm late,' Mitch said, heading towards them. His bottom half was in the white paper overalls while his top half was trying to catch up. 'We had an away game in Worcester.'

'Of what?' she asked as he drew alongside her.

'Dominoes.'

'Really?' she asked.

'Hey, we're top of the league.'

'There's a league?'

'There's a body as well when you two have finished,' Keats snapped.

'Double call-out. Testy,' Kim explained to the forensic techie.

'Got it,' he said, taking a good look at the body. 'Oh dear, this was no accident, was it?'

Kim stayed silent as he walked around the body.

'Anything touched?' Mitch asked.

Keats shook his head. 'Guy that found her touched nothing, and only photos taken so far.'

Mitch nodded his approval. 'Okay, I'm guessing we want the bag first?'

Kim nodded, hoping there was going to be some kind of identification in there.

Mitch donned his protective gloves and reached for an evidence bag. He clicked open the satchel, removed the poo bags and placed them into the evidence bag. Next item was pay dirt, a purse. He carefully opened it as Kim took out her phone.

He went to the front of the cards section and took out a driving licence. Kim read it while taking a couple of photos. Sandra Deakin, aged forty-one, with an address in Hawne, an area of Halesowen within walking distance of the church. She tried to force the image of the woman's face in the photo into her mind, to overlay the picture already in her head, but she knew that her initial visual of Sandra Deakin was the one that would stay with her forever.

'Thanks, Mitch,' she said as he placed the satchel on the ground and started to bag the hands.

She put her phone away and looked around for a face she recognised. A deeply tanned white-haired man was striding towards her.

'Better late than never, Planty,' she said to a police inspector she knew very well.

'At your service, Inspector.'

'Can I trust you to do the honours?'

He nodded sombrely as she held up her phone for him to read the address.

'I'll get right on—'

'Hang on just a bit. I'm hoping you'll be able to take the family dog back.'

He looked around but she didn't have time to explain.

'Are you done with me, Keats?' she asked.

'Overwhelmed with potential responses to that one, so I'll keep it zipped.'

'Good call,' she said, heading over to the group who'd been asked to remain.

She strode into the middle of them.

'Someone here found the victim?' she asked as the two constables stepped back.

A man with thinning reddish hair stepped forward. 'Father George Markinson,' he said, holding out his hand. 'Father George for short.'

Kim ignored it. 'You found her?'

He let his hand fall as he nodded to the guy in the cable jumper. 'No, that was Terence Birch.'

Kim glanced over the other five men. 'Anyone else see anything?'

They all shook their heads.

'No one went near the body or took photos?'

They all looked horrified as they again shook their heads.

Sadly, it was a question she had to ask these days.

'We've got all their details?' she asked the constables.

'Yes, marm,' they said together.

'Okay, you can all go for now, but please don't share what you've seen here with any press. Officers will come to take statements at your homes.'

They all nodded their understanding before filtering away.

'Okay, Mr...'

'Terence is one of our bell ringers,' Father George said. 'He was leaving—'

'Thank you, Father. Is Terence unable to speak?'

The clergyman's expression told her he didn't like to be challenged. She held his gaze for a second before turning to the man.

'Terence, can you tell me what happened?' she asked, touching him lightly on the arm. He hadn't yet looked at her once.

'So much blood,' he said, still staring at the ground as though the body was right there.

'You were leaving after ringing the bells?' she clarified, looking to where he would have exited the church. It was a good seventy metres away. 'You didn't head straight for the gate?'

To find Sandra's body he would have had to take a detour around the back of the building.

'I was checking.'

'For what?'

'Sandy. I saw her when I came in.'

'You know her?' Kim asked, hearing the distant peal of alarm bells herself.

Terence lifted his head and nodded. 'She's local. We all know her. She comes here a lot.'

'Yes, she does,' Father George added with a hint of irritation.

Halesowen wasn't a huge town. She shouldn't be surprised that the victim was known.

'Did she attend services?' she asked Father George.

'Goodness no,' he said. 'She came to the graveyard once or twice a week, walking the dog.'

Kim was unsure why a note of tolerance had crept into his voice, as though this was an activity he allowed her. If the place was open, where was the harm?

'And you saw her on your way in to ring the bells?' she asked Terence.

He nodded. 'Yes, she was here doing her thing.'

'What's her thing?' Kim asked.

'She walks around touching the graves. She stands there with her eyes closed just feeling the stones.'

Disapproval flitted over Father George's features but he said nothing.

'So you went to check on her when you'd finished?'

'Yes, I've had to walk her out a couple of times before. I'm a key holder. I lock up. I don't even know why I went that far out. I just had this feeling, so I kept walking and that's when I found...' He stopped speaking as the images returned full force, and his gaze once again went to the ground.

'Did you see or hear anything else at all?' Kim asked.

'Nothing. I just cried out then called emergency services straight away. I didn't touch her. I knew she was dead. I stayed with her until they came.' He raised his gaze again and his eyes were watery. 'Is that okay?'

'You did everything right, Terence,' she said. 'There was nothing you could have done to help her.'

A sob escaped from his lips. He'd had enough for one night.

'Go home,' she advised gently. 'Someone will be along to take a statement but thank you for checking on her. Finding her so early gives us the best possible chance of finding whoever did this.'

'I'll walk him to the car,' Father George said, guiding him away.

As she watched, she spied Inspector Plant getting into a squad car. She was pleased to see he was holding the lead of an excitable Labrador.

She took a last look around before heading back towards her bike. She glanced up at the bell tower, realising that the bells had been ringing above while Sandra Deakin had been fighting for her life.

THREE

'Hope you all had a good weekend,' Kim said, once her team was assembled. A group text message last night had instructed them to attend a briefing at 7 a.m. No further explanation had been necessary. They all knew what it meant.

'Felt like a mini holiday,' Stacey said.

Kim understood. Rarely did they have a weekend where no catching up on paperwork was required.

'Getting a bit bored to be honest, guv,' Bryant said. 'Jenny sent me out to the pub and told me not to rush home.'

'Yeah, that's just cos she doesn't like you very much,' Kim said.

'Fair point,' he conceded, safe in the knowledge he had one of the strongest marriages she'd ever seen.

They all looked to Penn.

'Lynne was working so I caught up on the housework.'

There was a second of silence before they all burst out laughing.

He shrugged as though he hadn't been able to think of anything better to do.

'Penn, I swear, if I wasn't gay and married, I'd snap you up tomorrow,' Stacey said.

'Yeah, I'd probably consider it as well,' Bryant offered.

'Okay, catch-up complete,' Kim said. 'I'm sure you've guessed that we have a victim.'

They all looked to the whiteboard where Kim had already written the details.

'Female victim named Sandra Deakin, forty-one years of age, stabbed eleven times while walking her dog. In addition, our guy gave her one last slash to the mouth once the job was done. Obviously a detail that will be withheld from any press releases. Photos should be through around 9 a.m. when Keats gets in. He had a heavy day. In the meantime, she's around five feet five, slim build with blonde hair.'

'Sorry, boss, can't get past the number of stabbings and the mouth thing. Very personal,' Penn said.

'Agreed. Nothing was taken. There was no evidence of sexual assault, so whoever she is, she's upset someone.'

'Or we have a crazed killer on our hands,' Bryant said.

'Great theory, but in all our investigations, when have we ever had a mindless crazed killer on the loose?'

Bryant shrugged. 'Could happen.'

'It could, but for now we'll focus on the likelihood it was someone she knew. She was murdered between 7 p.m. and 8 p.m. at St John's Church in town. Bell ringers saw her when they went in, and one of them found her on the way out. She's known to them. Seems she liked to walk her dog through the graveyard and would stop and touch the stones.'

'What was that now?' Penn asked, raising an eyebrow.

Kim shrugged. She had no idea.

'Inspector Plant is getting statements from the bell ringers and Father George Markinson, but, Stace, I want you to do a bit of background on the good clergyman and also the guy that found her, Terence Birch.'

Stacey wrote the names down.

'Also, I want you to find out everything you can about Sandra Deakin.'

'Got it, boss.'

'Penn, post-mortem will be 9 a.m. on the dot and—'

'On it, boss,' he said cheerily.

'Had I finished?'

'Sorry, boss.'

'Keats had another customer yesterday. Homeless man, no name. Pump him for info.'

Penn waited.

'Now I'm finished.'

'Okay, boss.'

'As ever, Bryant, you and I are going to start our day by speaking to a grieving family.'

He grabbed his jacket from the back of the chair. 'You know, for once I might want to swap with Penn. He gets—'

'Err... boss, one sec,' Stacey said as they headed towards the door. The constable turned her screen around. 'Is this our victim?'

'Bloody hell, Stace, that was quick,' Kim said, looking at what appeared to be a professionally shot photo.

'I'd love to take credit but she wasn't really that hard to find.'

'How so?' Kim asked, moving back into the room.

'Sandra Deakin aka local medium also known as Psychic Sandy.'

Kim heard a sound and realised that the groan in her head had found its way out of her mouth.

FOUR

'Not a believer in psychics, eh, guv?' Bryant asked as they headed down the stairs.

'Have you met me?' she answered, rolling her eyes.

Bryant said nothing as he buzzed them out of the building.

Although bright, there was a nip in the air as the mid-March temperatures struggled to get into double digits.

'Don't tell me you think there's something in it?' she asked as they approached the car.

He shrugged. 'I've seen too much stuff to rule it out. I've watched shows on TV and there's things that can't be explained away by the sceptics.'

'Cheap parlour tricks,' she dismissed, fastening her seat belt.

Bryant opened his mouth and then thought better of it, staying silent as they pulled out of the car park and headed towards the home of Sandra Deakin.

Hawne was a residential area approximately one mile from the town centre.

It was just after seven thirty and traffic was starting to build as they passed the site of Halesowen College.

Bryant took a left and then a sharp right through a set of

decorative iron gates with a post box on the right-hand side. He negotiated three wheelie bins along the wall to take the last space beside two other cars: an old E-type Jaguar and a Nissan Micra.

'Nice,' Bryant said as they got out the car.

He was right. It was nice but not spectacular, and Kim had the feeling of being underwhelmed after the promise of the ornate gated entrance.

They mounted the steps that led from the driveway up to a detached bungalow formed of orange brick and oak-coloured window frames. As she knocked, Kim could see that although the house was set in about half an acre of land, it was overlooked to both the rear and the left side.

The door was answered by a man in his mid-forties wearing jeans and a Weird Fish jumper. His eyes were reddened and numb.

'Mr Deakin?'

He nodded and moved aside for them to enter without bothering to look at the IDs they'd held up.

She stepped inside. 'I'm Detective Inspector Stone and this is my colleague DS Bryant.'

He closed the door behind them and pointed to a door on the left.

Kim took a seat on the sofa, and Bryant took a single chair.

'Mr Deakin, we're sorry for your loss,' her colleague offered as the grieving man sat down on the other single chair.

Mr Deakin rubbed at his face before his hands ran through his hair, leaving salt-and-pepper tufts. His chin was rough with stubble.

'There's a part of me praying that you're going to tell me there's been some kind of mistake, that you've got the wrong person, even though she still hasn't come home. I want you to tell me that she wasn't really dead, but the officer wasn't updated before he came here.'

He lifted his gaze to meet hers, waiting.

Kim said nothing.

'You know, I never knew just how cruel hope can be. It can kick you in the gut repeatedly,' he said, realising his prayers were not going to be answered.

She nodded her understanding. 'We will find whoever did this, Mr Deakin.'

'Will, please; I'm not at school.'

Seeing her confusion, he continued, 'I'm a teacher.'

'Got it,' she said. The man had kids calling his surname all day. 'Okay, Will, I'm really sorry that we have to intrude on your grief to ask you some questions but...'

'It's fine, go ahead,' he offered as the tension filled his face. 'The sooner you ask, the quicker you can catch the bastard who did this.'

'Okay, firstly, can I—'

'Just looking for a collar to take Pickles for a— Oh, sorry,' said a voice from the doorway.

'Detectives, Nic,' Will said.

Kim gave a reassuring smile to the teenage girl holding a dog lead. The girl put it on the table and sat on the arm of the chair beside her father.

She reached for his hand. 'Everything okay, Dad?'

'Just need to answer some questions,' he said. 'Sorry, this is my daughter, Nicola.'

Side by side, Kim could see the striking resemblance between the two of them. Will Deakin had given his black hair, green eyes and strong chin to his daughter. She was unsure what the girl had got from her mother.

'We're so sorry for the loss of your—'

'She wasn't,' Nicola said.

Kim waited.

'Sorry, that sounded rude,' Nicola added, when her father stiffened. 'I meant to say that Sandy wasn't my mother.'

'I see,' Kim said, now clear why the girl wasn't in a distraught, snivelling pile in a corner.

'Take the dog, love,' Will said, patting and then releasing her hand.

She hesitated then stood, before leaving the room.

'His old collar is in the utility room,' Will called after her. 'Forensic people had to keep his new one. There were some spots of...' His words trailed away.

'It's okay, Will,' Kim said as Nicola closed the front door behind her.

Kim wasn't sure how much had been shared with the family. The savagery of the assault was not going to help matters at this point, and the detail of the slashed mouth would be revealed to no one.

'Will, we have reason to believe this was a personal attack. That's to say that we suspect Sandra was the intended victim.'

He frowned. 'The officer last night said she'd been stabbed. I thought mugging or' – he swallowed – 'rape,' he whispered, struggling to get his mouth around the word.

Talk about giving with one hand and taking away with the other. She was able to assure him that no sexual assault had taken place, but she had to replace it with the fact that someone had most definitely wanted his wife dead.

'Sandra wasn't mugged and there's no evidence that she was sexually assaulted,' Kim said.

Inspector Plant had done the right thing. He hadn't lied but he hadn't told the whole truth either. It was her job to join the dots and add detail to the outline.

'Your wife was stabbed, and what I say next is going to be hard for you to hear. I'm afraid she was stabbed repeatedly.'

'How many times?' he asked, as though the number made a difference.

'Eleven.'

'Jesus Christ. Why? I mean did she suffer?'

Kim recalled the blood on her hands, on her face, in her hair.

'She fought her attacker valiantly. She didn't give up easily.'

Kim had learned over time that talking to the families of victims was an art in not lying but not presenting them with images that would haunt them for the rest of their lives.

He shook his head, as though trying to avoid such images from ingraining themselves on his brain.

'B-But why? She'd never hurt a soul.'

'Had she mentioned anything to you recently? Any threats? Strange incidents, anything unnerving?'

He shook his head slowly. 'I mean, nothing in particular. Her work attracted the occasional crackpot but she was used to it, keyboard warriors and all that. She'd block them and forget them.'

'Anything more threatening than normal?' Kim pushed.

'Not that she mentioned. I'm sure she would have told me.'

'Any disgruntled customers?'

'Absolutely not. You should read the testimonials on her website. She helps hundreds of people.'

Kim didn't trust the opinions placed on the website by the person being reviewed. She already had Stacey digging deeper on that.

'And how did Sandra conduct her business? Stage shows or...'

'No. She didn't do big venues. Too many voices, she said. She gave one-to-one readings and did small events: dinner parties and private functions. She wasn't keen on those and seemed a little unsettled after the last one. She had a couple of regular customers as well.'

He dropped his head into his hands and a sob escaped from his mouth. Talking about her in the normal context of her work and not her murder had given his brain a few seconds of relief before reminding him again that she was gone.

'It's okay, Will – take your time,' Bryant soothed.

Will took a breath, wiped his eyes and raised his head.

'Unsettled?' Kim asked. Anything out of the ordinary was worth pursuing.

'Just some spilled red wine or something. She didn't talk much about her work when she got home.'

'And she also had regular clients?' Kim asked. How many times did one need to go and see a psychic?

He nodded. 'Some people like regular guidance, support. I suppose I always thought of it like going to see a life coach or something. Sometimes she came back full of energy and other times it was like she just wanted to chuck it all in.'

'Will, is there any way we can get access to her client list, maybe her computer as well?'

'Of course, if you think it'll help,' he said, standing and leaving the room.

'Stepdaughter seems to have taken it remarkably well,' Bryant said, once the man was out of earshot.

'That's an understatement,' she agreed as the front door opened.

The Labrador she'd seen the night before came bounding into the room. The quick walk around the block appeared to have done little to burn off his energy.

'Gorgeous dog,' Kim said, stroking his head.

'He's mine,' Nicola said, unclasping the lead from his collar. 'My dad bought him for me when I was fourteen.'

And yet it was the stepmother who'd been walking him regularly, according to Terence Birch.

'Have you got them yet?' she asked as Pickles took a good sniff of Bryant's shoes. 'The person who did it, I mean.'

Kim admired her youthful optimism that they could catch a killer within twelve hours. Either teenage naïveté or watching too many police dramas.

'Not yet but we will,' Kim said as Will came back into the room.

'I'll put the kettle on,' Nicola said, hedging past her father. Pickles followed closely behind.

'Here, this is her laptop and work diary but...' He stopped speaking as he handed them over.

'But?' Bryant asked.

'I was going to say she'll need them back by tonight.'

'It'll take a while,' Kim said, passing the belongings to Bryant. She turned back to Will. 'Sorry but may I use the bathroom before we leave?'

'Of course – just down the hallway.'

Kim headed right for the kitchen.

'Oh, sorry, I was looking for the loo,' she said to Nicola's back.

'No you weren't cos you walked right past it.'

Pickles was busy munching his way through a bowl of food, and the girl was mixing batter for a waffle iron. A selection of berries and syrups were evident on the counter. Someone still had a healthy appetite.

'So, your dad bought you Pickles as a birthday present?' Kim asked as a warm-up.

'No, he bought him for me as an adjustment present when I moved schools to live here and lost all my friends.'

'Oh, I see.'

'Do you really?' Nicola asked, turning towards her. 'So, I suppose you already know that it was impossible to make new friends once anyone found out who my stepmother was. You know how it felt to have spooky noises called out at me all day? How everyone asked if I saw dead people too?'

Kim watched the multitude of emotions pass over her face. 'I'm assuming you never grew close over the years?'

'Tolerance is the best way to sum us both up. Sandy was only interested in my dad. I was the unfortunate baggage that came with him. She wasn't the maternal type, and I'd have rebuffed any efforts of that nature anyway. I had a mother. She died.'

'I'm sorry,' Kim said, hearing the pain in those last two words.

'Thanks, but you didn't know her. We were okay, Dad and me – we were getting through it. He was starting to smile again. And then he met her and everything changed.'

Kim couldn't help wondering if this was perhaps the longest tantrum ever recorded. Many people had other relationships after the death of a loved one. It seemed that a great deal of change had hit Nicola during adolescence. That had to have been tough, but it was surprising that the animosity hadn't diminished over the years.

'Your father appeared to love Sandy very much,' Kim offered gently. 'You don't begrudge him a second shot at happiness?'

'Of course not,' she snapped, pouring the batter mixture into the waffle iron.

Yet there was something that Nicola had been unable to forgive. She waited for the girl to continue.

'I never wanted him to be on his own forever. I don't begrudge the fact they met. I just hate the way they met. It sickens me to my stomach, and I could never forgive her for that.'

FIVE

'They met when she gave him a reading?' Bryant asked incredulously as they got into the car.

'Oh yeah, he was looking to communicate with his recently deceased wife, who met an untimely end in a hit and run.'

'How recent was her demise?' Bryant asked as Kim sent a text message.

'Two months.'

'Are you kidding?'

'Swing by the station,' she instructed. 'And no, I'm not kidding. Nicola is still angry. She feels Sandra preyed upon him and caught him at his weakest point.'

'Two months, bloody hell. Wonder if during the reading she told him he was going to meet someone new.'

'Dunno, but there is something a bit distasteful there,' Kim said.

Two months, eight weeks, approximately sixty days. Nowhere near long enough to grieve.

'Maybe wife one sent a message through wife two that it was okay for him to move on,' Bryant suggested.

'As long as it was with her,' Kim said.

'Ooh, cynical, guv. He clearly loved her so let's not be too judgemental, eh?'

Judgemental or not, there was still something tawdry about the whole thing, and it certainly gave her a clearer insight into Nicola's animosity.

She said nothing more until Bryant pulled up at the station, where Stacey was waiting at the front entrance.

Kim lowered the window and handed her the laptop.

'Pay close attention to the emails. Apparently, she did get threats and crackpots from time to time.'

'Nothing too incriminating on the background search yet,' Stacey offered as she took the laptop. 'She was named in an exposé piece written by another psychic in the *Daily Mail* a couple of years ago.'

'Okay, keep looking,' Kim said. 'Can't stop – Bryant's buying me coffee at Luigi's.'

Bryant's head snapped round at this new information.

Stacey made a face. 'Aww, have one of those to-die-for vanilla cannoli for me.'

Kim smiled as she rolled the window back up.

Luigi's was an authentic Italian restaurant that had opened on the outskirts of town. Superior products, excellent coffee and great customer service had disproved the people who said it would never work. It had become the team's go to place for a takeout treat given that it was just a couple of minutes away from the station.

'Mmm... I can taste it already,' she said as Bryant pulled up in the car park.

'Almost four quid for a cup of coffee,' he moaned as they got out of the car.

'Worth every penny you're gonna pay for it,' Kim said. 'Just black for me,' she added, taking a seat outside. Luigi's coffee didn't need anything else.

The outside seating had a good view of the dual carriageway that ran up Mucklow Hill, but she wasn't here for the urban scenery. She opened up Sandra's week-to-view diary. Immediately, Kim could see that Sandra used each small daily space for just about everything: dentist appointments, doctor's appointments, vet visits, notes on grocery items and social engagements. The pages were a blur of red and black pen. The personal entries were in red and the business entries were in black.

'Thanks, Bryant,' she said as he placed the tray on the table. Her eyes went to the plate nestled between the two cups of coffee.

'Err... you didn't have to take her literally,' Kim said, thinking of Stacey's instruction to have a cannoli. 'And what's that?' she asked, seeing a small brown bag, folded and taped.

Bryant shrugged. 'A sachet of coffee from Luigi to Stace. He specifically said it was for the "nice" police lady.'

'You're not funny,' she said, taking the package from the tray and bringing it closer to her. 'Right, from what I can see, Sandra's entire life was in this book. Some of the entries are sparse on information; it's probably best if we work backwards from the most recent engagement, which was on Thursday night.'

'You really think she was murdered in connection with her work?' Bryant asked, taking a generous bite of the cannoli. Flakes of fried pastry stuck to his lips.

'Jeez, I sometimes wonder how Jenny can resist you.'

He shrugged and took another bite.

'It's not exactly your normal profession, is it?' she asked. 'We know from the outset it attracts crackpots and haters, so it seems like a good place to start.'

'So, what we got for Thursday night?' he asked, taking a breather from his pastry.

'We've got the name Catherine, with a house number and a postcode. Not a lot but it's enough to make a start,' she said, wondering what exactly this visit would tell them.

SIX

Despite the boss's information that Sandra Deakin's post-mortem was starting at nine, Keats appeared to be well underway when Penn arrived at one minute past the hour.

'Sorry I'm late,' he offered, not wanting to upset Keats so soon.

'You're not. I decided to forego any trip home and get an early start.'

Penn's attention was instantly drawn to the woman's face. He'd seen a photo of Sandy prior to her murder, and the cut across her mouth added a macabre element. He pulled his gaze away and focussed on the boss's instructions. She had told him to get details of the unidentified homeless man.

'Boss said you had a busy weekend,' he said as Keats noted the weight of the liver.

'If only folks would stop dying out of hours,' Keats replied, placing the liver back carefully.

Penn had the sudden realisation that there was no need for that level of care and attention during this part of the process. The removable organs could be placed anywhere before sewing the body back up. Who would know? It was at times like this that he completely understood why people labelled him as weird and they weren't aware of half the crap that went through his mind.

'To summarise what we know so far,' Keats said, 'our victim was at a healthy weight for her height. She appears to have never smoked and there's no evidence of heavy drinking. Her last meal was some kind of chicken and pasta dish, which was consumed approximately one hour before her demise.'

Penn nodded, falling into step with the dance they did every time. Keats would begin by offering information that was absolutely no use to the investigation. Next would come the details of the injuries. And finally, he would deliver any nugget he'd found along the way.

'The wounds were counted correctly last night. A total of eleven, consisting of three that were primarily surface wounds, four that went deeper but didn't touch any major organs, three that would have been potentially non-fatal individually and a final one to the heart that no degree of medical intervention could have healed. The twelfth wound to her mouth was delivered post-mortem as suspected.'

'Mauling,' Penn said without thinking.

'Is that a CID technical term?' Keats asked.

'Sorry, just thinking aloud. It's like a predator softening its prey before the kill. Clearly, he knew how to deliver the fatal wound but chose not to do so until he was ready.'

Keats said nothing but didn't disagree.

'Anything under the fingernails?' Penn asked.

Keats shrugged. 'Samples have been taken and sent to Mitch, but with the amount of blood in there from clutching her wounds it's going to be hard to tell.'

Despite the brutality of the attack, it looked as though forensic evidence was going to be thin on the ground.

Keats appeared to wait to see if he had any further questions. Penn stepped from one foot to the other and said nothing. If there was a nugget to come, it'd be on its way right now.

'I did find one interesting thing though.'

'Oh, cool.'

'Nothing that's going to help your investigation.'

'Oh.'

Interesting to who? he wondered, if it didn't help them at all.

'I found a hairline fracture right at the back of her skull,' Keats said, pointing to the area on the back of his own head.

'Okay.'

'It's an old one, most likely from before the age of ten.'

'Not sure why I'm still listening,' he said.

'Do you think that's the incident that could have given her the gift?'

Penn allowed the puzzlement to show.

'Oh come on, many psychics, mediums, spiritualists claim that they began to see or hear things after a traumatic childhood event.'

Seeing the blank look on his face, Keats continued. 'You're not even mildly curious about her gift or if she even had any spiritual skills?'

Penn hadn't considered the question since learning of her career. It made no difference to him really.

'I suppose if I was to consider it carefully I'd wonder, if she was truly gifted, why she never saw it coming,' he said honestly.

'Oh, Penn, I'm not sure it quite works like that, but I can see I'm wasting my time trying to engage you in philosophical debate.'

'Maybe over a pint and a bag of scratchings. But in the meantime the boss said something about a homeless guy,' Penn said, realising there was nothing more to learn about Sandra Deakin.

'And did your boss ask you to grill me about him?' Keats asked as his mouth gave a knowing lift.

If in doubt of the right answer, go with the truth was his motto.

'Yes.'

'Let me finish up here and you can meet him if you like.'

Penn was confused by the smile of satisfaction on the pathologist's face. He had long since vowed never to involve himself in the dynamics between his boss and Keats. Why on earth they continued this hostile sparring when they had clearly grown to like and respect each other over the years was a mystery to him.

'Did you deliberately tell her it was a John Doe?' Penn asked, suddenly suspecting his deviousness.

'It might have slipped out; but obviously your boss can't look into it when she's just started a major investigation. It would be wrong to even ask.'

So, of course, he hadn't even bothered to ask. He'd just dropped the crumb that he knew the boss couldn't resist: *unidentified*. Keats, and everyone else, knew the boss had a thing about people who were nameless. Everyone deserved their own name.

'He wasn't murdered though, was he?' Penn asked. 'He doesn't need an investigation?'

Keats shook his head. 'No, he just needs someone who cares.'

And there it was. The trust and respect the man had for his boss that he would never admit to, even if his life depended on it.

One thing Penn knew beyond a shadow of a doubt. He wasn't the one who was going to tell the boss she'd been played.

SEVEN

Catherine Taylor lived in a semi-detached cottage on the outskirts of Kingswinford. According to Stacey's reverse search of the electoral roll, she was thirty-nine years of age and resided with her forty-one-year-old husband and fifteen-year-old twin boys. A Fiat Punto was parked in front of the house.

Kim knocked and the door was opened quickly by a woman who was clearly on her way out. One hand held her car keys and the other a slice of toast.

'I'm sorry but I'm late for—'

The woman stopped speaking as Kim produced her ID card and introduced them both.

'May we come in for just a minute?'

'Oh God, is everything okay?'

'Everything's fine,' Kim said as the woman stepped out of the way for them to enter.

Kim instantly noted that the rooms were small with low, beamed ceilings, and had been furnished sparsely.

There were also quite a few of them, she realised as the woman guided them to the rear of the cottage, where a sizeable extension had added a spacious and airy kitchen that belonged in a completely different house.

The woman threw her toast in the bin but didn't invite them to sit down.

'So, what are you...?'

'We're here about Sandra Deakin.'

Catherine started to shake her head. 'I don't know anyone—'

'Psychic Sandy,' Kim clarified. 'She was here on Thursday night.'

'That's right,' she said, frowning. 'But we didn't do anything illegal.'

'Of course not. I'm sorry to tell you that Sandy has been killed.'

'Wh... wh... what?' Catherine asked, losing colour. She looked to the head of the oversize dining table, presumably where the psychic had sat, then headed for one of the other seats and finally indicated for them to sit.

'How... I mean... where... bloody hell.'

'This isn't going to get any easier to hear,' Kim warned. 'She was murdered last night while walking her dog.'

Catherine's mouth fell open. Clearly the woman was shocked at the news but Kim had to forge ahead. This wasn't a family member or friend. She was a customer and she'd been the last customer to see Sandy alive.

'You were her last engagement, and we're trying to establish if there was anything strange in her behaviour.'

'It was my first time meeting her so I wouldn't know if she was acting out of character or not, but there was nothing that struck me as odd.'

'She didn't seem nervous or distracted?'

Catherine shook her head.

'You didn't see any strange vehicles before or after she arrived?'

'I wouldn't have noticed. The driveway was like a car park all night.'

'Why was that?' Kim asked. 'Was something else going on?'

'No, only the arrival and departure of the others and the mix up with Betts's husband.'

'There were others here?'

'Oh yes. Sandy wasn't only here to see me. It was a few of us from the yoga class. We thought it would be a bit of a chuckle. I can't recall who suggested it but Betts goes to see her all the time.'

'Betts?'

'Bettina. She goes to see Sandy often. She arranged it but I offered to host it here,' Catherine said with pride in her voice.

'So it was a group of your friends?'

Catherine grimaced. 'They're not really what I'd call friends. I mean, I haven't known any of them for a great length of time, but we all sometimes chat before and after class. The subject came up and I offered to hold it here. I'd already told them about my new kitchen.' She raised her eyebrows. 'And about the budget arguments Mark and I were having. So it seemed like a good opportunity to show them what all the fuss was about.'

To show off, Kim thought, catching the woman's vibe. So far she had mentioned the kitchen more than the dead woman.

'Can you give us the details of the other women present? Addresses and phone numbers.'

'Oh blimey. I don't have all their addresses but I have their numbers on my WhatsApp,' she said, reaching for her phone.

Bryant took out his notebook.

'Okay, so Bettina is a housewife with three young children, and she volunteers a few hours a week at the PDSA shop in Dudley,' Catherine said, before reading off her number.

'Got it,' Bryant said.

'Lisa Brown is a property developer or something. You can

find her breaking someone's balls at that building site over in Netherton.'

'The flats?' Kim clarified.

Catherine nodded.

Kim knew the site. It had been a small retail park just off the Cinder Bank Island that had planning permission for thirty new flats.

'Then there's Emily, a post-op cancer survivor,' she said, pointing to her chest. 'That's about all I know.'

Bryant took down the number.

'And finally, there's Rose who can't do a downward dog to save her life, although she does try, bless her. Maybe without those extra pounds but who am I to judge?'

And yet you seem to, Kim thought, letting the comment pass as Catherine read out Rose's number.

'And where might we find Rose?'

'That's a good question. I don't actually know anything about her except that she works in a hospital.'

'Okay, is that everyone that was here on Thursday night?'

'Yeah, unless you count two teenage boys who cut holes in my Egyptian cotton sheets to barge in making spooky noises.'

'Your husband?'

'Working late. He got home an hour after everyone had gone and wolfed down the leftover sushi.'

Bryant put his notebook away. They had everything they needed, but Kim was intrigued to learn more.

'Did the night go well? Did anyone learn anything?' she asked.

'Well no one's Aunt Mabel came through to tell them where the valuable brooch had been hidden, if that's what you mean.'

It wasn't exactly what she'd meant.

'To be honest, the whole atmosphere changed a bit after Betts's husband came. I mean Lisa was already seething after her reading. Seems she might have a little something in her past she doesn't really want broadcasted, so she didn't mind the distraction.'

'Of the husband turning up?' Kim clarified.

'Yeah, but Betts took him into the lounge. They had a private conversation but we knew he was just sitting on the drive waiting for her. Kinda made everyone feel like the night was over.'

'Other than that do you feel that everyone got what they wanted from the session?'

The question brought a slight tension to Catherine's jaw. 'Oh, no one expected to get anything serious out of it. It was just light entertainment. A bit of a laugh.'

The words and sentiment sounded totally convincing.

Except her expression said something completely different.

And it was that expression that stayed with Kim long after they'd watched Catherine get in her car and leave for work.

EIGHT

Stacey resolved to put the laptop to one side for a short time while she focussed on the two names she'd been given by the boss: Father George Markinson and Terence Birch. She decided to start with the man who had found the body.

Following her usual process, she typed his name into the PNC. The Police National Computer was a database used by the police and other bodies.

'Oh,' she said as his photo appeared on the screen, matching the boss's description. Rounded face, mid-thirties, brown hair and a small mole on his right cheek. The photo had been taken in his mid-twenties but everything else was the same.

Terence Birch had first come to the attention of the police when he was twenty-four years old. A neighbour, twenty-six-year-old Charlotte Danks, had reported him constantly standing outside her house.

Visit number one: Birch had been advised to stay away from the complainant.

Second report from victim of the same behaviour.

Visit number two: Birch had insisted that he wasn't going to stop because he liked looking at her. Officers had advised him of the changes in law regarding stalking, and had warned of arrest and a criminal record if his behaviour continued.

Stacey knew there were different types of stalker: ex-intimate, acquaintance or stranger.

Birch proclaimed they were acquaintances, but Danks insisted she'd never exchanged a word with him in her life.

The cat-and-mouse game continued for a couple of years. Just when Danks had gathered enough evidence and police were poised to arrest, he'd back off for a couple of months. Eventually he started turning up at Danks's place of work. Being warned off by male colleagues had no effect, and he always made sure he was on public property.

Four years in and he finally appeared before a magistrate. He was given a slap on the wrist and a stern warning.

From what Stacey could see, Charlotte Danks had done everything right. She'd kept diaries, taken photos and filed restraining orders, which he broke the terms of and thus eventually landed himself in prison for six months.

Danks moved house but didn't change jobs. The day after he was released, he turned up at her workplace. A year later and another stretch inside, and Danks had relocated completely to Somerset. Within a week, Birch found her and the pattern resumed. Last year, he did another term inside, and by the time he was released, Danks had gone again.

'Jesus,' Stacey said, wondering why Birch had failed to get the message.

There was a lot more to this bell ringer than met the eye.

Stacey knew she had to find a way to speak to Charlotte Danks. Even though the records didn't note it, she had to find out if Birch had ever threatened her with physical violence. Was there any chance that he'd transferred his feelings to Sandra Deakin?

She read through the entries again.

'Bingo,' she said, seeing Charlotte's sister listed as emergency contact. She rang the number for Ella Danks.

'Hello,' said a female voice on the second ring.

'Hi, my name is Stacey Wood from Halesowen CID. Do you have a minute to talk?'

'About what?' The tone was neither warm nor cold. It was wary.

'About your sister.'

'I don't have a sister,' Ella said.

Stacey was confused only for a second.

'Ella, I'm going to hang up now but would you please call my station and ask to speak to me so you know I'm telling the truth?'

Hesitation before the line went dead in her ear.

Stacey had no idea whether she was going to call back or not but she tapped her fingers on the desk in anticipation. After what her sister had gone through, the woman could be forgiven for thinking Birch had paid someone to make the call to get information on Charlotte.

The phone rang.

'DC Wood,' she answered.

'Okay, I believe you're who you say you are, but it doesn't mean I'm going to tell you anything.'

'I need to speak to Charlotte.'

'Not happening.'

'It's about Terence Birch.'

'Well, I'd worked that much out. Only dealings my sister had with the police were because of that bastard, but whatever it is, he is not getting near her now.'

'Ella, I have no intention of placing her in harm's way. I just need to talk to her.'

'It's never gonna happen. I am the only person in touch with her and you're not getting past me.'

'Maybe her mum...'

'Doesn't know and hasn't seen Charlotte for over a year, after the bastard managed to trick the last address out of her. Speak to my mum and I'll come for ya.'

'You're threatening a police officer?' Stacey asked.

'You contacted me, so if we're all done, I'll—'

'Wait,' Stacey said, wondering how it had got so hostile so quickly. Normally she would have reacted to the woman's rudeness and threats, but Stacey understood that she was just trying to protect her sister. And she wanted something from Ella that she wasn't obliged to give. She had to bring this aggression under control.

'Look, Ella, I'm sorry to bring this all back. I can't even imagine what Charlotte went through, or the rest of you. I don't mean to cause anyone any pain.'

A sigh.

'It's okay. I'm a bit overprotective. I don't want him anywhere near her again. Mum lives daily with the guilt of getting tricked. I really can't let you talk to Charlotte. She's finally recovering from her breakdown and any mention of that man will send her backwards. But I'll help if I can.'

Given what she'd said, Stacey wasn't prepared to push her any further and she'd take whatever she could get.

'Can you tell me about what happened?'

'I'm sure you can see the records.'

'Tell me what really happened.'

'The bastard became obsessed. Charlotte never spoke to him. I think she smiled at him once while putting her wheelie bin out. That night she caught him just standing outside her house, staring up at her bedroom window. It didn't matter what she did, he wouldn't stop. He took no notice of the police or the courts or the physical threats my boyfriend made. Even spending time in prison did nothing. He turned her into a nervous wreck. She couldn't eat or sleep for fear of what he was going to do next. She lived behind closed curtains and jumped out of her skin at any unexpected noise. She saw him every-where she went. He changed her life and her personality completely.'

'Did he ever actually touch her, hurt her?' Stacey asked.

'Do you think that makes a difference? It's not enough that he tortured her mentally for almost ten years? You'd have preferred him to physically—'

'No, that's not what I'm saying,' Stacey corrected quickly.

She remembered a time when she was about thirteen and the school bully, Kayla, had said she was going to beat her up. Stacey had been terrified and she'd waited for the beating every day. It turned into something she couldn't stop thinking about day and night, waiting, almost praying, that Kayla would get it over and done with so she could stop fearing it.

Eventually Stacey had walked home from school and timed it to be in Kayla's path as she and her cronies had passed the park; perfect opportunity. Just get it over with, her mind had screamed. Let me have some peace.

Kayla had walked past her without a second glance, and Stacey had realised it had been an empty threat that meant much less to Kayla than it had to her. It wasn't on the same level but she got it.

'Ella, I'm not minimising Birch's actions or the effect they had on Charlotte, but there's a reason I need to know for sure.'

'He's done it again, hasn't he? Only this time he's gone and hurt someone, just like she said he would.'

'Did he ever touch her?'

'No, but Charlotte felt it was only a matter of time.'

'She was really convinced he was going to hurt her?' Stacey asked.

'She'd just watched a documentary on Shana Grice who'd been murdered by Michael Lane in 2015.'

Stacey remembered the case. Lane had put a tracker on Grice's car which notified him every time it moved. One time he'd snatched her phone and grabbed her hair. Eventually he'd entered her home, slit her throat and set fire to her bedroom. She had been nineteen years old.

'But wasn't he an ex-boyfriend?' Stacey asked.

'He was, but that wasn't what frightened her. Shana Grice made her first complaint to Essex Police on the eighth of February. She was dead by the twenty-fifth of August.'

Stacey recalled that Essex Police had been heavily criticised for not taking Shana's claims seriously. The fact that he'd stalked thirteen other women should have highlighted just how dangerous the man was.

'So Charlotte felt that Birch could kill her?'

'No, she cut ties with her family and friends and moved halfway around the world for the fun of it.'

'Even though he'd never touched her?'

'She knew beyond a shadow of a doubt that if she stayed, he would eventually find a way to kill her.'

NINE

Kim stood at the metal fencing of the building site trying to get someone's attention. The signs she was trying to look around made it clear that she couldn't enter.

A lull in the sound of the diggers and loaders gave her an opportunity.

'Oi,' she screamed at the top of her voice.

'Impressive,' Bryant offered as a man fuelling up one of the excavators finally looked her way.

She beckoned him over.

'I need to speak to Lisa Brown,' she said.

He shrugged.

'The boss.'

'My boss is Derek so...'

'Big boss,' she said, doing a circle with her hand to indicate the whole thing.

'Oh, her, hang on,' he said, walking away.

He approached another man wearing the same uniform but with a different-coloured hard hat. She surmised it was probably Derek, who looked their way and then disappeared. The guy went back to filling up his excavator.

Kim stepped away as her phone rang.

'Go ahead, Stace.'

'Hey, boss, just to let you know Terence Birch might need a closer look.'

'Go on.'

'He's got form for stalking and we're not talking kiddy stuff. We're talking sustained obsession with one female that went on for years, despite court orders and prison time.'

'Any violence?' Kim asked, seeing the picture of Sandra's bloodied body.

'Not that I'm aware of but...'

But it still needed to be followed up.

'You still in the office?'

'Yeah.'

'Grab a car, go and do a follow-up, and we'll chat later.'

'On it, boss,' Stacey said before ending the call.

Kim returned to stand beside her colleague.

'Can you imagine managing this lot?' Bryant asked, looking at all the vans parked side by side. From the livery she could see there were builders, drainage firms, electricians and plumbers. All different contractors with different priorities, different rules, different bosses. Bringing it all together was no mean feat, and the person responsible was striding towards them.

At around five feet seven, Lisa moved with confidence around machinery, holes in the ground and stacked piles of materials. Her auburn hair was tied back beneath a yellow hard hat with the word 'Boss' written in marker pen on the front. An orange high-vis vest covered a black T-shirt and jeans.

She pushed the gate open, stepped out and closed it again before speaking.

'If there's been another noise complaint, we've made sure that no machinery is being operated before—'

'We're not from the council,' Kim said as both she and Bryant produced their IDs.

Lisa looked at them. 'You know, even though I know I've done nothing wrong, my mind is replaying the events of my day so far just to make sure.'

Kim understood. Sometimes they were like a moving conscience.

The woman looked back to the site and frowned. 'How can I help?'

'Not connected to your work,' Kim reassured her, moving around the side of the building as the excavator started up again.

The woman followed, looking even more confused. She removed her hard hat to reveal a red line that stretched across her forehead.

'You were at an event the other night, a psychic reading?'

Her eyes filled with amusement. 'Oh Jesus, Catherine didn't kill the psychic, did she?'

Kim and Bryant exchanged a glance but said nothing.

'I saw that. Wh... what's happened?'

'Psychic Sandy was murdered in a graveyard last night.'

'Jesus Christ,' Lisa said, reaching for the wall behind and leaning against it. 'You say she's dead?'

'Very,' Kim confirmed.

She shook her head a few times. 'You don't think...'

'The psychic party on Thursday was her final working engagement, so we're collating accounts from the last people to spend time with her.'

'She was fine, that I recall. She was a bit sheepish when she spilled red wine on Catherine's new rug. Catherine tried to laugh it off, but it was hollow if you know what I mean. Sandy offered to pay for professional cleaning, but I don't think Catherine could properly relax after that.'

Her gaze moved off into the distance. 'Sorry, I'm still trying to process that the woman is dead. I mean, to me she seemed fine. But Betts has known her for a while.'

'Catherine mentioned Betts's husband turning up. Some kind of miscommunication between the two of them.'

'Yeah, right,' Lisa said, rolling her eyes.

Kim waited.

'The only miscommunication between those two is Betts not yet having found the courage to tell him he's an insufferable, misogynistic, controlling arsehole.'

'And you know this how?'

'Officer, have you ever spent time with someone who tells you what's going on more by what they don't say than what they do?'

'Such as?'

'Looking constantly at her watch if we went for coffee after class and leaving dead on nine o'clock. Recounting her activities with no inclusion of any help from David. A couple of snide remarks from him about the baby weight. You get the picture?'

Yes, unfortunately she did.

'And it was Bettina's idea to hold the party?' Kim asked.

Lisa shook her head. 'Oh no, that was definitely Catherine. Betts mentioned that she'd been to see Sandy, but it was Catherine who suggested the get-together at her house for a laugh.'

That wasn't quite how Catherine had described it.

'And was it... a laugh, I mean?' Kim asked.

'It was for me. I had a great time. I don't believe a word of it, but it was very entertaining and that's what I took it for, an evening of light-hearted fun to switch off the work button,' she said, nodding back towards the building site.

'Catherine gave us the impression you heard something you didn't appreciate. Something in your past?'

Lisa's face hardened. 'Of course she told you that.'

'Anything you'd like to share?'

'Not really but seeing as you're the police and it's easy

enough for you to check, I'll admit that I have a record. Violence in my late teens.' She held up her hands. 'I learned my lesson and it never happened again.'

'Why would that bother you? It was years ago.'

'I don't know how Sandy came across the information but let's just say I don't advertise the fact.'

'Oh,' Kim said, now understanding the issue. She nodded to the site behind. 'It's not on your CV?'

'Nor the application form or the disclaimer,' she said honestly. 'And if Catherine had access to that information, it certainly wouldn't be staying in my past where it belonged.'

'You and Catherine don't get on?'

'Catherine likes to be top dog and something about me challenges that.' She shrugged. 'Like I don't get enough of that shit here.'

'Must be difficult,' Kim said.

'It is. That's why I go to yoga class. I bloody hate the pace of it but it does force me to slow down, which I'm not normally very good at. There's always...' She smiled as a figure at the gate motioned for her attention.

She held up her hand to indicate five minutes. He disappeared from view.

'If it's urgent, please...'

'It's not urgent. Kenny is a better plumber than he thinks he is. If I send him away for five minutes, he'll work out the answer on his own.'

'Is that your management style?' Kim asked, intrigued. 'Send them away until they find the answer themselves.'

'Management isn't about a single style, especially when you're a woman managing men, no offence,' she said to Bryant.

'None taken. I'd imagine you have to be quite tough to manage so many different personalities in this environment.'

She smiled. 'Is that your way of asking how a woman gets on

managing approximately a hundred men without wishing to sound sexist?'

Bryant coloured slightly. Kim liked the woman's directness and was learning about her by just witnessing the exchange.

'Pretty much,' Bryant admitted.

'I'd imagine your boss here would understand if I said it wasn't always easy. I quickly realised that men are people too. I'm not a raging feminist. I don't want to do better than men. Attitudes like that are divisive. I want everyone to have the chance to succeed. This position is about being fair. If someone drops a bollock, they get told in no uncertain terms. If they perform well, they get praised. It's not rocket science. Be fair and be consistent. Anything else?'

Bryant shook his head.

'You want a job or are you happy where you are?' she asked, pushing herself away from the wall.

'I'm good, thanks.'

'May I?' she asked, nodding towards the gates.

'One last thing,' Kim said as Lisa reached for her hard hat. 'Did Sandy seem genuine to you?'

She thought for a minute then shrugged. 'I dunno. I suppose I'm a sceptic and I'm convinced she knew of my past some other way. Some of the others were hanging on her every word and nodding vigorously at every sentence. I've seen things on telly that I can't explain but she didn't blow my socks off. I didn't feel she delivered any revelations, but others might disagree. Not fair of me to comment, especially as she's dead.'

Kim nodded her understanding.

'If I can help further just come back. Always here, and as we're behind schedule, I literally am always here.'

'Thanks for the offer,' Kim said, turning away.

'Hey, Inspector,' Lisa called.

Kim turned.

'That quip I made about Catherine killing the psychic. It was just a joke, you know.'

Kim nodded and continued to the car.

She hadn't thought for a minute it wasn't a joke. So why had the woman found it necessary to set her straight?

TEN

'Okay, so what do we know about him?' Penn asked, once John Doe was out of the fridge and on the table.

Keats pulled back the sheet. Penn took a closer look.

He guessed the man to be mid- to late forties with hair that was more grey than brown. He saw no piercings or tattoos or anything that would help identify him.

'He was found in the Stourbridge underpass, already deceased, and had been for a good twelve hours. Take a look and tell me what you see.'

'Average height, below average weight. I assume you've cleaned him up a bit?'

'Not as much as you'd expect,' Keats answered.

'Clean nails, clean ears. No bunions or corns from poorly fitting shoes.' He paused and looked up. 'May I touch?'

Keats handed him a pair of gloves.

He put them on and then gently turned over the man's hands. 'No calluses. Actually, his hands are pretty soft.'

Keats nodded. 'All organs are healthy with no signs of excess, but there's something a little more intriguing. Open his mouth.'

'Excuse me?'

'Okay, just lift his upper lip.'

Penn did so. 'Veneers?'

'The best,' Keats said.

Penn knew that dental care was not high on the list of priorities for people who didn't know how they were going to get their next meal.

'Hmm, doesn't present like your normal homeless person,' Penn acknowledged, feeling that first burn of curiosity that came with an anomaly.

'To summarise, this man is approximately mid-forties, reasonably healthy until the aneurism, definitely wealthy at some point but has not one shred of identification. Who was he? And where is his family? Because he might have been living on the streets, but he hadn't been doing it for very long.'

Penn wondered if the identification of this John Doe was really going to be as straightforward as his boss might have first thought.

ELEVEN

Bettina Ford lived in a new-build detached house on a recent development just out of West Hagley.

Despite being detached, the space between the house and its neighbour was less than the length of an average-sized person.

Kim remembered the placards mounted all around the development screaming 'affordable housing'. She knew that meant most of the properties would be upwards of three hundred thousand and approximately ten per cent would be below that figure.

The house she was visiting had a bay window next to the front door with two identical white uPVC windows above. A single car garage was tacked on to the side.

The door opened and a baby cried in the background before the woman opened her mouth.

'Sorry, can I help you?'

Her hair was fashioned into an untidy bun on top of her head, and her hands were covered in splashes of paint.

They both held up their IDs.

'Oh, goodness,' she said, looking along the road. 'Is someone hurt?'

Kim shook her head, 'No, it's you we've come to see. Bettina, isn't it?'

'Only if you're my mother and I haven't done my homework on time.'

Kim smiled.

'Otherwise it's Betts.'

'Okay, Betts, may we come in?'

'Please do, seeing as you know my name.'

They stepped into the house and followed Betts to the rear and into a sunroom.

A baby Kim guessed to be around six months old was making contented sucking noises as it slept.

'Oh, a great age,' Bryant said, smiling into the Moses basket.

'Yes, at this stage I can be sure they'll stay where I left them. The other two are at school so...' She indicated towards a small chest of drawers she seemed to be refurbishing.

'Your job?' Kim asked, taking a seat in one of the wicker chairs.

'Not really. I'm not confident enough to put myself out there so I just tinker.'

Although Kim didn't know much about restoration, it looked like Betts knew what she was doing.

'I don't have an actual job. I'm just a wife and mother.'

'Hardest job in the world,' Bryant said, glancing again into the Moses basket.

Kim had the feeling Bryant was getting broody for a grandchild, but his only child, Laura, was focussed on her midwifery career.

'We understand you attend a yoga class with a few other friends?'

'Not really friends, but yes, it's either one night a week bending myself into impossible positions or hitting the gin for a break. Actually, it's a good way to shift the baby weight,' she said, patting her stomach.

'A few of you had a psychic night recently?' Kim asked.

'Yes, Sandy came and did a reading for all of us.'

'And you knew Sandy quite well?'

'Oh yes, I visit her every couple of months for— Wait a minute. You just said knew, past tense. Has something happened?'

Kim took a breath. 'I'm afraid to say that Sandy was murdered late last night.'

'Wh... what?' she asked as her hand went to her throat.

'I'm sorry but it's true. There's no way to dress it up. It was a particularly brutal attack, and we understand from the others that you knew her the best.'

'I did, inasmuch as I'd met her many times before, but purely in a professional capacity. We weren't friends or anything.'

'Would you have known if she was acting differently, maybe if there was something on her mind?' Bryant asked.

'I don't think so. She was a little more distant than normal but that's because it was a group setting. Our one-to-one sessions were more intimate, but she was trying to devote time to all of us equally, except for Catherine, who was trying to hog the whole thing.'

'And it was Catherine's idea to hold the event?'

'Goodness, yes. She approached me before class a couple of weeks ago and told me what she was thinking of doing.'

In the space of a few hours, they'd gone from Catherine merely allowing the group to hold the event at her house to actively initiating the whole thing. Not a crime, so why lie about it?

'Were there any cross words with anyone?'

'Oh no, it's not like that. It's a calm environment. There was the usual bickering between Lisa and Catherine, which Rose defused as usual. She's the eldest and doesn't like conflict.'

Kim noted that fact for later.

'What was the bickering about?'

'Oh, everything and nothing as usual. Lisa advised Catherine how to get the red wine out the rug, and Catherine snapped at her.'

'There's tension between them?'

Betts pulled a face. 'Just sniping. They're not in each other's lives enough for it to be serious; weekly yoga class; an occasional coffee afterwards. They're very strong women and they both want to be in charge.'

'Of what?' Bryant asked.

'Exactly. There's nothing to manage so the rest of us just sit back and let them get on with it. Except for Rose, who steps in if it starts getting heated. Only those two could bring a negative vibe to such a positive experience.'

As though remembering the reason for their visit, her face fell. 'Is she really dead?'

Kim nodded. 'May I ask why you used her services?'

'Cheaper than a therapist,' Betts joked weakly.

Kim waited.

Betts shrugged. 'I dunno. I suppose I felt like she really knew me. She guided me well through difficult situations.'

'May I ask what?'

Betts swallowed. 'Between my second child and little Joseph over there I had a miscarriage. A late one, literally days after we told people the news.' Her eyes reddened but she continued. 'Sandy told me I would be pregnant again within a year and that it would be a boy.'

Kim's analytical and naturally sceptical brain turned that one over quickly. The woman before her was clearly fertile, given that she'd been on her third pregnancy. It stood to reason that they'd try again; and the sex of the child was always a fifty-fifty gamble. It wasn't a profound prediction.

'It gave me hope,' Betts went on. 'I was terrified I could have no more so the hope got me through the grief.'

Kim wondered what it was in people that made them want to know their fate or gain confirmation and validation of themselves through other means. Why give that control to someone else?

'And you say Catherine was hogging the session?'

'Oh yes, asking all kinds of questions about her future. I mean she wanted specifics: dates, times, places and names. Sandy kept trying to move on. To be honest, I could understand if it was Emily being as forceful as Catherine. Now there's a woman who could be forgiven for hogging the session and getting everything she could.'

'And why's that?' Kim asked.

Betts waved her hand. 'Not my story to tell. You'll understand when you meet her.'

Kim was intrigued. Emily was the next person on her list.

Kim opened her mouth as the front door burst open.

'Bettina, Bettina, why aren't you answering your—'

The man stopped shouting as he entered the room. His reddened face lost none of its colour as his gaze took in the visitors inside his home.

Kim was in no doubt that this short, raging, slightly overweight man was David.

'Who are you?' he asked, looking at Bryant.

The baby stirred at the sound of the man's voice.

Bettina gave him a look while rocking the Moses basket.

'We're police officers,' Kim said, standing and offering her identification. 'We're here to speak to your wife about Sandra Deakin.'

A look of satisfaction stole over his face. 'Why, what's she done now? I'm going to guess at fraud. She's taking people's money under false pretences and you're finally doing something about it. Am I right?' he asked, folding his arms and leaning against the door frame.

'David,' Bettina hissed.

'Sandra Deakin is dead, murdered,' Kim said, making no effort to soften the blow to someone who clearly disliked her.

'Oh. Oh, I'm sorry to hear that,' he said, letting his arms drop so that his hands fell into his pockets.

'You don't sound very sorry,' Kim observed honestly. 'We understand you came into contact with Sandy on Thursday night when you arrived early to collect your wife?'

'It was a simple error. Bettina told me to collect her at eight by mistake.'

'No, David, I didn't,' Betts said, stepping away from the baby, who appeared to have been lulled back to sleep. 'I said nine. It was your mistake.'

Betts spoke quietly but firmly. David's nostrils flared but he didn't pursue the disagreement further.

'That woman has put all sorts of ideas in her head,' he said, nodding towards his wife, whose cheeks were flushed in embarrassment. 'I've had all kinds of backchat from her since she started spending time with that fraud.'

'Backchat?' Kim asked. He sounded as though he was talking about a spirited child.

'You know what I mean. She's no longer the woman I married, and that bloody troublemaker has been encouraging Betts to start a business and make her own money. She's said things to me that she would never have said before.'

Kim was surprised at how open about his marital problems he was with a total stranger. It told her he felt justified in his dislike of Sandy and was trying to recruit others to his opinion. And, of course, Betts beginning to stand up for herself couldn't have been of her own volition, Kim mused as Betts put her hands on her hips.

'People change, David. I've already explained that I have to have something for me. Sorry, officers, you don't need to hear all this.'

On the contrary, Kim thought. The whole scene was very telling. This man was losing control of his wife and he didn't like it one little bit.

'She told Betts to leave me, find someone new,' he said, eyes blazing.

Betts threw her hands in the air and stormed from the room, while Kim tried to follow his logic.

'You're saying that Sandy encouraged Betts to end the marriage and that Betts did everything that Sandy told her to?'

'She was an interfering, poisonous—'

'So why is Betts still here?' Kim asked simply. 'If she did everything Sandy told her to do, why hasn't she gone?'

'She's planning to. Sandra has put her up to it and it's just a matter of time until she does what that crackpot said. I don't care if she's dead or not. I despise every single word that ever came out of her mouth.'

Kim's mind went straight to the vision of Sandra, lying amongst the gravestones, covered in blood, with a slash across that mouth that he so despised.

TWELVE

Stacey got out of the squad car and stood at the top of the street in Coombs Wood.

She knocked on the window and told the police officer to go. Never would she get over the guilt of taking up an officer's time to ferry her around. She resolved to take Devon up on her offer of free driving lessons.

After she reassured him she'd get an Uber back, he pulled away from the kerb.

She walked the narrow street taking note of the house numbers. She passed by number seventeen, the house where Charlotte Danks had once lived. She took another couple of steps and spied the house of Terence Birch across the road. The first thing she noticed was a midi skip in front of it, and the second was that the man had enjoyed a clear and unobstructed view of Charlotte's house from any one of his front windows. He hadn't needed to stand right opposite to see everything, so that action had been purely to terrorise her. A shudder passed through her but she pushed it aside. She wasn't here to judge him on his past crimes but to see if there was any link to the current one.

A man approached the skip with an old bedside cabinet. He hauled it in and looked her way.

'Terence Birch?' she asked, offering a smile. Remembering that was what appeared to have got Charlotte into trouble, she hastily tried to rearrange her face into total neutrality.

'That's me,' he said, wiping his hands on his jeans.

Stacey introduced herself. 'Just here to go over a couple of things in your statement, if that's okay.'

'You mean you've discovered my history and now I'm a suspect. I bloody knew this would happen,' he seethed, hitting the top of the skip with both hands.

Stacey was caught off guard by his sudden rise to anger. She took a half step back.

The boss had described him as meek, non-threatening and a bit of a drip.

'I should have just left her. Someone would have found her eventually.'

'May we step closer to the front door, Mr Birch?'

Normally she would have asked if they could talk inside but the thought made her uneasy.

'No, we may not,' he said, planting his feet firmly. 'I'm a bit busy clearing out my dead mother's belongings.'

'I'm sorry for—'

'No you're not, so keep your platitudes.'

Stacey wondered how they had reached open hostility so soon and how the hell she could bring it back. Trouble was, he was bang on the money about the reason for her visit.

'We understand you knew Sandra Deakin,' she said, forging ahead. She needed to ask the questions whether he was hostile or not.

'I've seen her in the graveyard a few times. We're not friends or anything.'

'But you've spoken to her a couple of times?'

'Yeah, so?'

So it took a lot less than that for you to become fixated on one of your neighbours, she wanted to say.

'I just wondered what you talked about.'

'None of your fucking business, and if you're not having this same conversation with every other person she ever spoke to, I'll be suing you for harassment,' he said, taking a step towards her.

Stacey stood her ground, wishing for just a minute she'd let the squad car stay.

Well, temper wise he was already at DEFCON 2 so she had nothing left to lose.

'There's no chance that you'd become fixated on—'

'Oh, piss off, you stupid cow. If you're trying to pin this on me cos of my relationship with Charlotte, you can go fuck yourself,' he said, glancing down the street.

Stacey held firm.

'It wasn't really a relationship though, was it, Mr Birch? Whatever your feelings were, Charlotte didn't return them. You were very slow in getting that message so I can't help but—'

'Sometimes people are slow to understand who they are meant to be with. Charlotte is my soulmate and eventually she'll realise that too.'

Stacey was glad that Charlotte had moved far away because this man was not going to give up while there was breath in his body. Not one of the deterrents had quashed his belief.

'So don't even think about comparing my feelings for Sandy to my devotion to Charlotte.'

Stacey quickly realised that her best interviewing technique right now was to stay quiet.

He'd just admitted to having feelings for Sandy.

'You lot had no business getting between me and Charlotte. It's because of you that she's left the area again. She wasn't gonna keep waiting around while you lot trumped up crimes and kept sending me away. If it wasn't for you, we'd be together right now.'

How was it possible for two people to have such opposing views of the same situation? Stacey wondered. Charlotte had moved continents to get away from this man, and he was convinced she was going to return to him one day, to live happily ever after.

She couldn't work out if he was delusional or mentally ill.

She was tempted to ask how many times she'd visited him in prison or if he'd kept her letters, but she suspected greater minds than hers had tried to unclasp him from his obsession.

'She'll be back when she realises fate is on our side, so why would I ruin that by cavorting around Hawne after some random psychic, eh?'

'Mr Birch—'

'Enough,' he said, throwing his hands up in the air. 'I'm not saying any more. You wanna talk again, fucking arrest me. Otherwise leave me the hell alone.' He turned and stormed back up the garden path.

He'd admitted having feelings for Sandra Deakin and had also made it clear he knew where she lived.

Stacey had paid him this visit to rule out any emotional connection to the victim and to cross him off as a suspect.

She was leaving unable to do either.

THIRTEEN

The small storefront in Dudley High Street was sandwiched between a pound shop and a women's boutique.

Kim got out of the car with the vision of David's apoplectic expression and Betts's humiliation still at the forefront of her mind. The air had been charged when they'd left the house, and even if Betts hadn't been thinking of leaving the man before, there was a good chance she was considering it right now.

There was no doubt in her mind that David had turned up at Catherine's house early to curtail his wife's exposure to a woman he hated with a passion. The fact that Betts had finished her evening while he waited in the car was a testament to the woman's growing strength. Regardless, Kim had fired off a text to Stacey, instructing her to do background checks on both David Ford and Lisa Brown.

She stepped into the small space and was hit with the smell of jasmine incense and the sound of pan pipes.

On her left was a selection of tie-dyed clothing which gave way to crystals and jewellery, then self-help books and CDs. There was one other customer, and with her and Bryant, the store felt cramped.

To make space, Kim edged her way around a display cabinet holding coloured stones, to get to the till. A woman appeared from nowhere and Kim realised she'd been sitting down.

'Emily?' Kim asked.

The woman nodded and Kim introduced them both. The door closed behind the single customer as she left without a purchase.

'Gee, thanks, guys, only my third customer of the day.'

'Sorry about that,' Bryant said as Kim took a moment to appraise her.

The woman was painfully thin with a pale complexion. It dawned on Kim that the turban she wore wasn't for fashion purposes, and now she understood what Betts had meant when she'd said that Emily could have been forgiven for wanting to hog the reading and gain insight into future events.

'Can we talk?'

'Not sure what I've done but I can't shut the shop. I need all the customers I can get.'

'No problem.'

'But you can come back here while I make myself a cuppa.'

They followed her through an arch to a small kitchen and store room from where they could still see the front door.

Emily indicated to them to take the two seats at the table.

They both remained standing.

'Please,' she insisted. 'I try to stand for a little longer every day. Get my strength up.'

They both sat.

'Anyone want one?' she asked, holding up a box of lemon tea.

They both shook their heads.

'Emily, we need to talk to you about the psychic party you attended a few nights ago,' Kim said.

'Did we break any laws?' she asked with a half-smile.

Of all the people they'd told, this was going to be the hardest. Kim really didn't want to add any more negativity to this woman's life.

'I'm sorry to tell you that Sandy was murdered on Sunday night.'

Emily's mouth fell open. 'Murdered?'

Kim nodded. 'We're speaking to everyone at her last work engagement.'

'Oh goodness, how awful. Her poor family. Who on earth could have wanted her dead?'

'That's what we intend to find out.'

'You can't suspect anyone at the party?'

'No,' Kim said, holding up her hand. 'We're just trying to get a feel for her demeanour, her mood and to find out if anyone saw anything strange.'

'I came with Rose and left with her. She took me right to my door so I didn't see Sandy arrive or leave.'

'Seems a friendly group at this yoga class,' Kim stated.

'There are others in the class but we're the only original members from the start. We call ourselves the OGs. We see each other once a week, sometimes have a coffee afterwards, cos Betts will do anything to string out her one night of freedom. An occasional message or joke through the WhatsApp group. I've missed a few sessions during treatment but I'm in remission – again,' she said, holding up crossed fingers.

So this wasn't her first battle with the big C.

'And you had a good night?' Kim asked.

'I took it for what it was, Inspector. A laugh, entertainment, a distraction from my life and keeping this place afloat.'

'You didn't take it too seriously?' Bryant asked.

'God, no. Any answers I want aren't going to come from a bloody psychic.'

'Did she offer you any info that was useful?'

'No, just told me how strong I was and that I had many

more experiences ahead of me. I had more fun watching everyone else's reaction to the whole thing.'

'You mean Catherine?'

'Yes, especially Catherine. She was hilarious,' Emily said, laughing. 'Sorry, that's inappropriate in the circumstances but I'll take any laugh going.'

Kim couldn't blame her. This woman was staring death in the face every single day.

'What was so funny about Catherine?'

'Well, who would invite a psychic into their home and then argue with them?'

'About the wine spillage?'

'Oh no, about the reading. I don't know what answers Catherine was seeking but she wasn't getting them from Sandy.'

'What was Sandy telling her?' Kim asked, intrigued. Catherine's name had come up in every conversation so far.

'That there were big changes ahead but that she'd meet them with fortitude. Catherine pressed her as to what changes. She wouldn't elaborate further, but I think Catherine took it as a negative. She also told her that an unknown woman was going to become prominent in her life. Catherine demanded to know who she was talking about. Every time the poor woman tried to move on, Catherine asked her another specific question. When it became clear Sandy was going to say no more, Catherine sat there glaring at her until the session was over. I don't think Sandy could leave quick enough. It was a bit intense for a while.'

Sounded like Catherine had organised the evening under false pretences and then proceeded to spoil it for the rest of them.

'Sorry I can't help any further. Only Betts knows Sandy well enough to judge her mood or state of mind.'

Kim realised that the woman looked exhausted. It was

barely three in the afternoon but Emily looked like she was done for the day.

The shop door opened and Emily's face broke into a smile as an attractive brunette in her early forties with a freshly blow-dried tidy bob entered and closed the door behind her.

'Let me guess, DI Stone and DS Bryant from Halesowen CID?' the woman asked before anyone had a chance to speak.

'Are you psychic?' Bryant asked.

'No, Betts put a note in the WhatsApp group about an hour ago.'

'Rose Foster, I presume?' Kim asked.

Rose nodded as she stepped around them and went to Emily, taking her hand. 'Just came to check you were okay.'

Emily nodded and squeezed her hand in return.

'May we ask you a few questions while you're here?' Kim asked, seizing the opportunity.

Rose nodded. 'Of course. It's all absolutely horrific. It still hasn't sunk in properly that she's dead, and I didn't even know her. It's just that surreal feeling of someone that you recently spent time with now gone – and murdered of all things.'

Rose had had a bit longer to get used to the news and appeared to have given it some thought.

'And did you get what you wanted from the evening?'

'Yes and no. I had an evening's entertainment and the company of some acquaintances, but I didn't get any news of anything more permanent coming my way.'

Kim waited.

'A man, Inspector. I've been on my own for a while now. The old-fashioned way of meeting someone has been replaced by swiping left or right or something. News of the arrival of my Prince Charming and happy ever after was not forthcoming. If I'm honest, I did consider a one-to-one session with her, but clearly that's not going to happen now.'

'We hear that you broke up a bit of a tiff between Catherine and Lisa,' Kim said.

She rolled her eyes. 'Nothing new there. If they both had dicks we'd be sick of the sight of them.'

Emily laughed out loud, and Bryant hid a chuckle behind a cough. Even Kim appreciated the woman's no-nonsense attitude. Having just a few years on the others seemed to give her the wisdom to tell it how it was.

'And Lisa's reaction to her reading?'

'Well, she wasn't thrilled. There were no details or anything, but Sandy did refer to not repeating past mistakes, as next time she wouldn't be so lucky. Lisa was pretty quiet after that.'

'And you saw David Ford when he came early to collect Betts?'

Rose rolled her eyes. 'He's a knob but she stood her ground.'

'You heard the conversation?'

'Yeah, my chair was nearest to the lounge. He ordered her to get in the car and told her she was to have nothing more to do with "that woman". I wasn't sure exactly which one of us he meant, but a few minutes later he was back in the car and Betts had returned, albeit looking a bit strained.'

'You took Emily to the function?' Kim asked.

'And brought me back,' Emily confirmed. 'I nodded off in the car.'

'Before I could even ask her if she'd seen the shenanigans outside. She was asleep in seconds.'

'Outside?' Kim asked.

'Yeah, I was clearing away the nibbles plates when Catherine was seeing Sandy to her car.'

'And?'

'Oh, they were going at it. Actually, that's unfair. Only one of them was going at it. Sandy was just trying to leave.'

'Catherine was shouting at her?'

'Oh yeah. Her arms were gesticulating all over the place. She was in quite the rage, and the more Sandy ignored her, the more animated Catherine became. Sandy finally managed to edge her way into the car without touching Catherine, who unceremoniously kicked the car and gave the middle finger salute as Sandy headed out the drive,' Rose said.

Kim was now sure that they would be paying a second visit to Catherine. It was time for the host of the evening to explain exactly what had happened on Thursday night.

Kim stood. 'Thank you both for your time. If we need anything—'

'Hang on, guv,' Bryant said, standing. 'I just need to have another look at that crystal in the corner. It's the wife's birthday next week and she loves this stuff. May we?'

'Of course,' Emily said, switching on the kettle as Rose took a seat.

Kim followed Bryant back into the shop.

'That's the one I was thinking of,' he said.

It was a purple quartz piece shaped like an armchair.

'Nice,' Kim said.

'I'll take this one,' Bryant called out.

'You sure?' Emily asked doubtfully.

'Absolutely – my wife will love it.'

Emily packaged it carefully and charged him.

Once outside, he placed the crystal carefully onto the back seat of the car.

'Head to Mackie's – I'll shout you a late lunch,' Kim said.

'Blimey, that's a turn up,' he replied, starting up the car.

Some days her colleague reminded her what it was to be human.

He'd bought the most expensive piece in the shop and it wasn't Jenny's birthday for another five months.

FOURTEEN

Penn parked his car about forty metres from the homeless shelter in Stourbridge. It had been the obvious choice as a place to start after leaving Keats at the mortuary. John Doe's body had been found only metres away.

It wasn't even 4 p.m. but a line was beginning to form. To his knowledge they didn't start serving food until around 5 p.m.

He walked the line thanking his lucky stars for his own lot in life. Seeing these folks made him eternally grateful that he'd never had to worry where his next meal was coming from.

At the head of the queue was a bearded man in his late twenties, sitting on the ground with a terrier cross lying by his legs.

'I'm not podging,' Penn said, knocking on the window.

'I should think not, mate, looking like that. This lot will have you kicked across that road in seconds.'

A quick look down the line confirmed that there were some curious glances aimed his way. He didn't think telling them he was a police officer would help his case.

He knocked again.

'They're not gonna answer,' said the man as the dog finally

looked up. His hand left his pocket and rested on the dog's head, which went back down.

'I'm not trying to get a meal. I need to talk to someone in there.'

He shrugged. 'They don't know that. They don't open them doors early come hell or high water. They're out back. They can't hear so you're just gonna have to wait until five o'clock like the rest of us.'

Damn it, he really needed to get an identification on this John Doe the boss was worried about. Once he had a name, he could make sure the family was informed and get back to work on the main case.

He had a sudden idea and took out his phone.

'You got a minute...'

'The name's Jericho and let me just check my schedule.'

Penn struggled to make out his expression beneath the bushy beard but he saw amusement in the eyes. He scrolled through his photos of John Doe to find the one that looked the best, though it was hard to get a good one in his current state.

Penn leaned down, and the dog growled.

'It's okay, Kizzy,' Jericho said, patting her head.

The dog settled back down.

Penn held out his phone. 'Do you know this man?'

'Jeez, is the guy dead?'

Penn nodded.

'Coulda warned me, dude. I'm about to have my tea.'

'Sorry. Do you know him?'

'Course I know him. That's Dan. Shit, Dan's dead?'

''Fraid so,' Penn answered, nodding across the road. 'Found yesterday morning in the underpass. Aneurism.'

'Shit. Sorry to hear that.'

'Do you know Dan's last name?' Penn asked, unable to believe he'd struck gold on his first try.

'Nope. Don't know his first name either. Dan's his street name, after Dan Ackroyd.'

Penn was confused.

'Just cos of *Trading Places*, the film – you know it, right?'

'Yeah, but I don't get it.'

Jericho rolled his eyes. 'Let's just say that being on the streets was a new experience for him. He fell a long way. Ain't got a clue on his real name.'

Penn should have known he wouldn't be that lucky.

'How long had he been out here?' he asked.

'Sorry, mate, ain't got my diary on me. It's back at the office with my Rolex and Lamborghini.'

'Roughly?' Penn asked, ignoring the sarcasm.

'Maybe two years or so. Could have been longer. I was in Rhyl. Kizzy here likes to travel.'

Although the guy had managed to make him feel like an idiot a few times, there was something likeable about him.

'Talk to him much?'

'Now and again. We were next to each other in the queue sometimes.'

'And?'

'We sipped lattes and discussed our secrets.'

'Secrets?' Penn asked.

'Oh yeah, we all got 'em. But I was being sarcastic. Again.'

'Yeah, I caught that. Was he an alcoholic?'

Jericho shook his head.

'An addict?' he asked. He knew of many men and women who had lost everything through substance abuse.

'Not like you're thinking.'

'Go on,' Penn urged.

'Bloody hell, mate, for this much probing you could have bought me dinner.'

Penn laughed.

'Dan was a gambler. He couldn't help himself. He'd offer a

bet on anything. I watched him lose his shoes on a bet with one of the others on which raindrop would travel down the glass quickest. He bet a meal on whether the next person to give Reggie a quid would be a man or woman. He lost and had to sit and watch Reggie polish off two portions of hotpot,' he said, nodding inside. 'He couldn't help himself. I mean, he won sometimes as well. I saw him earn himself an overcoat and two pound coins. It was some kind of compulsion. He had to be betting on something.'

'Anything else?'

The man shook his head.

'Thanks, Jericho,' Penn said, rising to his feet.

'You're welcome.'

Penn started to walk away and then walked back.

'And there'll be a breakfast bap waiting in the morning at Merry Hill Costa.'

'Cheers, man,' Jericho said as his face lit up.

The least he could do was offer the man a meal he didn't have to worry about.

He now knew that John Doe had likely been wealthy and two years ago he'd lost it all. He also knew that the man was a hard-core gambler.

He didn't yet have an identity for the boss, but he did have a place to start.

FIFTEEN

It had taken Stacey a while to throw off the unsettled feeling she'd had following her meeting with Terence Birch. She'd gone to see him as a 'rule out' exercise. A precursor to rubbing his name off the board. What had unnerved her the most was the speed with which his rage had accelerated from zero to sixty in less than a second. It wasn't hard to imagine him snapping and stabbing someone repeatedly. Perhaps he'd fixed his attention on to Sandra Deakin, and she'd rebuffed him, bringing back his constant rejection from Charlotte. And that was why his name remained on the board.

Penn's entrance distracted her from her thoughts. 'Hey, buddy, didn't realise you'd taken the day off.' He'd left just before nine. It was now after five thirty and the boss had already thrown an extra couple of names at her.

He smiled as he whipped the tie from around his neck and placed it in his drawer. It was like he couldn't be held within its constraints for a minute longer than necessary. She sometimes felt the same way about her bra.

'Tell me about it, Stace. Not the most productive day.

Nothing new on Sandy and still no name for the John Doe, although I do have a lead from a guy called Jericho.'

'Jericho?'

'Just his street name,' Penn said, logging into his computer. 'And how's your day been so far?'

'Bit weird. Our Terence Birch is a stalker, hard core, with a quick, fiery temper.'

'Possible suspect?' Penn asked.

'Person of interest,' she said. No blood had been visible on the man at the scene and he was the one who had raised the alarm, although it wouldn't have been the first time that the person calling the police and the murderer were one and the same.

'Where's the boss?'

'Return to the start. Do not collect two hundred pounds.'

'She's playing Monopoly?'

'Good guess but no. She's on her way back to the first woman she spoke to, who appears to have been less than truthful.'

'Shocker,' Penn said, starting to type.

'Hey, you gonna get into that laptop of Sandra's?' Stacey asked.

'Yep, in a bit. Just gotta check out this lead on our dead guy.'

'The one that died of natural causes as opposed to the murder victim who was stabbed eleven times.'

'Yep, that's the one,' he said, ignoring her sarcasm.

She shook her head in despair and continued her background checks on Father George Markinson. So far she'd established that the man was fifty-seven years of age and by the timeline she'd managed to sketch out, he'd worked in thirteen parishes in twenty-seven years.

1995 – 1997 Nottingham

1997–2000 Leeds

2000–2001 Ilfracombe

2001–2003 Preston

2003–2006 Isle of Wight

2006–2007 Gloucester

2007–2009 Chester

2009–2010 Norfolk

2010–2013 Leicester

2013–2017 Islington

2017–2018 Bedford

2019–2021 Stratford

2021–Present Halesowen

Stacey's head was spinning. She didn't change bed sheets as often as that. For comparison, she took a look at St Luke's in Cradley Heath. Father Derek Wilmot had presided there for over seven years. His previous stint had been nine years in Coventry. She tried another. Father Michaels from Old Hill. The website said he'd been there for eleven years. Before that thirteen years in Liverpool.

She understood that clergymen were moved around on occasion and they were required to go wherever they were sent, but already she was beginning to smell something fishy. Getting to the bottom of this was going to take some work.

'Listen, Penn, I need some—'

'On it, Stace,' her colleague said, reaching for Sandra's laptop.

She smiled her thanks.

The boss was going to want a report on any potential threats to Sandra by the time she got back.

SIXTEEN

Bryant pulled up in front of Catherine's house just as she was getting out of the car. She stood at the top of the drive waiting for them.

'Back so soon?'

'Just another couple of questions, if that's okay.'

'You've spoken to the others?' she asked, unlocking the door.

'We have.'

Catherine kicked off her heels the second she was inside. Next, she put down her bag and removed her jacket. 'Boys,' she called up the stairs, but the house appeared to be silent.

They followed her through to the kitchen, which was not the same photoshoot-ready room they'd seen that morning.

'Bloody hell,' Catherine said, gathering up all the empty wrappers and crisp packets. Pot Noodles had been made and appeared to have been the ammunition in a food fight. There were noodles stuck to every surface, cupboard and all over the floor. The initial anger in her face had been replaced by weariness as she took a wet cloth and started to wipe down surfaces.

Kim couldn't help but feel a bit sorry for her, but ultimately there were questions that needed answering.

'Sorry to go over Thursday night again but we understand you weren't particularly happy with Sandy.'

'She spilled some wine. I probably reacted a little ungraciously, but everything is brand new.'

Probably shouldn't host an event, Kim thought, until the newness had dulled a little bit.

'It was sorted. No harm done.'

'That's not exactly what I was talking about,' Kim said. 'We understand you weren't happy with your reading.'

'Don't be silly. It was a bit of fun. I wasn't expecting anything.'

Kim was beginning to see that Catherine didn't realise when to stop lying.

'I'll be clear,' Kim said, adding a tone of firmness to her voice. 'We've spoken to everyone and we know you haven't been entirely truthful with us. The evening was your suggestion. You planned it and you arranged it.'

Kim noted that although Catherine's back was to them, her movements had stalled.

She continued. 'We know that you tried to monopolise the evening and treat it as a one-to-one session. We know that you weren't happy with what Sandy told you, and you even had words with her outside before she left. Harsh words.'

Catherine turned. Her eyes blazed. 'And my friends told you all this, did they?'

'Acquaintances,' Kim said, reminding her of her own description earlier in the day.

'What's going on, Catherine? What are you not telling us?'

Catherine attempted to stare her down, but Kim's gaze was going nowhere and neither was she until she had answers.

Catherine sighed heavily. 'My husband is having an affair,' she blurted out.

'Oh,' Kim said, unsure what to say.

'I know it and I'm pretending I don't know it because I don't want to lose my family.'

As she said the words, she used her arms to indicate the space around her. Kim was unsure if she was more upset at losing the family or the home.

'I asked Sandy to come for reassurance that my life was going to continue. Then I'd know the affair will fizzle out and I can pretend it never happened.'

'But that's not what she said?'

'No. She told me there would be great change in my life and that an unknown woman would play a huge part. What does that sound like to you?'

Kim said nothing, beginning to understand the importance people placed on this kind of divination.

'It's like she threw the grenade and left the room. She confirmed my worst nightmares and then refused to give me anything more concrete. I just wanted to be ready but she moved on to the next person.'

'And the discussion outside?' Kim pushed. Rose had recounted quite the animated exchange.

Catherine had the grace to colour slightly. 'Not my finest moment. I was asking her if she was a fraud. I wanted her to say yes. I wanted to believe she'd got lucky with her general statements. I asked her if she was just making it all up.'

'And what did she say?'

'She said, "I think you already know the answer." And then she got in the car and left.'

Kim chose not to mention the kick to the car or the one-finger wave.

'I'm not proud of myself,' Catherine repeated. 'Especially now.'

'It wasn't quite the light-hearted, fun evening you told us about, was it?' Kim asked. She now understood the situation but Catherine wasn't completely off the hook yet.

There was a reason for the saying 'Don't shoot the messenger'.

'Not for any of us, Inspector,' Catherine said, taking a seat. 'We all wanted to know something, and if the others told you otherwise, they're lying.'

'Go on,' Kim urged.

'Lisa's a pretty confident woman. She has a job with great responsibility. She's well paid and she enjoys the fruits of her labour. Maybe a bit too much. She's been living beyond her means for months, maxing out credit cards, and her project is overbudget and behind schedule.'

'She's worried about her career?' Bryant asked.

'And her mortgage, and her car and her reputation. All of which will be gone if she gets the dreaded call to head office.

'Then there's Betts, constantly trying to find meaning in her life. She married a controlling man who is a raging misogynist and won't allow her to consider any opportunities beyond the home and children.'

After meeting David, there was nothing there she could disagree with.

'Abusive?' Kim asked.

'Not physically, as far as I know, and she won't have a word said against him.'

Kim waited.

'And then there's Emily. Oh, poor sweet Emily. She knows she's going to die and wants reassurance of what she'll find on the other side.'

'She's in remission,' Kim argued.

'Did she look in remission to you? It's what she's telling people but it's not true. She's made the decision to end treatment. She can't take it any more.'

Kim couldn't help the sadness that washed over her.

'And then there's Rose, still trying to make contact with her dead son.'

'What?' Kim said. Rose had claimed she wanted to know about the future of her love life.

'She didn't tell you?'

Kim shook her head.

'Her son was kidnapped and murdered when he was fifteen years old.'

Kim played out the day she'd had and wondered if she'd met with anyone who hadn't outright lied to her.

SEVENTEEN

'Okay, team, quick recap before I set you free for the night,' Kim said, pouring coffee from the pot. Even though it was almost seven, she wasn't going home for a while yet.

'Okay, I'll start,' Stacey offered. 'Terence Birch is a volatile, aggressive guy who could quite easily have stabbed Sandra eleven times without a shadow of a doubt.'

'You sure?' Kim asked. She hadn't got that impression from him outside the church, but she hadn't got the impression he'd done serious time for hard-core stalking either.

Stacey shrugged. 'Boss, I like to think I'm not that easily intimidated but my heart rate leaped up a few points while talking to him.'

If Kim had for one second suspected this kind of behaviour, she'd never have suggested Stacey question him alone.

'Did he ever touch his victim?'

'Not that I know of; but the threat was real enough for Charlotte to leave her family and move halfway around the world.'

'Okay, keep him current.'

'Still working on Father George Markinson. Something

dodgy there. Doesn't stay in one place for very long, so more work to do.'

Kim nodded. 'Sandy's laptop?' she asked, looking from Penn to Stacey, unsure who had taken on the task.

Penn put his hand up. 'Mixed bag on social media. Some folks love what she does and others troll her. She didn't respond to the negative comments. She just blocked them and moved on. Her inbox hasn't thrown up any serious threats but I need more time.' He paused to signal a change in subject. 'Nothing that we didn't know from the post-mortem except that Sandy might have had an accident when she was a kid.'

Kim deliberately donned her 'are you kidding me?' face.

'Keats was very interested as to whether the childhood accident gave Sandy her gift.'

Kim almost spluttered her coffee all over herself. 'Keats believes in psychics?'

She didn't have that on her bingo card.

'I think he'd like to be convinced,' Penn answered.

Just went to show that no matter how much you thought you knew someone, they could always surprise you.

'Okay, and our John Doe?'

'Got a couple of leads that I'd like to follow up tomorrow, if that's okay?'

'Yes. Give the man his name to be buried with and his family some closure.'

Kim knew that now his death had been ruled as due to natural causes, he would be quickly released to what was once called 'a pauper's funeral' but were now called public health funerals, carried out by local councils.

A public health funeral took place for people who had died alone, in poverty or who were unclaimed by their relatives. The service included being provided with a coffin, a funeral director to transport them to the cemetery with dignity and a short service at the graveside. There were no flowers, viewings, obituaries or transport for family members, and burials took place in an unmarked grave, often shared with other people.

If he had family, they should at least know about his death and have the chance to bury him.

'Okay, good work. We've learned that the psychic reading on Thursday wasn't the fun night out we thought but we'll go into detail on that tomorrow. Go home, eat food, give your wife an early birthday present.'

Stacey and Penn exchanged a look while Bryant chuckled.

'But get some rest and be back by 7 a.m.'

'Got it, boss,' Penn and Stacey said together as they stood.

Stacey offered Penn a questioning look.

'Come on – I'll drop you off as long as you give me a good rating on my driver profile.'

They laughed as they walked out the door.

'What do you reckon about today, guv?' Bryant asked, grabbing his coat.

'Too many people trying to hide too many secrets,' she said, waving him out the door.

All the women appeared to have ulterior motives for attending the psychic night: abducted kids, criminal records, controlling husbands and dying wishes. Their lives were filled with personal issues and questions that might or might not have been answered by the psychic on Thursday night. Had they been secretly disappointed, embarrassed, angry? Enough to harm her? How much emotional investment had the women had in the readings? she wondered.

And more importantly, did any of it have anything to do with the murder of Sandra Deakin?

EIGHTEEN

'It's a bit dark,' Stacey said, looking out the window of the first-floor flat.

'That's okay – we've got headlights,' Devon answered.

'Looks like rain,' she said.

'Luckily, the car has a roof.'

'Dee, I think I'll give it a miss for—'

'Nope. Not a chance,' Devon said, pulling on her boots. 'When you walked into the flat an hour ago, you asked me to do this, and you specifically said I was not to let you wriggle out of it.'

'I feel sick.'

'Then grab a paper bag on your way out. It'll be fine. I know a place that will be pretty dark and quiet by now.'

'Oh yeah,' Stacey said, offering a cheeky wink.

'Nice try, and any other night I'd allow you to distract me, but you were resolute so this time I'm holding you to it. Jeez, I've had the L plates in the car for over a year.'

Stacey felt her stomach lurch at the prospect and wished she'd never said anything. But the truth was that she was getting sick and tired of relying on other people to get around.

After a few bad starter lessons, she'd developed an irrational fear of the gearstick, which had grown mightier as time went on.

'I'll drive us there then you can go at your own pace, got it?'

'Okay,' Stacey said, rushing to the front door before she changed her mind. Devon locked it behind them.

'Just remember that I'm not going to shout at you, I'm not going to lose patience and I'm dead proud of you for trying.'

As ever Stacey wondered what the hell she'd done to deserve Devon.

They got into the car and Stacey envied the ease with which her wife did everything. It was as though she was on automatic pilot, muscle memory that required no thought at all. She watched as her hand slid to the gearstick as her feet did something else and at the same time she steered and checked her mirrors.

She felt beads of sweat break out on her forehead. There was no way she'd be able to do all that. She was going to let Devon down and that thought made her feel even worse.

'Okay, just down here is a trading estate that's only got one circular road. Nothing is open now but there's decent lighting. Okay?'

Stacey wasn't okay but she nodded anyway.

Devon stopped the car on a straight stretch of road.

'I'll fix the L plates while you get comfy in the driver's seat.'

As they crossed at the boot, Devon squeezed her hand. 'Don't look so frightened. No one's gonna die.'

Stacey squeezed her hand back and allowed some of the tension to leave her body.

She slid into the driver's seat as Devon got in beside her.

'Okay, first make sure your leg room is comfortable and you can reach the pedals.'

As she and Devon were around the same height, it felt fine.

'First thing, always, before you even start the car?'

'Seat belt,' Stacey said, reaching for it.

'It's a good habit to form,' Devon said as their hands clashed at the clasps between them. 'Okay, start her up. She's in neutral so she's not going anywhere. Just listen to the sound of the engine. Get to know it. Now put your foot on the left pedal and move the gearstick into the first position. Don't worry – you're not going to move.'

Stacey did as she was told and heard the engine change.

'Put your right foot on the far-right pedal but don't push down. Now release the handbrake and press gently on the accelerator pedal.'

The car moved forward and Stacey instinctively removed her foot.

'It's okay. There's nothing else around. Do it again but don't panic when the car moves. You're in control. See my hand?'

Stacey looked to the gap between then.

'I'll stay in control of the handbrake and if I think there's a problem, I'll pull it up, okay?'

Stacey nodded without speaking and repeated the process.

When the car started to move, she gripped the steering wheel hard and kept her foot in place.

'That's it. Just focus on the steering for now. Add weight to the pedal whenever you're comfortable to increase the five miles per hour you're currently doing.'

Stacey was perfectly happy at the speed she was moving. She resolved to increase pressure once she'd steered around the bend.

An hour later, feeling euphoric that she had mastered the gear change from first to second, she undid her seat belt as Devon parked the car outside their flat.

'Well done, babe,' Devon said, holding up her hand for a high five.

Stacey got out of the passenger side as Devon turned off the engine. In spite of herself, she was pleased with what she'd done. It was a small step but a step all the same.

She jumped back as a shadow moved at the side of the house.

'Dee,' she said as Devon came around the car.

'Wassup?'

'There,' Stacey said, pointing. 'I think there's someone behind that bush.'

They started moving towards it. Stacey's heart was hammering in her chest.

She heard a crunch before a shape came hurtling from behind and knocked them both to the ground.

'Jesus Christ,' Devon said, stunned.

'You okay?' Stacey asked, hearing the sound of shoes on pavement as the figure ran away. She pushed herself to her feet but knew there was no point giving chase.

'What the hell was that about?' Devon asked as Stacey helped her to a standing position.

She had a sneaky suspicion she knew but for once she hoped to God she was wrong.

NINETEEN

Barney wasted no time in jumping up beside Kim on the sofa once he'd finished crunching his supper treat of a carrot.

'Not the easiest thing to read, boy,' she said, absently stroking his head.

Since getting home, she'd thrown the ball for him outside before giving him his tea. They'd returned from their night walk at just after twelve, and he knew that the carrot meant wind-down time.

With plenty of coffee in the pot, she was ready to try and decode Sandra's system. She already had the colour coding sorted. Personal was red, business was black. She couldn't help noticing the ones marked as 'date night' with little hearts and the notes of anniversaries, theatre trips and dinner parties they were attending. Those entries made her smile. The couple had clearly still been very much in love. Other red entries were spa days or shopping trips with an N next to them. It didn't take much working out that the N was for Nicola. She guessed they were bonding trips, opportunities for the two of them to get to know each other. Many were crossed out, cancelled she guessed, wondering who had pulled out.

Sandra's whole life was contained in this book and Kim had the feeling that her murderer was hiding in here somewhere.

She started at the beginning and worked through by process of elimination, waiting for something to jump out at her.

About two weeks in she found it. On 14 January was a blue pen mark; neither business nor personal. It was a capital M in a circle but with a cross-out line.

She continued leafing through the weeks, still looking for anything unusual but also hunting for more blue Ms. A few weeks later she found another one. Again with a line going through it.

Another one three weeks later, again with the line.

Kim could only surmise that they were meetings that had been arranged but had never taken place.

Except there was another one. In the diary two days before she was murdered. Only this M didn't have a line through it.

TWENTY

Terence's heart was still beating out of his chest when he closed the front door behind him.

If his mother was still alive, he'd be forced to run upstairs to his room and compose himself in private, but her recent passing from a stroke meant he could express himself in any room of the house.

And right now he was exhilarated.

He had known it would happen one day. He'd been sure that someone else would come into his life with whom he would feel that instant connection. For a while he'd wondered if Sandy could be the one, but he'd seen something cold in her eyes when she looked at him: distaste, repulsion. It had angered him, and now she would never look at anyone like that again.

It was anger that had driven him to *her* home earlier. He'd wanted to frighten her for implying that his love for Charlotte had been anything but pure.

He had known from the moment he'd seen Charlotte that she was the one for him, and he'd done everything within his power to show his devotion.

That first smile had beguiled him. It had captured him in its thrall. He had felt a frisson of excitement, an electricity burn through his body. That one smile had thrown a collar around his neck and bound him to her for eternity.

Immediately, he had begun trying to prove his love for her. He had watched her house so that whenever she looked outside, she would see him, know that he was there protecting her.

She had noticed his presence and closed the curtains. He had breathed a long, contented sigh of satisfaction that she had known she would never be alone again. That she could sleep soundly in her bed.

It hadn't been enough for her. She had wanted him to prove himself worthy and he understood that. From that point on, everything had been a test. A hurdle for him to clear to show his affection.

The game had begun.

She had left clues in her rubbish for him to follow. A ripped-up telephone bill that he'd been able to painstakingly tape back together. A letter from her employer detailing the annual rise to her salary. Receipts that told him where she liked to eat, what she liked to buy from the supermarket. All breadcrumbs left specifically so he could prove his commitment to her.

From the pieced-together phone bill he'd got her number. She had read the first few texts but not replied. With each unanswered text, he had tried harder to communicate his devotion. When she'd blocked his number, it had just meant that she wanted him to try harder. That was okay. She was worth the effort.

When the police had arrived and advised him to stay away from her home, he had known she was pushing him to see how far he would go.

When he'd been arrested, he'd tried to explain to the police how she was using them to demonstrate her love.

They hadn't understood. Neither had the judge or his

fellow inmates. It didn't matter. He stopped trying to explain it to them. As long as she knew, it was fine.

He remembered how shocked he'd been when he'd been released from prison to learn that she no longer lived at the same address. The rage had filled every fibre of his being. He hadn't been there to protect her from whatever had made her leave her home. The idiot police had been too busy incapacitating him, and she'd suffered in his absence.

Luckily, he had known where she worked and had been able to find her again. He hadn't shown himself to her immediately. He had wanted to wait until he'd been able to follow her home, so that he could reassure her he was back and that he would never leave her again.

His heart had soared when she'd looked out of the bedroom window and their gazes had locked. He had known in that moment that he would do anything, climb any mountain, cross any sea to show his worthiness of her love.

She needed more and he was prepared to give it.

He messaged her. She blocked him. He bought another phone. He messaged her. She blocked him. He sent her flowers. She threw them out. He sent her different flowers. She threw them out.

The dance continued until one day she was gone.

She no longer worked at the same office and she no longer lived at the same address. Overnight she had been taken away and no one knew where she'd gone.

His heart had broken and he knew that wherever she was, she was feeling the exact same way. He had done everything he could to protect her, to show his love and prove himself worthy, but somehow she'd been taken away.

He'd always known that it was only a matter of time until another would take her place.

It hadn't been hard to find out where she lived. She'd given him her full name and he'd just searched the electoral register.

He'd already been waiting when her colleague dropped her outside the house. He'd watched from across the road as she'd fiddled with her keys to let herself inside.

When he'd seen her and the other woman leave the house, he'd expected them to be gone for longer. Their return had taken him by surprise, but he'd managed to grab a handful of rubbish from her bin, which he would forensically dissect later. Even though he had brushed past her, he was sure she hadn't recognised him, and he was glad. It was too soon.

He hadn't expected the complication of someone else being in her life, but no matter; she wouldn't be around for long and then he'd have her totally to himself.

He put his stolen booty on the dining table and switched on the kettle, relishing the feeling that was growing inside him.

There was no doubt in his mind. He had finally met the love of his life.

TWENTY-ONE

'Everyone have a good night?' Kim asked as her team assembled for the 7 a.m. briefing.

'Cinema,' Penn said. 'New Marvel film.'

'Jasper or Lynne?' Stacey asked.

'Both.'

'I spent the night looking up the various meanings of crystals,' Bryant said.

'Jenny liked it then?' Kim asked.

'Loved it. Apparently, it's amethyst and is known for protection, cleansing and intuition.'

'Maybe you should have left it in the car,' Kim offered.

'Talking of cars,' Stacey said, 'I went on a driving lesson with Devon.'

Three heads turned towards the constable.

Kim broke the silence. 'Sorry, you two, but Stacey is our winner. How'd it go?'

Kim knew Stacey's terror about learning to drive was real and it was growing worse the longer she avoided it.

'If I can drive round in circles in first gear, I'm good to go.'

'Keep at it now you've started,' Kim said.

Stacey nodded.

'Right, anything on David Ford?' she asked.

Stacey shook her head. 'Not a sausage. He's either incredibly clean or very careful. Looks like he and Bettina have been together since high school. He's worked at the same builders' merchants chain since he left college and has been slowly promoted to assistant branch manager. No complaints and no scandal.'

Not exactly what she'd been expecting for a man with such a big mouth, unless he reserved his bullying for his wife alone.

'And Lisa Brown?'

'One conviction for breaking another girl's nose on a night out in Birmingham. The girl barged her out of the way in a bar and came off worse for it. Suspended sentence and community service, which she completed, and no trouble ever since.'

For some reason she wasn't surprised at that result. Lisa's problems weren't what she had done wrong in the past. It was what she'd risked by lying about it. She couldn't imagine that the investors in the building project would be overjoyed at having a convicted offender running the show, although Lisa probably had more to worry about with Catherine knowing her business. Now, if she turned up dead, Kim might be tempted to take a closer look at the project manager.

'Okay, plan for the day. Stace, I want you to go deeper with Father George Markinson so we can rule him out. I'd also really like to know why he can't stay in one place barely longer than the travelling circus. Back off Birch for now. If he's threatening us with harassment, we need something forensic to link him before we speak to him again.'

Stacey looked as though there was something she wanted to add but changed her mind.

'Okay, boss,' she said, looking away.

'You sure?' Kim asked.

'Yep, all good.'

'Sticking with you, Stace, I also want you to dig deeper on Sandra. See who she knows whose name begins with the letter M. Find out about wider family and if there were any issues.'

Stacey nodded.

'Penn, I want you to take that laptop apart looking for potential threats. I've checked and she never reported anything, but if there were any serious threats that frightened her, she would have kept a record somewhere.'

'Got it, boss.'

'Oh, and get your man a name.'

'Will do.'

'And if that wasn't enough, wade in and help Stace with the digging.'

He nodded.

'Okay, now we all know what we're doing, I'll catch you all up from yesterday. What seemed like a light-hearted social event between a group of friends was anything but. They're not friends and I'm not even sure they like each other all that much.

'The whole thing was Catherine's idea because she wanted divine confirmation of her husband's affair and potential leaving date. She wasn't overjoyed with Sandy's confirmation of it. Although I do wonder if she's more worried about custody arrangements for the new kitchen.'

'Sandy really confirmed the affair?' Stacey asked.

'Lucky guess. But all of them had questions they wanted answered. Lisa is facing financial ruin if it gets out about her earlier conviction. Betts is looking for direction, and her husband makes no effort in hiding his hatred of Sandy. Emily is dying and wants comfort, and Rose is apparently looking for love or her dead son, based on who you believe.'

'Got a full house there,' Penn said.

'Of what?' Kim asked.

'Reasons why people go and see psychics: love, money, health and comfort. All the key reasons.'

'Says who?'

'Local author whose book I read a couple of years back. Clever guy, explains all about the psychology of the client, cold reading, lucky guesses and other techniques.'

'What the hell is cold— Never mind, we're getting off track. I'm struggling to believe Sandy was killed cos she gave someone a bad reading.'

'That's a mistake, guv,' Bryant said quietly.

'Go on,' she urged.

'You're minimising people's reasons for going to see a psychic. Their problems might not seem real to you, but they're all-consuming to the person seeking the guidance. Given that level of intensity, who knows what someone might do if they don't get the answers they want.'

'But it's a con,' she argued.

'To you it is because you don't believe, which is why you've never been to see one. But very few people who go to see psychics are doing it to disprove them. They're going because they believe. The psychic is powerful, so it's important what they say and how they say it.'

Kim looked at him. 'You sure you didn't sneak that crystal in your pocket?'

He laughed, and she nodded in his direction to say that he had a good point and she'd taken it on board.

'Okay, guys, let's get cracking. Our murderer isn't going to catch himself.'

TWENTY-TWO

'So who chose last night's film?' Stacey asked, once the boss and Bryant had left the room.

'Both of them,' he said, rolling his eyes. 'Not sure how I feel about how well they get on.'

Stacey knew he was joking and that he was thrilled at the bond between them.

'Lynne and I have even talked about taking it to the next level,' he said, taking the tie from his drawer.

'Marriage?' she asked, eyes wide.

'Bloody hell, Stace, we've only been going out a couple of months. No, I want her to come over more, spend a few nights, just when she wants to, have the run of the house and treat it like her own. I wanna ask her but I can't find the spare key.'

'Get another cut,' Stacey said logically.

He shook his head. 'Nah, can't have spare keys floating about. Might need to change the locks if we can't find it.'

'Penn, do you ever think that your anal retentive...'

'Hey, leave me alone, Stirling.'

'Huh?'

'Stirling Moss?'

'Nope, still not getting it.'

'Way to make me feel old, Stace. One of the greatest racing drivers who ever lived.'

'Oh, okay,' she said, sitting back in her chair. 'Come on, you know what I'm going to ask. Are you a believer in this psychic stuff or not?'

Stacey liked to believe that the boss and Bryant had similar conversations in the car.

He also sat back and twirled a pen in his fingers.

'Keats was trying to discuss the same thing yesterday and the answer is, I dunno really. The realist in me thinks it's a crock of you know what, but there's a part of me that wants it to be true, that there is a mysterious realm and untapped powers. I suppose I'm waiting to be convinced. I'd like to be convinced. How about you?'

'Actually no. I believe half of them know they're talking rubbish and are actively deceiving people and the other half genuinely think they have a gift but they don't.'

'Okay, explain Nostradamus.'

'He wrote everything in riddles,' she countered.

'Quatrains,' he corrected.

'Gobbledygook, which leaves it open to interpretation. I think events have been made to fit the vagueness of his so-called prophecies.'

'You're really very closed off to the possibility, eh?'

'I think it can all be explained,' she said, sitting forward and hitting her keyboard, bringing her screen back to life. 'And on that note, I'm going to dig deeper on Father George Markinson and see why he moves around more often than an army wife.'

Penn followed suit and took his headphones from the drawer.

On her way into work, Stacey had resolved not to mention what had happened once they'd returned from her driving lesson, because right now she couldn't even be sure of what she'd seen.

Shaken up at the time, she had been convinced that she'd recognised the form of Terence Birch, but as the hours had passed, her mind had rationalised it to a random stranger either casing the joint or taking a quick pee around the side of their building. The nagging doubt in her mind would disappear in time, she thought as she grabbed her list of moves for Father Markinson.

The more she looked at it, the more she realised that there was something very wrong with this picture. In some instances, he'd barely had time to unpack before being shunted off to somewhere else.

She decided to search his name connected to some of the local areas. Especially the ones where he'd been for the shortest time.

The first search got a result. She read the newspaper report in the local *Echo*.

'No way,' she said.

Penn took no notice of her outburst, but she could barely believe what she was reading.

During his one-year residency in Bedford, from 2017 to 2018, the Church had received a formal complaint that Father Markinson had flatly refused entry to his church to a same-sex male couple. The young professionals had gone to the press about his conduct.

She went back further, to Norfolk, where he worked from 2009 to 2010. This one was easier to find. A choirboy in his late teens had been discovered molesting his younger sister. It came out that Markinson had received two complaints from younger members of the choir about inappropriate touching, and he had failed to act.

Stacey was aghast at his failures of safeguarding, but she continued to search. Next was Gloucester between the years of

2006 and 2007. This one was harder but Stacey was convinced there was something to be found.

She was right. The article she discovered wasn't about him but his name was mentioned. A fifteen-year-old boy struggling with his gender identity had sought private counsel with the clergyman. After two sessions, the boy had taken his own life with an overdose of paracetamol. That was bad enough – Stacey could only imagine what advice he'd given during those sessions – but most chilling was Father George's statement on hearing the news of the boy's suicide, which had been: 'the boy's fate was God's will and now he's at peace in God's loving arms'.

'Bastard,' Stacey said as she realised that such a bigoted, narrow-minded, intolerant person had no place in the Church. He was a bloody liability.

A thought occurred to her. She searched the incident log and found the number she was after.

Will Deakin answered on the second ring.

'Mr Deakin, it's DC Wood from Halesowen CID. I'm sorry to disturb you at this painful time but we're just trying to tie something up.'

'Of course, Constable. Anything I can do to help.'

'Thank you. Did your wife have any dealings with Father George Markinson at St John's?'

'Unfortunately, yes.'

'Why unfortunately?'

'I'm afraid to say they didn't get along very well. He objected to my wife's gift and labelled her a blasphemer.'

'And they had words about this?'

'Oh, many times, until he took action.'

'What kind of action?'

'He banned her from St John's. He told her that if she ever set foot in the church, he would physically remove her himself.'

TWENTY-THREE

Kim hadn't expected to be visiting the Oldswinford home of Rose Foster after their conversation at Emily's shop, but she was intrigued to know why the woman hadn't told them the truth about her son's death.

The woman opened the door wearing joggers and a T-shirt. Her brown hair was wet after a recent shower.

'Come in – I've been expecting you.'

'Don't tell me, Catherine posted in the WhatsApp.'

'Not specifically,' Rose said, guiding them into the lounge. 'She just posted that we were all a bunch of bitches for pointing the finger at her and making her look bad. She's finding another yoga class and she's left the group.'

Rose didn't seem particularly heartbroken about it.

'May we?' Kim asked, pointing to the sofa.

'Of course. I'm not due at work for a couple of hours and I'm happy to answer whatever you want to know.'

'Why did you lie?'

'I didn't,' Rose said, sitting on the sofa but at the edge of the cushion.

Kim found herself doing the same thing. This wasn't going to be a long visit.

Rose folded her hands together and placed them in her lap. 'I just didn't tell you the whole truth. I would like to find someone to share my life with. Yes, my son was kidnapped and murdered ten years ago. Did a part of me wonder if there was something in it?' She shrugged. 'Maybe. But I wasn't overly surprised that she gave me a reading I could get from a decent horoscope.'

'I'm still not sure why you didn't mention it,' Kim pushed.

'You wanted to ask me about Sandy and the events of Thursday night. I don't find a way to insert the most painful part of my life into every conversation I have. Do you?'

Kim took her point.

'What happened to your son?'

Rose sighed heavily. 'It was a normal morning. He was riding to school with his friend. Brad, my son, was ahead. They often raced through the woods. By the time Josh caught up to where Brad should have been waiting, a white transit van was pulling away at speed. Poor Josh had no clue what had happened and thought Brad had just carried on racing. He didn't raise the alarm until he went into first class and realised Brad had never made it to school. He remembered the white van and told his teacher, almost half an hour after Brad had been taken.'

Kim remembered hearing about it now. She'd been stationed in Digbeth, Birmingham at the time. She remembered the photo that had been passed around for observations.

'I kept the hope alive for a year, until they found most of his clothing in a secluded area on Cannock Chase. Police dug up a couple of mounds but they never found him.'

Kim noticed that Rose's voice had grown quieter.

'I was told by the detective chief inspector that they had

concluded that Brad was no longer alive, and that he was likely buried somewhere on Cannock Chase, but obviously...'

Kim understood. She knew that the Chase was famous for the bodies of three young girls found in the late sixties. She also knew it covered 26 square miles, making it impossible to search for a body.

'It took a while but I finally accepted that he was dead. Of course there's no closure without his body.'

'Of course,' Kim said, feeling sorry for stirring up her pain. It was as though they were speaking to a different woman than the one who had answered the door. She had fallen back against the cushion, and her hands were rubbing her upper arms in what Kim knew to be a self-comforting gesture.

'We're sorry for your loss, and we appreciate you being honest with us.'

'Not sure it'll help Sandy, but it is what it is.'

Kim headed for the door and sighed heavily when it closed softly behind them.

'Jesus, Bryant, can you even imagine not having the remains...'

'Don't do it, guv,' he said, unlocking the car.

'What?' she asked innocently.

'It's not our case. It was never our case and we've got no business meddling. You can't solve everything. You've already got Penn following up on some John Doe that Keats got you riled up about. We have our own murder to solve and now you want to give this woman her son's body to bury.'

'You're right,' she said, putting on her seat belt.

'I am?'

'Absolutely,' she said as her phone began to ring. 'Go ahead, Stace.'

'Father Markinson, boss – he's a bigoted, judgemental, authoritarian scumbag excuse for a human.'

'Okay, thanks for that,' Kim said, putting her on loudspeaker.

'And I think he's worth a visit.'

'Go on,' Kim said. The constable's task had been to rule him out of the investigation.

She listened with a growing sense of outrage as Stacey listed his placements and what appeared to be the reasons for his many transfers.

'Okay, so he's also intolerant but why does that make him interesting to us?'

'He and Sandy had words a couple of times. He'd actually banned Sandy from the church.'

'What?' Kim asked. She didn't know they could do that. Wasn't God's house always open?

'Hang on, there's more. Mavis the cleaning lady witnessed him pushing her forcefully out the door.'

He'd actually put his hands on her. That altered things as far as she was concerned.

'Okay, Stace, we're on our way,' she said as Bryant pulled away from the kerb. 'Oh, and while I've got you, do me a favour when you get a minute – pull the files on Bradley Foster, fifteen-year-old abducted and killed ten years ago.'

Bryant groaned beside her.

'Will do, boss,' Stacey said, then ended the call.

'What?' she said to her colleague, who was shaking his head.

'I thought you said I was right.'

'You are. Still doesn't mean I'm gonna listen.'

TWENTY-FOUR

Penn had searched Sandy's laptop with a fine-tooth comb.

In the deleted file of her emails he'd found a few rude and insulting messages that went back a year or so.

Most were complaints about her stage show and not having been chosen for a reading. A few called her a fraud for not having picked up on their dead relative, or for not doing a longer show to give them a chance to come through, as though it were a supermarket and the spirits were just waiting in line to be served.

None of the messages, while rude, were threatening or aggressive. None were repeated and none were responded to. They were just ordinary complaints from dissatisfied customers, which were far outweighed by the messages of support and gratitude.

So would she have filed more sinister messages in the same place? he wondered.

He had done a keyword search of her whole computer hard drive using words like 'kill', 'murder', 'stab', 'death' and even 'hate', but he'd found nothing.

Her email system was broken down into many sub categories from the inbox, and then further sub categories from those. He had no choice but to examine every one. In the absence of a file marked 'death threats', he had very little choice.

He'd followed a line of sub folders originating from household bills through all utilities until he came to a folder marked 'misc'. From what he'd seen, there was nothing left to be filed under a cover-all category.

He clicked in and a list of more than twenty emails filled the screen.

'Got it,' he said.

'Got what?' Stacey repeated.

'Emails, threats,' he said, scrolling to the bottom of the list. 'First one was sent almost two years ago, all from the same email address.'

He opened the first one and read it out loud.

'"You are disgusting. You are a manipulator and a liar. Stop taking people's money and get a real job."'

'Okay, not nice,' Stacey said. 'But probably not uncommon in her line of work.'

Penn agreed, so why had she kept them all?

He worked his way up the timeline and noticed something as he went.

First of all, this person hadn't just sent a nasty email and then forgotten about it. They had made a concerted effort to share their thoughts regularly over a couple of years. Sandra had ignored the messages, but the sender hadn't got bored and gone away. If anything, the lack of response had fuelled their fire.

The final message received just ten days earlier was a little different.

'Stace, listen to this one,' Penn said. '"You are a repulsive creature still taking money and defrauding people. You are a user and a repugnant slug that should never have been born. You have no ability so that makes you a thief. You are targeting people at their most vulnerable times and making money out of it. I hate you and you need to just die a long and painful death so you can feel the suffering you inflict on other people. Enjoy your time, Mrs Deakin, because you don't have much of it left.'''

Stacey frowned. 'Same person?'

'Oh yeah.'

'Bloody hell.'

Yes, his thoughts exactly. Although the messages had begun quite tame, they had become progressively more menacing and finally led to full-on death threats.

There was no question in Penn's mind that the author of these messages had seriously wanted Sandra Deakin dead.

TWENTY-FIVE

'You're not going to treat him like a suspect, are you, guv?' Bryant asked, parking the car outside St John's Church.

Two squad cars and a forensics van were still in attendance.

'Why do you get antsy when we speak to anyone in authority?'

'Well, see, there's this story about a china shop and a bull...'

'I'm going to treat him no differently to anyone else,' she said, ducking under the cordon tape.

'That's what worries me.'

'You think he should be treated differently?' she asked.

Bryant shrugged with a pained look on his face. 'He's a man of the cloth, a man of God. Surely that deserves some kind of... I dunno... respect,' he said as she headed up the path towards the church entrance.

She was saved from replying when Father Markinson met them at the door.

'Ah, Officer, I assume you've come to give me my church back?'

'It's Inspector and I'm afraid that's a little premature, until the forensic technicians advise accordingly.'

He looked beyond her, and she tried to quell her immediate dislike of the man. In him she sensed an entitlement, an expectation of obedience, an obvious reverence for his position, as though he viewed everyone as his inferior. She tried to shake away the thoughts. She hadn't spent enough time with him to make those judgements.

'It's quite inconvenient, you see. The church needs to be open to the community, especially now when everyone is feeling vulnerable and frightened. The church and the comfort it offers needs to be available to everyone.'

'If the archbishop himself wanted to visit, it'd be a no. But not everyone is welcome to enjoy the comfort of the church, are they, Father George?'

Sensing he was getting nowhere with his pleas, his expression changed from irritation to tolerance.

'If you're referring to Sandra then I assume you've heard about our disagreement,' he said, making no attempt to invite them inside. Clearly this church was not open to everyone. Only the people admitted by its caretaker.

'We have. Would you like to elaborate?' she offered, waiting to see the emergence of discomfort, even shame, at having been caught refusing someone access to the house of God.

'Absolutely. I asked her not to attend this church any more.'

'You banned her?' Kim clarified, seeing no remorse on his face.

'This isn't some council-estate pub where people are barred for unruly behaviour. She was asked not to attend because of the effect she had on the congregation.'

'And she obliged?' Kim asked.

'Not initially, no.'

'Not until you physically removed her from the premises?' she asked, tipping her head. He'd made no mention of physically engaging with Sandra.

'Where I'm from we call it gentle persuasion.'

'Where I'm from we call it assault,' Kim said.

His face hardened. 'You're being ridiculous. I simply placed my hands on her upper arms and guided her towards the door. Hardly assault,' he scoffed.

'If she'd made a complaint, that would have been decided in court, but as she didn't, I'll have to be content with your explanation as to why you felt it necessary to physically remove her.'

'She was unsettling,' he answered.

'Unsettling how?' Kim asked.

'Inspector, there is no such thing as communicating with the dead or foreseeing the future. The spirit leaves the body and is delivered into God's safe hands. There is no wish or need to try to continue life on earth. Only God can foresee events in His great plan, so any claim to be able to do such things is pure blasphemy.'

Kim chose not to mention that religion on a whole was based on belief in something that you can't see. She knew there was no point sharing her thoughts on his faith. She only wanted to know how his convictions related to one person.

'Do you not believe in forgiveness and acceptance? You think God would approve of your actions?'

'I absolutely do. Not only was she peddling lies but she was charging money to intrude on people's grief and misery.'

'Okay, I understand the difference of opinion between you and Sandra Deakin, but I'm sure your opinions differ with those of your congregation on many things. I'd like to understand what was unsettling about her presence. Did she do readings in the middle of your service?'

'Of course not.'

'Did she actively disrupt any other church activity?'

He shook his head.

'Father George, you're going to have to help me out. What exactly did she do?'

'Her presence upset many members of the congregation.'

'Written complaints?'

'No. Unease doesn't have to be formalised.'

'Surely it does for action to be taken. Quite frankly, people eating anything with horseradish makes me uneasy, but I wouldn't ask for them to be banned from Starbucks.'

She felt rather than heard Bryant's groan beside her. Father George was oblivious and all his attention was on her.

'Inspector, you're trivialising the effect of her presence on the good people of—'

'Okay, fair enough,' she conceded. 'Give me the names of the people she offended and I'll have a quick chat with them directly.'

Bryant took out his notebook and they both waited.

'I'm not going to share—'

'Father, I don't think there's anything to share. I believe your decision to exclude Sandra Deakin from the church was a personal choice based on your own prejudices about her career choice.'

'Inspector, that is absolute—'

'Is it? It's not the first time you've granted yourself divine right to judge who the good people actually are.'

He said nothing.

'Your perpetual move from parish to parish appears to coincide with questionable decisions made in relation to the not-so-good people of your congregation.'

'I do God's work, Inspector.'

'Even if the Church has moved on and views things differently?' she pushed.

'The Church buckled under pressure and popular demand. God did not, and I continue to follow the teachings of—'

He stopped speaking as her phone rang from her back pocket.

The caller was Keats.

Shit.

She stepped away.

'Stone,' she answered.

'Bridge House, Waterfront. Be quick.'

The line went dead.

'Bryant, we gotta go.'

He nodded his understanding.

'Sorry we have to cut this short, Father George,' he said. Bryant was ever the professional with enough good manners for them both. 'Because,' he continued, 'I was looking forward to the part where I got to say that you do not represent any God in which I believe.'

Kim hid her smile as she and her colleague headed back to the car. There was no time to express her pride in him.

A call like that from Keats could only mean one thing.

They had another victim.

TWENTY-SIX

'Well?' Stacey asked, when Penn returned from the canteen with snacks.

'Lemon meringue is all gone.'

'Penn,' she pushed. He'd been sent to the canteen to find out what the boss was heading towards. Although she wasn't going to turn down the piece of fudge cake he'd put on her desk.

'Not getting a lot of detail from uniforms. Been told I should keep the radio on.'

Although they weren't obliged to carry a walkie talkie, most stations managed to free up a couple of hand-held units for the CID team. Bryant was pretty good at keeping one around but not while they were interviewing.

'Didn't the boss say anything?'

Stacey's one trip to the loo had meant Penn took the call.

'Only that Keats had called and they were on their way to Bridge House, Waterfront. I barely managed to tell her I'd found the threats on Sandy's computer.'

'Jeez, Penn, you couldn't have interrogated her a bit more?'

'Firstly, no, cos she's the boss, and secondly, you know when she's done talking and that weird thing happens when—'

'The line goes dead,' she finished for him. 'Okay, fair enough, but bloody hell, Penn, I'm dying here.'

'Best just crack on and wait until we're needed then, eh, which for me is going through the missing persons reports to identify our John Doe.'

Stacey watched as he gathered up all the paperwork relating to other tasks he'd completed into neat piles. He always did this before starting a new task, as though the act was a refresh button on his mind.

She continued her own task of finding out as much about Sandra Deakin as she could, which included a lot of trawling.

She opened her mouth to speak to her colleague, but he'd already donned his headphones.

Despite the string of emails from one particular person, Stacey wasn't finding a whole lot of negative press about the woman. There were no forums discussing her abilities or labelling her a swindler or fraud. There was nothing overly positive either. Although she'd done a few shows at small venues, she seemed to favour the dinner-party environment and one-on-one readings. She'd appeared on local TV and radio, but her reach didn't appear to stretch beyond the borders of the Black Country.

Her website wasn't sensationalised, nor did it make extravagant promises. On TripAdvisor the shows got a rating of 4.4 or higher. Stacey had read all of the negative comments, which ranged from Sandy not being on stage long enough to poor seating to having trouble hearing some of her comments, but there was nothing vicious or threatening. Most people who had attended her shows had enjoyed the experience. And, so far, she hadn't come across anything to connect Sandra to anyone with a name beginning with M.

The articles containing anything to do with Sandy were growing more and more sparse as she scrolled through the

Google search. There were articles about other Sandras and other Deakins but very few that now contained both names.

'Hang on,' she said as she almost scrolled past an archived article printed in the *Daily Mail* almost eighteen months earlier.

She clicked in and started reading.

Within seconds her mouth had fallen open. It was a hit piece exposing all so-called bargain-basement psychics.

The article laid into every psychic she'd ever heard of and a few that she hadn't. Derek Acorah, Colin Fry, Sally Morgan, Sandra Deakin and a couple of others got a roasting. The article was savage and called for the general public to boycott these charlatans. The piece was vicious and went low in places, alleging family collaboration and knowledge of perpetrated fraud. The tone and the content read as though the author had rolled out of bed in the bitchiest mood imaginable and had put pen to paper before even a sip of coffee had passed their lips.

Stacey scrolled to the end of the lengthy article.

The author was named as Monty Dunhill, a self-proclaimed psychic to the stars.

Seemed to her that the only psychic Monty Dunhill had any respect for was himself.

TWENTY-SEVEN

Bridge House was a modern four-storey building at the heart of the Waterfront commercial area of Brierley Hill, built on both sides of the Dudley No. 1 canal.

Kim showed her ID to two security checkpoints before she reached the police cordon.

It was an officer that knew them, and he lifted the tape on seeing the car.

Bryant parked behind the waiting ambulance. They both jumped out of the car and pretty much sprinted around the L-shaped raised flower beds to the group gathered at the corner of the building.

Keats appeared to her left.

'Same killer?' she asked before setting eyes on the body.

'Your job not mine,' he said. 'But the manner of death is definitely the same, as is the calling card.'

Kim groaned as she turned to where the majority of the group had moved away.

'Jesus Christ,' she said, seeing all the blood that had pooled around the victim.

A woman to the left gave a loud cry as the body became visible again.

'His boss,' Keats offered. 'She found him.'

'Can someone get her out of eye line?' she snapped. Bloody hell. It was a sight the woman was never going to forget, but she didn't need to be reminded.

Bryant immediately headed over to the police officers and the witness.

'Good God,' she said, working hard to keep out of the blood pools.

'How old?'

'Nineteen,' Keats offered.

He looked barely that. She guessed him to be of Indian descent. He was of a slim build and wore black trousers and a mustard polo shirt.

'Azim Mahmood,' Keats offered. 'It's on the lanyard we've already removed. His name was the only thing visible. We'll let you know more once we've cleaned it up.'

'He worked here?' she asked, nodding towards the building.

'Second floor,' Keats confirmed.

Kim took a look around the immediate area. It was a bin store and what looked to be the unofficial smoking area. She could see one CCTV camera that was pointing the other way. This was a dark corner, completely out of sight, and the intention was to avoid the camera. She knew the uniforms would already be requesting a CCTV check from the control room.

'Number of wounds?' she asked, looking back at the victim, who appeared to be growing younger by the minute. He was little more than a child.

'Nine, I think. I'll let you know for certain once I get him back. Less stabs but more violent by the looks of it.'

Judging by the amount of blood, she thought so too. Just like Sandra, Azim's hands were covered in blood where he had clutched his wounds. A couple of light nicks of the blade had caught his right forearm, indicating that he had tried to fight back. And exactly like Sandra, his mouth had been slashed into a gaping hole across his face. The rage was growing inside her. There was no such thing as a good victim but this was a lad barely out of school.

What the hell could he have done to have deserved this?

'Only turned nineteen last week, guv,' Bryant said, appearing beside her with his notebook open.

Seemed to her they'd gone down the wrong line with Sandra's work and her murder had nothing to do with her being a psychic at all. This boy had either been attacked by a random knife bandit who was killing indiscriminately, or they were linked for some other reason.

'Sergeant Lewis has been despatched to inform the parents. Address supplied by the boy's boss over there,' Bryant said.

'Who would want this kid dead?' Kim asked, struggling to make sense of it.

'He's a decent guy, guv, according to his boss. He's respectful, polite, hard-working. He'd finished working a night shift and was having a smoke before getting in the car; his brother's car. Family doesn't know he smokes.'

'What time did he finish?'

'Seven this morning. His day shift boss came over here for a mid-morning cig and discovered him. She's in a pretty bad way and not a speck of blood on her.'

Looking at the scene before her, Kim knew that was a total impossibility if she'd had anything to do with it.

'Jeez, Bryant, why?' she asked, shaking her head.

'Well, guv, it might be linked to his job. Azim worked on the second floor. It's a call centre.'

'And?' she asked, waiting for the punchline.

'It's a hotline,' he explained. 'A psychic hotline.'

TWENTY-EIGHT

It was twenty minutes later that Kim and Bryant mounted the steps to the second floor of Bridge House and the premises of the psychic hotline. They'd given Azim's manager a little time to get herself together before asking her any further questions.

A petite blonde woman was waiting to keycode them in to the office space.

'I'm Helen Leonard. Marina's out back and not really in any fit state to talk. Her husband is on his way to pick her up. I hope that's okay.'

Bryant had made sure they had her details for any follow-up, but Kim didn't think the woman had witnessed anything that would help them. The killer had been long gone when she'd discovered Azim's body. This conversation was to establish if they could identify the young man's killer another way. Although she didn't want to be talking to someone who knew Azim only as a person at a desk.

'You knew Azim well?'

She nodded. 'I was his direct supervisor for almost a year before my promotion.'

'That's fine,' Kim said.

'Do you mind if we talk here?' Helen asked, guiding them over to a horseshoe-shaped sofa placed around a couple of coffee tables. 'Everyone is unsettled enough without me walking you through.'

Kim nodded her agreement and took a seat which gave her a full view of the phone floor.

She could see five rows with seven or eight desks to each row. Less than half seemed to be occupied.

'Our quiet time,' Helen said, following her gaze.

'There's a busy time?' Bryant asked.

Helen nodded. 'We get busier throughout the day and then we're fully staffed by 8 p.m. for the peak hours of nine until two in the morning.'

'That late?' Kim asked.

'Yes, callers have had a drink or two, partners are in bed, it's a long and lonely time of the night. A time when we all tend to evaluate our lives.'

'And they call a psychic hotline?' Kim queried.

'Most are seeking comfort, reassurance.'

'For an extortionate rate per minute,' she said before she could stop herself. Kim couldn't help but think it cost nothing at all to call the Samaritans.

'We're a business,' Helen said, with a slight edge in her tone. 'We're providing a service.'

'But you're not really though, are you?' Kim asked. She had no problem with an exchange of goods for money, even high-priced ones. If anyone knew what she'd recently paid for an authentic Vincent Black Shadow carburettor, they'd think she'd lost her mind, but it was a genuine part that was now in her hand. 'You've not got real psychics on the end of every phone line?'

'We give comfort and reassurance and ensure we don't say anything that can negatively impact the caller.'

Kim marvelled at the human capacity for justification.

Helen shifted uncomfortably. 'Is this what you wanted to talk about?'

It wasn't.

'Would you have been made aware if Azim had taken a bad phone call?' she asked.

'Every phone call is recorded.'

Kim felt a surge of hope. 'So if Azim had a hostile caller, it would be saved somewhere.'

'Of course.'

'Did he make you aware of any such call, of any threats or aggression?'

Helen shook her head.

'Do your callers have to identify themselves?'

'Our operatives only know the caller by their first name, and they give a false first name so it's unlikely that Azim was specifically targeted.'

'But there's a chance that one of your people spoke to someone who became irate and...'

'Of course, but you have to understand that the calls don't come locally. Callers ring a national line, and the calls are farmed out to call centres like this around the country. At any one time there's in excess of two hundred people taking an average of three calls per hour, more than that for the peak hours I've already mentioned.'

Kim's quick calculation told her that was more than fourteen thousand calls per day. There was no way they could investigate on that scale. Her mind tried to find alternatives.

Okay, maybe the calls couldn't be interrogated, but perhaps there was another way, she thought as she heard the low hum of voices speaking into headsets as work on the call floor restarted. She supposed business didn't stand still for long.

'But these callers have to register payment details: debit cards, bank accounts?' she asked, pulling herself back.

'Payment information and personal details are kept in a

separate database at headquarters, in Leeds. We don't have access from this office.'

'But we could search them?' Kim asked with a growing excitement.

'With a court order you could certainly search the payment details of almost two hundred thousand people, especially if you knew what you were looking for.'

The futility of that exercise hit her like a wrecking ball.

Kim had no doubt that their killer was in there somewhere, but with those kinds of numbers, she had no choice but to accept that this was not how they were going to find them.

TWENTY-NINE

Penn had removed the headphones just long enough to wolf down the sandwich Stacey had generously shouted him for lunch. It wasn't that he hadn't wanted something warm like the cottage pie his colleague had eaten, but he needed something quick that he could eat while continuing to work.

He had a lot to thank John Montagu, the 4th Earl of Sandwich for, except the earl had wanted a hand free to continue gambling, instead of trying to identify a John Doe. Although, he could see the irony that the man he was seeking had liked a bet or two.

Jericho had told him that Dan had appeared approximately two years ago, so he'd worked chronologically backwards from around eighteen months. So far he'd ruled out more than twenty possibilities.

'Next,' he said to himself as he clicked to the next record. He stared at the screen. 'Shut the front door.'

Stacey looked up.

He dropped the headphones on the desk. 'I think I've got my man.'

Stacey got up and came around to look over his shoulder.

He took out his phone and scrolled to the photo he'd shown Jericho.

Stacey took a look with him.

'Oh yeah,' she said, returning to her desk. 'That's your guy.'

Penn studied the two photos and saw very little had changed. Yes, the man's skin looked a little more weathered, he had stubble, the circles beneath his eyes were a little darker and there was just a shade more salt and a bit less pepper in the hair. Penn had once been told that you age at twice the rate on the streets. He wasn't sure if he believed it and definitely not in the case of Barry Sharpe, he thought as he was finally able to give John Doe a name.

Penn hadn't been far off in the age department. Sharpe had been fifty-four years of age when he went missing.

'It's not a long report though,' Penn said, in case Stacey was still interested.

She waved her arm to indicate she'd moved on, and he supposed he'd be able to do the same soon.

He read the report and learned that Barry had gone missing twenty-two months earlier. The report had been made by his wife, who hadn't registered him missing until five days after he'd last been seen. A bit strange, but if he'd been working away it could have been unclear when the last sighting had actually been. His job as regional operations manager for one of the top fuel suppliers may well have taken him on the road.

The report filed by Janice Sharpe, his wife, only contained the bare minimum of facts: visual description, age, dates and times. Further investigation by the officers had turned up nothing in addition, but judging from the thickness of the report, he wasn't sure how hard they'd tried. There were no rumours of affairs and all had been well the last time his wife had seen him. His love of gambling had been mentioned a couple of times, and his details had been logged with all the local bookies and casinos. All of whom he was known to.

The more he read, the deeper he felt the frown forming on his face. Something wasn't adding up. A prolific gambler didn't just stop like that, unless he'd received some kind of specialised treatment. The fact he'd still been trying to bet on anything that moved until his death said the treatment, if received, had not worked.

He scrolled through the sparse information again, and something else struck him. His wife had given the leanest of information and there were no follow-up logs. No further calls or visits from his wife chasing progress, wanting updates. In his experience that was virtually unheard of.

It was almost like she'd reported him missing because she had to.

He shrugged the thoughts away. He had an identity for the man and all that was left was to inform the family.

And then his work on this case was done. He was sure of it.

THIRTY

The news of her son's murder was barely an hour old when Azim's mother opened the door to them. Her eyes were red and bloodshot, and Kim could hear crying from beyond the door.

The woman stepped aside for them to enter and pointed to a door on the left. Two girls were seated on the sofa. Their hands met across the divide that Kim guessed had been occupied by their mother prior to answering the door.

The room appeared to have been two reception rooms now knocked into one large lounge, with an archway into the kitchen. A dining table bridged the gap between the two spaces, which looked as though it doubled as a workspace for the family; a laptop at one end and textbooks at the other. Kim nodded at the two girls. She guessed one to be mid-teens and the other early twenties.

Mrs Mahmood re-took her seat on the sofa. Both of her daughters immediately clasped one of her hands and held on tightly.

'We are desperately sorry for your loss, Mrs Mahmood,' Kim offered, taking a seat on the single chair. Bryant lowered himself onto a foot stool to the right of her.

'Meera, please,' she said. 'This is Navi and Satya,' she added, pointing to the older and then the younger sister. Meera's orange and red sari was a splash of colour between her daughters' Western wear of jeans and T-shirts.

'He's a good boy,' Meera said. 'A nice boy,' she repeated, clutching her sari and touching her forehead with the fabric as though it would ease her pain. 'Who would do this?'

'We don't know, Meera. His colleagues have nothing but good to say about Azim.'

'Then why?' she howled.

Navi, the oldest daughter, pulled her mother close but spoke to Kim. 'He never hurt anyone.'

'We don't believe he did,' Kim said. 'We believe it may be connected to his job.'

Meera pulled away from Navi and looked at Kim in horror, obviously wondering how something as trivial as his job could lead to his death. How could she possibly have lost one of her children because of what he did for a living?

'He hated that job,' Satya whispered, before burying her face in her mother's arm.

Navi nodded her agreement. 'He was only doing it because of his trip.'

'Trip?' Kim asked.

'My brother was saving for a month-long visit to India. My mother and father came to England when Rishi, our older brother, was two. Azim had never been. He worked the night shifts because they paid more money so he could go sooner.'

'Why did he hate it?' Bryant asked.

'He felt bad for some of the people that called in. The call handlers had instruction lists, predictions to follow, what to say. There were different variations depending on the sex and approximate age of the caller. Azim said many of the callers were desperate people. Heartbroken people looking for comfort, reassurance and for someone to listen. Regardless of the reason for the call, the aim was always the same – keep the caller on the line for as long as possible. Azim got told off a couple of times for not stretching calls.'

'Did he ever mention any specific incidents where someone got irate with him?'

'Sometimes,' Navi answered. 'But the operators were never identifiable.'

'He was driving his brother's car?' Kim asked.

'Azim couldn't afford his own car yet,' Navi explained. 'Rishi is on holiday so doesn't need it.'

'And he doesn't mind his brother using it while he's away?'

Navi managed a smile. 'In our culture we view possessions more communally. Although it belongs to Rishi, he has no use for it while he's out of the country. It would not sit idle in the street when other family members have no transport.'

'So it's like a pool car?'

'I suppose so but we know no other way.'

With no further questions, Kim didn't want to intrude on this family's grief any longer.

'Meera, a family liaison officer is being appointed to assist—'

'No strangers please,' she said, shaking her head. 'We have each other,' she added, squeezing her daughters' hands.

Kim nodded her acceptance of their request. She was guessing that there was no longer a Mr Mahmood senior, as there had been no reference to him. It was understandable that the woman didn't want strangers traipsing in and out of her home.

'Is Rishi contactable?' Kim asked.

Navi nodded. 'He will be home this evening.'

'We'll contact you tomorrow about identifying Azim.'

Navi stood to see them out. Her puzzlement turned to understanding. Kim had deliberately avoided using the word body, and the delay would give them time for the horror to sink in and to decide who was best able to carry out the unenviable task.

As Navi gently closed the door behind them, Kim felt as though the grief of the family had attached itself to every fibre of her being.

She couldn't give them Azim back, but with every breath in her body, she wanted to give them justice.

THIRTY-ONE

Not one word had passed between her and Bryant since they'd got back in the car.

Stacey had sent her the link to the article written by Monty Dunhill that mentioned Sandra Deakin, along with his address in Bromsgrove, but she hadn't yet even looked at it.

Still on her mind was the image of Meera Mahmood, surrounded by her daughters as they tried to come to terms with their loss.

'Need to get prepared, guv,' Bryant said as they approached a traffic island.

She accepted the prompt and took out her phone. She read the article that Stacey had included.

'Bloody hell, this guy doesn't pull any punches,' she said, bringing both herself and Bryant back to the investigation. 'This article is filled with contempt for what he calls the frauds and charlatans that give genuine sensitives a bad name. Wanna guess what he does for a living?'

'If I say psychic does that make me gifted too?'

'Probably more lucky than gifted. But yes, you are correct.'

'Do you think Monty Dunhill is the M in Sandra's diary?'

'Not sure, but the fact he's written an article with such venom, and that our first victim's name is in said article, makes him worth talking to,' she said as Bryant started to slow the car.

He turned onto a redbrick drive of a detached property on Herbert Austin Drive in the Marlbrook area of the district. Properties on the Lord Austin Estate sold for upwards of a million and enjoyed exclusive access to the communal 26 acres of land, tennis courts, six-tee golf course and children's adventure playground.

'Guv, we are definitely in the wrong business,' Bryant said, guiding the car to a stop outside one of the bay windows.

A man opened the front door dressed in sky-blue trousers, white shirt, dickie bow and white deck shoes. His hair was jet black but the smattering of grey in his moustache wasn't in agreement.

He was flanked by two Great Danes that reached his waist.

'Mr Dunhill?' she asked, taking out her ID.

'I am he – please come in,' he said, taking only a cursory glance at her warrant card.

The dogs faithfully followed their owner into the lounge, a formal space fashioned of dark wood and variations of cream furnishings.

Kim sat where he had pointed, which gave her a clear view of his photo wall.

Each photo was exactly the same size, all in gold frames and hung in a grid-type pattern.

He watched her eagerly. Waiting for her to acknowledge his wall of fame.

She turned towards him. 'Mr Dunhill, we're here to talk about Sandra Deakin.'

Disappointment and then irritation flitted across his face. Kim guessed immediately this was a man that liked to be feted, admired, envied. Unfortunately, she had never been impressed by celebrities. They had no bearing on her life or her job.

'Well of course you are,' he said, recovering quickly as a Great Dane placed itself at his feet. The other lay in front of the fire. 'I wouldn't be much of a psychic if I hadn't been expecting that.'

'Quite,' Kim said, unsure what supernatural ability was needed given they were in the same profession and therefore it was fair to assume their paths might have crossed.

'You wrote quite a scathing article a while back. Her name was mentioned.'

'And I stand by that. Dead or alive makes no difference to the fact she was a fraud.'

Kim said nothing.

He continued. 'Please let me be clear: I despise people who make a laughing stock of our profession. They invite the doubters and the sceptics, who then come sniffing round us all for a scandal to fill their seedy little newspapers and clickbait articles. These charlatans give us all a bad name, doing these stage shows and television programmes. It makes a mockery of those of us with a genuine gift. Real psychics don't whore themselves out for after-dinner entertainment.'

'I'll assume you feel the same way about phone psychics?' she asked.

'They are the soil on which the worms slither, Inspector. There is no worse kind of fraud than the people behind a psychic hotline.'

'And you're different?'

'Oh please. I'm sure I don't have to explain the difference between steak tartare and a carnival hamburger. You can see for yourself the calibre of clientele that I work for,' he said, nodding towards his wall of fame.

'I'm sorry but I don't know who those people are,' she said, almost honestly. A couple of faces were vaguely familiar, but she couldn't have put a name to them if she was being held at gunpoint.

His face showed his displeasure at her lack of deference and awe.

'Inspector, you may not know it but there are some very important people there; elegant, sophisticated, educated people who want genuine guidance through the obstacles of their lives, not members of the great unwashed who want next week's lottery numbers. Real psychics don't do tawdry stage shows. They have no wish to try and entertain. They wish only to offer guidance and reassurance.'

To people who can afford it, she almost tagged on to the end.

'So you place yourself in a different class to other psychics?' she asked.

'Only the fraudulent ones.'

'But your gift is genuine?'

'Absolutely, Inspector. I had a terrible fall as a child. I was seven years old, and for a few minutes I actually died. I could see myself on the ground; my parents running towards me. There was panic, screaming, chaos, emotion. I felt nothing. I was serene, floating; more at peace than I'd ever been. It's a tough one to explain if you've never been through it.'

She had but she hadn't experienced anything like that.

'Go on,' Kim urged.

'The next thing I recalled was regaining consciousness. My first emotion was pure disappointment. Then I became aware of hushed voices talking around my bed. Lots of them. The voices grew louder. The content was no clearer but the volume increased. I opened my eyes and the room was empty. Except I could still hear the voices.'

'Must have been frightening for a young boy,' Bryant said.

'It was, but more frightening was the reaction of my parents and the doctors when I told them. It was eventually concluded that it was a temporary state due to my having died for a while, and the matter was never discussed again.'

'You never told your parents you could still hear voices?' she asked. Truthfully, she didn't believe it, but she felt that he believed it.

'No. I could tell that the very subject scared my mother to death. So I secretly learned how to tune out the noise, to hear past the crowd and focus on one single voice at a time. I realised that communicating their wishes was what I was born to do.'

'Okay, but how do you know that Sandra didn't possess that same gift?'

'Firstly because she's dead and she should have seen that coming.'

'And secondly?' Kim prompted.

'Because I tested her,' he answered.

'You did what?'

'I got the idea from an American woman who carries out stings on fraudulent psychics.'

'How?'

'I had a friend of mine, let's call her Jayne, set up a fake profile on social media. She filled it with a false life of two grown-up boys and a husband to whom she'd been married for twenty-seven years. Jayne joined a couple of diabetes groups, liked some poetry appreciation pages and listed academic credentials. Once the profile had been running a few months and Jayne had a few friends, she rang Psychic Sandy and arranged a consultation. The money was taken for the session around ten minutes before it started.'

'And?' Kim asked. She had to hand it to him and his skill in setting a scene. She was now invested.

'Everything Sandy said was aimed at the personality of the fake profile. Her first stab was that she was sensing loneliness. Decoy Jayne's youngest child had just gone off to university. Real Jayne has no children and has never wanted them. She has more friends than Mark Zuckerberg and is definitely not lonely.

'She spoke of Jayne's literary interest. Real Jayne couldn't form a five-line limerick. Next, Psychic Sandy expressed concern for her health. She even took a stab at something to do with sugar levels that might need checking. She told Jayne that she saw travel in her future and bright lights. Decoy Jayne had shown interest in a resident show in Vegas. Real Jayne holidays on a beach in Turkey. Her insights focussed on a thirst for knowledge and self-improvement. Real Jayne likes to read the trashiest romance novels she can find.'

Kim waited for more, and Bryant's expression told her that he was equally entranced.

'Those are the highlights, but suffice to say she picked up not one link to the real Jayne and only drew from the personality that had been fabricated.'

'Did you share this with Sandy?'

He nodded. 'I did, and I advised her to cease trading or I would expose her deceit.'

'And?'

'She asked to meet to discuss it, begged me not to publish anything until she'd explained.'

'Did you meet her?'

'No. We made a few arrangements but things would come up, so I had to cancel a couple of times.'

Kim had counted four broken appointments. She suspected he'd enjoyed the power he'd wielded; the influence over Sandy's career. He had dangled her on a string for his own amusement and ego.

'You had a meeting planned last week,' Kim noted.

'Did we? Oh, something must have come up. I certainly wasn't able to make it,' he said, inspecting his nails.

'So, if you're the genuine article, why don't you read for me now?' Bryant asked.

'Because I'm not a trained monkey at your beck and call. And anyway, I suspect that you couldn't afford me.'

'You may be wrong,' Bryant challenged as Kim got to her feet.

'Well, come back with your chequebook and then we'll talk.'

Dunhill stood and Bryant did the same. The two Great Danes were up and beside their owner in a flash.

Kim allowed herself to be shown the door despite a vague unease in her bones.

She had the feeling that Monty Dunhill had just told them an outright lie. The latest M in the workbook hadn't been crossed out. The meeting had not been cancelled.

She suspected that Monty had met with Sandy just a few days before she died. But if so why not just admit it?

What exactly was he trying to hide?

THIRTY-TWO

Penn pulled over as his phone began to ring. He was close but he wouldn't risk driving while on the phone.

'Yeah, boss,' he answered.

'Your man with the book, local author guy, what's his name?'

Penn had to search his memory for what she was referring to.

'Oh, the sceptic guy?'

'Yep.'

Penn pictured the book on his shelf.

'Richard Blake – lives in Kinver, I think.'

'Thanks, Penn,' she said, before ending the call.

'Aha,' he said, spotting the property he'd been searching for. It was an end terrace on the very edge of the Hollytree Estate.

Outside was a battered Fiesta that didn't look as though it would make it to its next MOT never mind pass it.

The door was answered by a woman in her mid- to late forties with tied-back blonde hair. Her eyes were immediately suspicious.

'May I help you?' she asked as the fresh scent of lavender travelled through the house towards him.

'Janice Sharpe?'

She nodded.

He took out his ID. 'DS Penn. May I come in?'

'What's it about?'

'Your husband.'

She hesitated before moving aside for him to enter.

He stepped to the left into a small lounge that was made all the smaller by the ironing board and piles of clothing scattered around the room.

'Feel free to have a seat, if you can find one,' she said, taking her position behind the ironing board. 'I can't stop. These are all due back today.'

Close to each pile of clothes was either a laundry basket or a bag with a handwritten tag on it. Clearly it was how the woman made a living.

'Out with it. What's he done this time? And whatever he owes I can't pay it. We're divorced.'

'Mrs Sharpe, I'm afraid I have some bad news for you. Your husband died a few days ago.'

'Wh... what?' she asked, setting the iron upright.

'He suffered a brain aneurism and died in the Stourbridge underpass.'

She just stared at him as though he was speaking a foreign language.

'What was he doing there?'

'It's where he was living. Your husband has been homeless for the last couple of years.'

A shadow of regret passed over her face but she shook it away. 'So that's why no one could find him.'

'You reported him missing?' he asked.

'Only because my daughter, our daughter, insisted. In all honesty I didn't care where he was.'

That explained the lack of follow-up calls.

He noted that the woman hadn't sat down but hadn't continued ironing yet. It was as though some part of her wanted to react to the news but another part of her wouldn't allow it.

'Did he suffer?' she asked, staring beyond him and out of the window.

'I don't think so,' Penn, answered, feeling it was the kindest thing to say. The man had died alone in a rubbish-infested, urine-stained underpass.

'I didn't know he was homeless,' she said. 'When he disappeared, I assumed he was couch surfing, to keep out of the way. I didn't want him back. It was a good job he didn't come back then or I'd have killed him myself.'

Her gaze fell on the mountainous piles of ironing yet to do. It galvanised her into action and she took hold of the iron again.

Penn wasn't sure exactly what he'd expected. His task was complete. The homeless man had a name and his family had been notified. And yet his curiosity got the better of him.

'May I ask what led to your husband becoming homeless?'

'The same thing that led to his wife and daughter being put in that position. It was a bet, Officer. He was a gambler. I always knew it but it grew worse and worse. I thought I was being clever in controlling the purse strings, so that I could make sure everything got paid on time, but maybe I did it all wrong. Maybe if he'd had more money...' Her words trailed away as though she'd processed the 'what if' scenarios a hundred times. 'But I didn't. He found a group of extreme gamblers online. It went from horses to dogs to just about anything.'

He said nothing and she continued speaking while she ironed.

'It wasn't until it was too late that I realised money wasn't necessarily the currency. One time he had to go and labour for a builder for two days straight because he'd lost a bet. Another time he turned up with a Jack Russell puppy he'd won from a local breeder.'

She sighed heavily. 'And then one day a firm of solicitors turned up to tell me that we no longer owned the house I'd lived in for seventeen years. He'd gambled it away on the results of a local football match.'

'Was that legal?' Penn asked.

'Yes, it was all official. He'd signed transfer papers. He was never one to go back on a deal. And that's when he disappeared. I was given a month to vacate. I spent the first two weeks using up what I had left in the bank seeking legal advice. The agreement was binding. We had nothing, Officer,' she said as the pain filled her eyes. 'My fifteen-year-old daughter and I were left homeless and penniless and I never saw Barry again.'

'I'm so sorry,' he said, wishing now he hadn't forced her to relive it. There was nothing he could offer to help.

It was as though his kind words and gentle tone put a pin in her.

She sighed heavily and sat down. 'I know that I must seem unfeeling to you but his gambling has been a part of my life for so long.'

'Did he ever get therapy?' Penn asked.

'I certainly did,' she said. 'He tried once. Well, one session actually. I carried on going and learned a lot. I found out that there were three types of gambler: professional, social and problem. I knew immediately he was a problem gambler when the therapist explained that they try to pass themselves off as either of the other two types. Barry was actually a compulsive gambler. It's called ludomania. I mean, every gambler is willing to risk something of value in the hope of getting something of even greater value. Except I learned that it's not quite that simple.'

'How so?' Penn asked.

'Gambling can stimulate the brain's reward system, like

drugs and alcohol, so you're continuously chasing bets, using savings and creating debt. The therapist told me the signs, and Barry showed every one. He was always preoccupied with gambling and how to get more money. He needed to up the stakes, the value, to get the same thrill. He was restless or irritable if he was asked to cut back. He was always chasing his losses and trying to get his money back, but it was the thrill of the bet itself he needed. For that high, he lied to his family. He risked losing every important relationship.'

'How did he get hooked?' Penn asked.

'Horses. In the good old days he'd go to the betting shop a couple of times a week, but you don't even need to leave the house any more. It's everywhere. You can bet on anything from reality gameshows to who will finally find life on Mars.'

'I can't even imagine what that must have been like to live with,' Penn offered.

'I was constantly trying to get him to stop. He would soft soap me with success stories like the guy from Kent who sold all his possessions, bet over seventy thousand on one roll of the roulette wheel and won. I argued that he would never know when to walk away. I read of one guy who collected his welfare cheque in Vegas and gambled it to win a million dollars. He didn't know when to stop and lost it all in the same day. It wasn't about the money. It was his compulsion to bet that lost us our home.'

'That must have been very difficult for you both.'

She sat upright. 'We're both fit and healthy and for that I'm grateful. But please understand that I am not a good enough person to forgive him yet, even in death.'

'I understand,' he said, standing. 'I'm sorry if I've caused you any pain, and I'll see myself out.'

The woman thanked him and he could swear he heard a quiet sob as he closed the door behind him.

'No don't shut— Never mind,' said a voice from the other side of the hedge.

A white-and-tan Jack Russell appeared before a teenage girl holding on to the lead. It was clear who had been in charge of the walk.

'And who are you?' she asked, walking down the path towards him. Now home, the dog appeared to have calmed down.

'Is this about my dad?' she asked before he had a chance to speak.

'I've just had a conversation with your mum,' he said, feeling the news would better come from her.

'I'm nearly eighteen and she won't tell me anything. We both have to act as though he doesn't exist.'

'I'm sorry but your mum should be the one to—'

'To what? Oh no... Tell me... He's dead, isn't he?'

Penn nodded as her eyes filled with tears.

'I knew it. I knew I'd never see him again.'

The tears escaped from her eyes and rolled over her cheeks. 'Did she know where he was?'

Penn shook his head.

'Whatever she told you, he was a good dad. He loved me. I didn't want him to stay away. I loved him,' she sobbed.

'I'm sorry, I—'

'Did someone hurt him?' she asked.

'No. He died of natural causes.'

'Where?'

'Stourbridge,' he offered vaguely. He didn't want to put the picture in her head of him being on the streets, alone. Her mum could do that if she wanted to.

'Can I go to his funeral?' she asked, wiping away the tears.

'We'll inform your mum once we have the details.'

'No. She won't tell me. Will you take my number and let me know? I need to be able to say goodbye properly.'

He took out his phone, opened it and passed it to her.

'Put your number in. I'll let you know.'

'Thank you,' she said, adding herself as a contact.

This girl was an innocent in all this.

'Do me one favour though,' he said. 'Go easy on her. You might not agree with everything she's done but she was the one who kept you safe.'

She nodded and he stepped aside for her to get into the house.

Penn knew his work here was over. The man had been identified and his family had been informed. And yet his gut was telling him that he hadn't done enough.

THIRTY-THREE

Between Penn's memory and Stacey's ability to bend the electoral register to her will, Kim now had an address for Richard Blake in Kinver. Given that Azim's murder was linked to the psychic community, she was hoping that the man who'd written the book could help them understand a bit more about how psychics operated and give them an insight into the type of people that used them.

The cottage lay on a narrow lane at the edge of town, with cars parked end to end, except for a skip outside their target property.

Bryant followed the winding road to a pub car park and pulled up opposite three white Transit vans emblazoned with the same livery.

'Hope he's not going to mind us just popping in,' he said, locking the car.

'I shouldn't think so,' she said as he fell into step behind her. There was no footpath so it was either the middle of the road or single file between the houses and the parked cars.

'He's a writer and we're going to be asking him questions on his chosen subject of interest. Bit like asking you to wax lyrical about *Strictly*.'

'Really, guv?'

Just because she hadn't teased him for a while didn't mean she'd forgotten that he and Jenny still took the ballroom dancing lessons.

'Bloody hell,' she cried as a loud bang sounded behind her as she knocked the door.

She stepped back and looked up. The front bedroom window was open and a builder stood with a piece of wood poised to follow what he'd already thrown.

'Sorry, love, didn't see you there.'

She took out her card and held it up to him.

His colleagues who had been laughing suddenly silenced.

'You can arrest me any time, darlin',' he said to groans in the background.

She beckoned for him to come down. Before he got there, the door opened to reveal a man in jeans and a sweatshirt. His hair was sandy blonde and contained a pair of glasses that had been pushed up onto his head.

'Mr Blake?'

'Indeed,' he answered.

She held up the ID that was still in her hand.

'Ah, excuse me one minute,' she said as the builder appeared, wearing an apologetic, cheeky grin. 'Yeah, that might work on your mother or your girlfriend, but not on me, fella. Put your hands out. Bryant, cuff him.'

'What are you doing?' the builder asked, panicking.

'Fulfilling your dreams, buddy,' she said as Bryant produced the handcuffs.

Her colleague stepped forward as Richard Blake watched with amusement.

'Of course, there is one way to get yourself out of this predicament,' she said, before the cuffs touched his skin.

'Like what?' he asked eagerly.

'You can make sure that by the time I leave here, the skip is cordoned off and made safe before you go throwing anything else out of bedroom windows.'

'Okay, will do,' he said, rushing past Richard Blake and back into the house.

'DI Stone and DS Bryant – may we take a minute of your time?'

'Normally not without a phone call, but after that performance, how can I possibly refuse?' He stepped aside. 'Please mind the mess.'

They followed him through to the rear of the cottage past dust-sheet-covered furniture and stacked boxes.

A small round table was his current working space, where he had a stack of books, a notepad and a laptop.

'I'd offer you a drink but I let the guys have the kettle during the day. Small price to pay for not having them in and out my office every five minutes.'

The space was chaotic and filled with displaced items.

A loud crash sounded overhead followed by feet thundering down the stairs.

'We're fine. You've got enough on your plate,' Kim said.

'We're turning the smallest room into an en suite, and in the process they found a good infestation of termites. The wife has gone to stay with her sister in Lyme Regis, but I stayed put for brownie points and eternal martyrdom.'

Kim smiled at his expression, but quite frankly she was on the side of his wife.

'You're working through this?' she asked, nodding towards the table.

'Trying to. Publisher deadlines don't care too much about home improvements or termites; but please, satisfy my curiosity and tell me why you're here. Actually, is there any chance of me being locked up in a quiet police cell?'

'No.'

'Pity. How can I help?'

'May we?' she asked, pointing to the chairs around the table.

'Of course,' he said, pulling them out and taking a seat himself.

'We're here because of your book about fraudulent psychics.'

'I wasn't expecting that. May I ask why?'

'Not right now but we need to pick your brains about the whole thing.'

'Okay, fair enough. I'm happy to share. I'm a psychologist by trade.'

'We won't hold that against you,' Kim said, deadpan.

He smiled and sat back in his chair. 'It's a subject I started studying around ten years ago, after I treated a client who had become so caught up in his psychic's predictions that he wouldn't make any decision about his life without her counsel. And she was doing quite nicely out of it, thank you. I wanted to study how a person had become so entranced with the notion of divination they had lost their ability to function fully of their own cognition.'

'So you don't believe in psychics?' she asked.

'If they exist, I've never met one,' he said. 'What I do believe is that there are many tricks used for frauds to appear to be genuine psychics.'

'Go on,' Kim said.

'The psychic's first gift is the subject themselves.'

'How so?' Bryant asked.

'When life is good people go out and party. When it's not they seek advice, guidance and reassurance from other people. A psychic's subject is already in the market for what the psychic is peddling.'

'But they must be doing something right,' Bryant said. 'There's a massive market for it.'

Kim watched as Richard sat back and took a good look at her colleague.

'We've never met before, have we?'

'Absolutely not,' Bryant answered.

'Okay, I'm gonna say that travel is in your future, somewhere hot, probably November. You're a solid dependable guy with a good portion of tolerance. You welcome all nationalities and have no bias. You've been married twenty to twenty-five years, and you love your wife as much now as you did when you married her.' He tipped his head to the side. 'I'm gonna say you tried to master a musical instrument in your youth.'

'All true,' Bryant said with wide eyes. 'But how could you know all that?'

'It's called cold reading and it's achieved using an array of techniques. You have a decent job and work hard but you're not rolling in it. You'd like a week or two in a hotter climate to relax but you go out of season because it's cheaper. You have little or no bias because a female is your superior and you are perfectly at ease with that. You have the most perfect creases in your trousers, unlikely to have been put there by you, so you clearly have a wife who loves you very much. Safe to assume you feel the same way.'

'But how could you know about the guitar?'

'I didn't specify which instrument. Statistics say that seventy per cent of males tried to master a musical instrument in their teens.'

'Bloody hell,' Bryant said.

'See the effect. You actually wanted to believe that I could know all that about you.'

'So that's cold reading?' Kim asked. 'Observations and process of elimination?'

'Oh no. It's much more than that. The fraudulent psychic is incredibly clever and skilled. Cold reading dates from the late 1940s and is used to convey paranormal insight into the client's personality, current life situation or future. The techniques can be used with crystal balls, palmistry, cards, tea leaves, all of which are merely props.

'A satisfactory reading must touch on the subject of interest to the particular individual. The first and very important requisite is an accurate, detailed observation of the person's physical appearance from head to toe including jewellery and accessories, and their mental attitude. From this we can get a determination about personality and situation. Are they serious, worried, sceptical? What type of work do they do? What is their financial situation? The approach is based on the fact all of us have four major interests in life: ourself, someone else, our possessions and our ambitions. A few leading questions determine which interests the subject the most.'

'Hang on though,' Bryant said, butting in. 'I've seen a guy read someone thoroughly accurately while blindfolded.'

There was challenge in Bryant's voice but Richard looked unruffled.

'Give me the circumstances.'

'It was my cousin's birthday party. About twenty-five of us. The psychic mingled for abut twenty minutes and then he was seated in a chair and blindfolded. He couldn't possibly have known who was going to be chosen.'

'I'm assuming the subject was then seated opposite the psychic. About as far apart as we are now?'

Bryant nodded.

'Cheap parlour trick, my friend. It's all down to the shoes. He would have been looking down and recognised the shoes. Everything he needed to know was acquired in that twenty minutes of idle, harmless socialising. That's when he would have been doing his best work.'

Bryant looked deflated, as though someone had just told him all the secrets of the Magic Circle.

'There are some sure predictions for anyone. You'll receive

an important letter in the next few weeks. A lucky influence is coming your way. A sudden trip is in your future. A new and valuable acquaintance is coming into your life. Beware of insincere friends. Watch out for bad advice. You will hear from someone very unexpectedly. Stock in trade predictions.'

'And the subject believes them?' Kim asked.

Richard nodded. 'The type of psychic you're dealing with has a huge effect on believability.'

'Type?' Kim asked.

'Oh yeah. Three main ones. You've got the compassionate healer. They're empathetic, understanding and create a warm, cosy environment, self-help books, big comfy chairs, scented candles, soft lighting. It's like entering a kingdom of kindness. They're part mentor, part parent. A soft, comforting voice, gentle eye contact, agreeable smile. There will be flattery and they will be endearing.'

'People don't see through the act?' Kim asked.

'Not if the psychic is any good. The second type is the polar opposite. Straight shooting, no sugar-coating. They're stern and serious. Good for people who like tough love. There'll be no candles here. There'll be psychic science books and framed diplomas. No niceties. It's not a social visit. It'll be a take it or leave it approach with an air of authority.'

'People pay for that?' Kim asked.

'Of course. The subject feels as though they're in strong and capable hands. Most of us will accept extreme forms of treatment if we believe it's in our best interest. That ultimately the person is looking out for us. That's why boot camps exist.

'And finally, you have the middle-ground psychic who will mix tough love with compassion. There'll be incense burning but any books on show will be neutral, like dictionaries. They will postulate solutions based on common sense using gentle truisms about human nature. They'll identify with the client using compassion and empathy but also offer hard-hitting advice. They'll use more humour than the other two.'

'You mentioned that you kept your statement vague about Bryant's musical instrument. So how do people believe if they're so vague?' Kim asked.

'Because they want to believe. Did you notice how he gave me the information? I said instrument, he remembered guitar – that's what psychics call a hit.'

'What about a miss?' Bryant asked.

'Oh believe me, there are plenty of techniques for getting around those, but you're not allowing for the Barnum effect.'

'The what?'

'It's a technique for convincing people something is true when it's not. You see, people tend to accept vague and general statements as unique to them. In 1947, Ross Stagner, a psychologist, gave a personality test to his students. He ignored the answers and presented them all with the same evaluation. He achieved an accuracy rating of 4.2 out of 5. The test has been repeated hundreds of times since and always achieves an eighty-four per cent accuracy rate. He actually used a newsstand astrology column.'

'How is that possible?' Bryant asked.

'Because people tend to be vain and optimistic. Let's look at a couple of typical Barnum statements: "when confronted with restrictions you feel upset and fearful" or "while you do have a few character weaknesses, your positive qualities more than compensate for them" or one of my favourites, "sometimes you question whether you made the right decision".'

'Don't we all?' Kim asked.

'Exactly. Statements that are positive and flattering are easy to accept. Psychics trade in emotions. They bank on uncertainty and hope. Most subjects want to be comforted.'

Kim said nothing as she tried to process this level of gullibility.

'I can see your doubt but clients that visit psychics do so because they already believe. They need solutions to their problems.

'It's all so carefully choreographed from the second the subject enters the space. There'll be a warm greeting and an educated guess on the reason for the visit.

'Again, this is based on statistics. Different age groups are worried about different things. But instead of choosing one thing they might say something like "I sense you're here to talk about relationships or your job but I'm also sensing some grief". People will hear what they want to hear and discard the rest. For someone worried about their boyfriend cheating, that would be a direct hit. The reading must seem specific but remain general. Cold reading in a nutshell is how to talk to people so they think you're psychic. And of course, it's well worth the effort perfecting the art.'

'How so?' Bryant asked.

'In a recent study it was reported that the US market alone was worth two billion.'

'Okay, if that's a cold reading, what's a hot one?' Kim asked.

'That's when the psychic has prior knowledge or contact with the subject.'

'And what—'

'Inspector, I don't wish to hurry you along but...'

'I'm sorry,' she said. 'We have taken quite a bit of your time.'

'I've enjoyed chatting but I really must get back to the day job. Hard enough trying to work amongst this bombsite.'

Kim knew she had to leave but she had so many more questions, so much more she wanted to learn.

The answer slapped her in the face.

She had an idea that could be a solution to both of their problems.

THIRTY-FOUR

Stacey turned to the next job at hand. Do some digging around the disappearance of Rose Foster's son.

She typed in the details from the boss and refamiliarised herself with the case.

Fifteen-year-old Bradley Foster had been riding to school with his friend Josh Adams, as he always did. His mother claimed there was nothing out of the ordinary. He'd done his half wave from the gate before setting off with his friend.

From Josh's point of view, they'd been riding together on their way to school when Bradley called out to race to the end of the woods. Not unusual. They'd often punctuated the three-mile journey with short races. Bradley had sped off, and while changing gear Josh had slipped his chain, forcing him to get off the bike and reattach the chain before making chase. He'd exited the woods to see a white Transit van pulling off the pavement and speeding away.

He'd found it a bit strange, also that his buddy hadn't waited for him. It was only when Bradley was nowhere to be seen at school that Josh remembered the white van and raised the alarm.

Extensive searching had been carried out for weeks with hundreds of volunteers coming out to help. Not one thing was found and the team was eventually broken up and reassigned. Just over a year after his disappearance, his clothes, bike and a patch of blood had been found at the northern edge of Cannock Chase.

Cadaver dogs were utilised but hadn't come up with anything. Obvious new mounds in a half-mile radius had been checked but nothing further had been found. No similar incidents had been reported by other police forces, so the DCI heading the case had concluded that Bradley was buried somewhere on the Chase but was unlikely to be found. The case was still active but everyone had accepted that Bradley Foster was dead.

From what Stacey could see, the investigation had been thorough and well-managed. There was nothing untoward, and all officers appeared to be above reproach.

She was about to start a short report when the boss walked in the door.

'Where's Penn?' she asked by way of a greeting.

'He's just—'

'Right here,' Penn said, a few paces behind.

'Good,' the boss said, taking off her jacket.

She looked accusingly at the empty coffee machine, but Bryant was already en route to fix that particular problem.

'Just checked out the Bradley Foster case, boss,' Stacey said, getting in first. 'All in order. Nothing doing.'

'Told you,' Bryant said, emptying the water into the back of the machine.

The boss ignored him and looked towards Penn. 'John Doe identified and the family informed?'

'Done,' Penn answered.

'Care to elaborate?' asked the boss.

'Sorry. Yes, Barry Sharpe, ex-husband of Janice Sharpe and

father to Tanya. The guy was an extreme gambler who basically lost their house on a single bet. He ran away rather than face the music and left his wife to deal with it. She now lives on the edge of Hollytree, taking in other people's washing to make ends meet. She was pretty cold to the news of his death, but Tanya misses her dad terribly and was broken up at the news. She'd like to attend his funeral.'

'Good job, Penn,' she said, and Stacey noted her satisfaction that the man would not be buried without his name.

'I'm sensing a but though,' the boss said, folding her arms.

'I'm gonna just inform this one guy who seemed quite concerned and then I'm gonna leave it alone.'

'What's the choice? There's nothing left to do.'

'Just feels shit, boss. How can it be legal for him to have signed away the house without her knowing?'

Stacey understood his hesitation. In solving one mystery he'd uncovered a misdeed, and it was natural for every police officer to want to right every wrong that crossed their path.

'I assume she got legal advice at the time?' the boss asked.

He nodded.

She opened her hands. 'It's done, Penn. Tell your guy the outcome and put it to bed.'

'Okay, boss,' he said.

'Does anyone wanna know what the guv has been doing this last half hour?' Bryant asked.

'Of course,' Stacey answered.

'She's been bending the law of the universe to her will. Basically overriding protocols and regulations to get her own way.'

'And?' Stacey asked. Sounded like a typical day so far.

'She's fast-tracked someone onto the approved list of consultants, forced him to the front of the vetting queue, all for her own convenience while also convincing the guy she's doing him a favour. My head is still spinning.'

'And who might the expert be?' Stacey asked, chuckling.

The boss opened her mouth to speak but Bryant was having way too much fun.

'His name is Richard Blake, an expert on fraudulent psychics who happens to be in need of somewhere quiet to work on his next book,' Bryant said, pointing to the spare desk.

The boss shrugged but didn't disagree.

'Do we really need an expert on fraudulent psychics?' Penn asked, mirroring her own thoughts.

The boss gave him a knowing smile. 'Okay, meet him and then you tell me.'

THIRTY-FIVE

Kim had just finished updating the activity log when she got the call that Richard Blake was being escorted up to the office.

'Okay, guys, he's on his way up but don't bombard him with questions. You all understand that with the murder of Azim, the focus has shifted away from the dinner party, towards the broader subject of psychics and their customers. We can gain a lot of insight from Richard, but give the man a minute to get settled in.'

'Got it, boss,' Stacey and Penn said together, while Bryant waved his understanding.

'Come in, Mr Blake,' Kim said as a constable deposited him at the door.

'Richard, please,' he said, following the direction of her nod towards the spare desk. He placed his laptop on it and took a seat, then smiled around the room.

'Stacey,' the constable said by way of introduction.

'Penn,' the sergeant offered, wheeling across with his hand outstretched. 'I've read your book.'

'Oh, you're the one,' he said, smiling.

Kim appreciated his modesty but she'd checked his reviews

on Amazon. The book had been very well received by readers but probably not so much by the psychic community.

'Thanks for letting me get some peace and quiet. The mid-afternoon karaoke had just begun.'

'If we could pick your brains a bit before you start, for the benefit of Stacey and Penn? I've summarised our chat from earlier so if there's more you can offer, that would be great,' she said, taking her mug to the percolator. 'Oh, and help yourself.'

He took a bottle of water from his bag and held it up to signal that he was good.

'Maybe if I tell you a bit about the psychics themselves?'

Kim nodded and sipped her coffee.

'Okay, so even though people who visit psychics are believers, during the warm-up phase of a reading, a psychic will admit that even psychics make mistakes. They prep the client for errors so the client forgives them immediately and moves on.

'There are seven themes most people want to talk about: love, health, money, career, travel, education and ambitions. The cold reader relies on a simple psychological idea that human beings have the ability to make sense of data, no matter what it is. They bank on the client's willingness to find more meaning in a situation than there actually is, and to connect the dots to make sense of it for themselves.'

Stacey held up her hand.

Richard laughed. 'It's not school. Ask away.'

'Are you saying that it's all down to a technique?'

'It's all down to a mixture of techniques, body language, shrewd observation, fishing, vagueness and gullibility.'

Stacey looked doubtful.

Richard tipped his head to the left.

'There's a heart problem around you. I'm sensing an older male. I'm feeling chest pain. It's either your father, grandfather or an uncle that—'

'My uncle died of a—'

'The month of June is important to you...'

'I got married in—'

'Why am I seeing water, a pool, a beach...'

'We honeymooned in—'

'There was a problem at the airport when you came back...'

'We couldn't get a taxi,' Stacey said as her eyes widened. 'But how could you know all that?'

Kim was amazed at how quickly Stacey had become caught up in the process, giving her a good idea of how effective the technique was on someone who believed.

'What I just did was called shot-gunning, which is offering a series of vague statements. I actually got four hits and no misses. Pretty good result.'

'But how?' Stacey insisted.

'Mainly because of you. Firstly, there are very few families not touched by heart disease – it's the number-one killer for older men. I named pretty much every older male relation you could have.'

'How did you know I got married in June?'

'I didn't. I said June was important to you. Statistically it's a very popular month for weddings, events and parties. You then offered the information of the marriage, so it's not too much of a leap to think you'd gone somewhere warm with water.'

'The airport?'

'Everyone has a crappy time at the airport when they're coming home. You had to wait for a taxi, no big deal, but you recalled it as a problem because you were tired, jetlagged, miserable because you were home. But here's the thing. I was prepared for your answers either way.'

'I don't believe that,' Stacey said, shaking her head.

'Wanna try it again but with negative responses?'

Stacey nodded.

'I sense a heart issue with one of your older male relatives.'

'All healthy.'

He frowned and shook his head. 'I think they need to go get checked. The sooner the better.'

'Okay.'

'I'm sensing June is important to you.'

'No.'

'Aah, wait a minute. Something important is going to happen in June.'

'Okay.'

'Why do I see a pool and water?'

'No idea.'

Richard raised a hand to his mouth. 'Oh dear, I may have ruined a surprise. Scrub that. Pretend I never said anything.'

'Bloody hell,' Stacey said.

'I know,' Bryant answered, having experienced the same thing earlier.

'I wouldn't have asked the airport question, obviously, but I'd have substituted it with a Barnum phrase.'

'What's a—'

'I'll explain later,' Kim offered.

'And now I have you back in the room,' he said, smiling. 'Or I could have tried what they call a rainbow ruse, which is a statement and its opposite. I sense you're a very considerate person but just occasionally you have a selfish streak.'

'Who doesn't?' Penn asked.

'Exactly. A good psychic always has an extensive knowledge of trivia. Most people have a box of old photos, old medicines, toys or books, items of jewellery or war medals. Gender specific, most men have worn a moustache or beard.'

Both Penn and Bryant nodded.

'Most men over thirty have an old suit that no longer fits. Most women own a piece of clothing never worn. Most women carry photos of loved ones. Most women have long hair as a child then adopt shorter styles. Most women have an odd earring. There are hundreds of these trivial facts that can be adopted to make a connection.'

Kim could see that her whole team was as interested in what he had to say as she was. She hoped the knowledge they were gaining would bring them closer to finding a motive for their killer.

'Introducing such trivia is especially dramatic in stage shows. Victoria Sykes uses it effectively. I went to see her in Birmingham last year.'

'Another name from Dunhill's hit list,' Kim noted as Stacey frowned and started tapping something into her computer.

'Oh, you've met him,' Richard said. 'Pleasant chap.' The roll of the eyes that accompanied the words told her everything.

'Your thoughts?'

'Only ever does private readings. He's a purist and despises pretty much everyone else. Obviously, I've had no chance to observe him. He does have some rich and famous customers, but he's probably very good at what he does because he totally believes in his gift.'

He sure does, Kim thought.

'Boss, I thought I'd seen the name Victoria Sykes other than in Dunhill's article.' Stacey turned her screen. 'She's performing at the Grand in Wolverhampton tonight. Event sold out weeks ago.'

'We need to go,' Kim said. They needed to see this deception and its effects up close. The woman needed to be warned and, finally, their killer might even be there. 'Stace, get the manager on the phone.'

'Victoria Sykes is very popular. She uses an element of drama in her shows. She doesn't do private readings, I believe,' Richard offered, while Stacey rang the theatre. 'But she is very good at getting the confidence of the crowd.'

'Here you go boss, Teresa Williams,' Stacey said, handing her the phone.

'Ms Williams, DI Stone of West Mids police. I need tickets to tonight's event.'

'Impossible,' the manager blustered. 'It's been sold out for weeks.'

'I need tickets,' Kim insisted.

'Unless someone is selling them on eBay, you're out of luck unfortunately. I can't allow your standing as a police officer to influence fire regulation limits. I'm sure she'll tour again at—'

'It's not a social engagement, Ms Williams. We need to observe the show in connection with an ongoing investigation.'

The woman was silent for a minute. 'How many tickets do you need?'

'Five,' Kim answered.

'Impossible,' she repeated. 'I can maybe manage two if I revoke the staff passes.'

Kim didn't have the luxury of feeling guilty for the two staff members who wouldn't be able to go.

'I'll take them,' Kim said.

The woman gave her instructions on getting the tickets when she arrived.

'Okay, guv, who's the lucky person going with you?' Bryant asked.

'Before you make your choice,' Richard said, 'if you really want to see how the deception works, you have a better chance of success if you've got a level of vulnerability. There are some tricks I'm happy to share with you, but no offence, they're not going to work on you. You don't look anywhere near naïve enough to be approached.'

Yes, she could see his point, but she definitely needed to be one of the two.

'With that in mind, which one of us are you going to take?' Bryant asked again.

She looked around her team and made a decision.

'I'm not taking any of you.'

THIRTY-SIX

Kim was already waiting in the locker room when she heard the unmistakeable voice talking to a colleague.

'Hey, Tink,' she said, stepping forward.

Tiffany's face froze in surprise as her colleague continued walking.

Kim saw their history together play out in the young woman's eyes.

The first time they'd met was when Tiff had assisted them with data mining on a child genius case, because Penn had been temporarily seconded back to West Mercia. The second time had been when Tiff went undercover into a cult they'd unearthed and very nearly lost her life.

Warmth filled the woman's eyes and Kim had to pause. That the young constable was so pleased to see her, given that every time she gave them a hand she got in some kind of shit, was a testament to her generosity of spirit.

'Hiya, boss.'

Tiffany was a person of unflinching positivity who whistled and hummed show tunes when she was deep in thought. She was sweet, naïve, trusting and bubbly. On paper Kim should have found her very presence annoying. She didn't.

'Need your help, Tink,' she said, using the nickname she'd awarded the girl because she reminded Kim of the cartoon fairy.

'Okay, boss. I'm off shift in...'

'It's been cleared. I can steal you right away.'

A quick call to Inspector Plant had secured her release.

'Wanna go see a psychic show with me?'

'A wh... what?'

'A psychic stage show over in Wolverhampton?'

Tiff fell into step beside her as she headed for the stairs up to the CID office.

'You've got a fifth ticket and you're inviting me?' she asked in wonder.

'No, I've got one spare ticket and I'm inviting you,' Kim said. 'It's work, and I really need someone with your skills.'

Kim was sure Tiff's face fell slightly, but it perked right back up again.

'Whatever you need, boss,' she said, following Kim into the squad room.

'Hey, Tiff,' everyone said with genuine warmth.

Her face coloured slightly as she gave them all a little wave.

'Perfect,' Richard muttered under his breath.

Kim wheeled her chair out of the Bowl and pointed for Tiff to sit.

She sat.

'Tink, we have two dead psychics and we're trying to find out why. There's a show at the Grand tonight, and we're both going so we can better understand psychics and the people who use them. We need to see the level of deceit, the influence they exert and the aftereffects of the process. Richard here is going to give us some tips.'

'Okey dokey,' she said, as though Kim had just said they were all going out for pizza.

'Right, Tiff, is it?' he asked.

'Or Tink,' she answered, shrugging.

'Okay, well, you're going to need to look as vulnerable as you can. Ideally, you'll stand alone and if you can look a bit upset, all the better.'

'How obvious?' Kim asked.

'Don't overplay it. If she looks vulnerable, they'll find her.'

'Who?'

'I call them the stooges. They won't arrive with the psychic and probably won't go anywhere near her, but they will be in contact. The stooges play two parts. First they work the foyer, looking for targets. They want someone who will pull on the heartstrings, someone genuine who will unknowingly convince the rest of the audience that the act is real. They'll find a clever way to get your story, normally by sharing theirs, and they will also want to know where you're sitting. The better your story, the more chance of the psychic hitting on you. As I've already said, it's all about emotion and they want the maximum pay-out.

'The person who you talk to will most likely be called upon too. His or her story will be rehearsed and practised and between the two of you, you'll make it very convincing for everyone else.'

'Anything else?' Kim asked.

Richard shook his head. 'That's enough to get noticed.'

Kim checked her watch.

'Come on then, Tink. Time for us to go talk to the dead.'

THIRTY-SEVEN

They arrived at the venue just as the doors opened and the queue began to move.

Tiff had got out of the car already pale and shaken, stating she'd been in high-speed car chases that had been less stressful. Although there were many things about Kim that had improved over the years, clearly her driving wasn't one of them.

They had separated as soon as they'd neared the theatre, to avoid being seen together. It was important for the charade that Tiff appeared to be completely alone. She was currently four people back and already looking vulnerable and out of place.

Kim reached the door in minutes, gave her name and explained that her colleague would collect the second ticket.

Once inside, Kim spied a good viewing spot and nestled herself at the far end of the bar, partly obscured by a stone pillar. Trying to witness the fraud was only one of the reasons for their visit this evening. Kim's two main priorities were searching the crowds for anyone that looked familiar or suspicious, and to get a meeting with the psychic herself after the show.

Without directly watching Tiff, she tried to keep her in her peripheral vision as the constable approached the bar, ordered a drink and then placed herself in the far corner of the room.

Kim's first reaction was to motion to Tiff to move somewhere more visible but quickly realised that the girl was doing exactly what she'd been told to. Richard had said that if she fitted the profile, they'd find her.

Kim busied herself looking around the crowd that was building nicely. The sound of excited chatter was all around her. The audience seemed to be made up of small groups and couples. Most were dressed up as though going to the theatre in the West End, but she supposed in a way they were.

As the crowd thickened, groups of people moved closer to Kim, partially obscuring her view. Some people appeared to already know each other and others were just chatting to pass the time with people they'd been shoved up against.

She was still trying to spot anyone who appeared to be acting unnaturally, but the melding of parties and natural movement of the whole crowd was making it impossible.

'Have you seen her before?' asked a woman in a group of four right in front of her.

Her husband was hugging a pint of something, trying to look attentive as his wife held court with two women who looked like sisters.

'No, we've never been to see a psychic before.'

'Oh, you're in for a treat. We saw her in Birmingham. She was marvellous. I went because my father hadn't long passed and, well, you know.'

'My brother died a year ago,' the woman answered. 'He was very sick. We wanted to see if he would come through.'

'Oh, I'm so sorry to hear that. Losing a person so young is just heart-breaking.'

'He was our older brother,' the woman clarified. 'He was sixty-one.'

'Still such a loss though, isn't it? My dad had suffered with his heart for years.'

'Yes, Tony had already fought cancer twice, but it finally got him.'

Kim was now totally invested in the conversation, amazed at the detail people were willing to share with complete strangers. Without realising it, the second woman had given away enough detail for a very convincing reading in two sentences.

She pulled her attention away and glanced over at Tiff as the crowds began to move subconsciously towards the doors as the start time grew closer.

She was still in the same spot, sipping her drink but looking beyond it as though completely caught up in her own thoughts.

The crowd was slowly moving away from her but no one was paying any attention to the lone figure in the corner.

Except for a blonde male in his late twenties standing at the bar.

No, no, no, Kim thought. This was not a good time to get picked up.

Damn it. If the blonde guy went over to talk to her, their trip would be a waste of time.

Kim growled in frustration as once again Tiff became obscured from her view.

THIRTY-EIGHT

By her count, the man at the bar had been watching her for a good five minutes.

Tiff hadn't noticed where he'd come from, but she had seen him do a quick sweep of the room before settling his attention on her. She'd continued with her act and had been careful not to look in his direction. It was more of an effort to look miserable than she'd realised, and her facial muscles were aching. Her natural resting face was quite open and relaxed with wide eyes and the hint of a smile.

She was saved from analysing herself any further when the bar guy appeared in front of her.

'Hey, are you okay?'

She allowed herself to offer a small, tight smile and a nod.

'My mum told me never to talk to strangers but you looked safe enough,' he said.

In spite of herself, Tiff laughed.

'I'm Neil,' he said, offering her a nod.

'Tiffany,' she answered.

'And just like that we're not strangers any more. My mum can rest easy.'

The smile grew on her face.

'That's better. It can't be as bad as that, eh? Tonight's supposed to be a bit of fun – at least that's what I'm hoping. You on your own?' he asked, looking around.

She nodded. 'Yeah, but I haven't come for fun. I'm hopeful. Are you on your own?'

'I am indeed. I got these tickets for my mum's birthday. She loves this kind of stuff but she came down with flu yesterday. She insisted I use the tickets, and surprisingly none of my mates wanted to tag along.'

Again, Tiff chuckled. He was very personable and she suspected he wasn't the stooge, but just like serial killers, who knew what one looked like?

'So, you hoping for contact from a loved one?' he asked, his voice softening with sympathy.

Oh well, she had her story. She might as well use it.

'My grandma. She died recently.'

'I'm sorry. Were you close?'

Tiff nodded and the tears pricked her eyes. She had been close to her maternal grandmother and had decided to stay close to the truth.

'We were. She was more like a mother to me. We used to watch musicals together. She took me to amateur productions of shows when I was a kid.'

All true. As was the fact that her grandmother had stepped in when her own mother had been consumed with caring for her brothers, always the priority.

'She sounds amazing but I suppose age gets us all.'

'Oh no, it wasn't old age,' she said, realising how easily she was sliding into the detail. 'She had a fall, down the stairs. Fractured skull.'

'Oh, how awful. So you never got the chance to say goodbye?'

'I never had a chance to put things right.'

'An argument?'

'Yes. We had a row just a few days before. It was over something silly. I was late to pick her up for bingo so she refused to go. I shouted at her for being stubborn, and then I showed the exact same trait by not giving her a call to patch it up.'

'That's so hard for you, but if you were close, she knows you're sorry, and I'm sure she wouldn't want you to beat yourself up.'

'Oh, I hope so,' Tiff said, with a small smile.

'I was never allowed to call my grandma that, as she said it aged her too much. She was Nana June until the day she died.'

'Mine hated the name Hilda,' Tiff said, realising she hadn't meant to give away her gran's first name.

The crowd suddenly began to move as the doors to the theatre opened.

'They're going in. Whereabouts are you sitting?'

'A seven,' she said.

'Don't worry, I'm not some kind of stalker guy, but maybe we could compare notes at half-time. I'm in C nine.'

'Okay,' Tiff said, moving forward with the crowd.

'Oooh, nature calls,' he said, edging away. 'See you later.'

Tiff offered him a little wave as she attached herself to the back of the crowd.

The boss was bound to ask her if she'd been primed or not.

Right now she honestly had no answer to give.

THIRTY-NINE

Kim found her seat and within minutes Tiff was sitting beside her.

'Anything?' she asked, leaning her head over while still searching the crowds around her. Their killer could be in this very theatre.

Tiff shrugged as music started to play and the lights went down.

For a few seconds, the theatre was plunged into darkness before blue lights began dancing on the stage.

Kim could feel the atmosphere building through the crowd; that air of expectation and excitement as the music increased in tempo and the lights skipped around to the synth beat playing.

It built over the course of a couple of minutes, the beat coming underneath her feet, urging her to bang her foot or clap her hands.

A screen lit up on the stage. The word 'louder' was projected there in capital letters.

The crowd obliged, including Tiff, who was stamping her feet and clapping her hands.

Kim was trying to remain objective but she could certainly

see the appeal. The audience had been drawn in immediately.

The huge projector screen changed and read, 'Louder – wake up the spirits'.

The crowd obliged and the theatre was a cacophony of stamping, clapping and shouting. It reached a crescendo with the synth music, then silence, and darkness. The crowd quietened with awe before the lighting hit back in and a single figure was revealed on stage.

Her hair was red, long and wavy. She wore black leggings with high-heeled boots and an oversize white shirt that almost reached her knees. Her head was bowed and her hands posed in front of her in a prayer position.

The crowd was silent.

Eventually her head came up and her gaze swept around the theatre.

'Thank you, Wolverhampton, for allowing me a moment of prayer and reflection before we begin.'

The crowd clapped vigorously, but this time she quieted them.

'Thank you, thank you. You've been more than kind. I know you're all here for different reasons. Some of you are hoping to hear from a loved one, some of you may be at a crossroads in your life, some of you might be looking for love and some of you might be here because the other half has dragged you along.'

The crowd laughed.

'For those people, I'll be as quick as I can and you can get the football on catch-up.'

Another laugh and already the room was enraptured.

'For those of you who've seen me before, you know how this works, but those of you who haven't, shame on you.'

The crowd roared.

'Just joking. I tend to move around the stage wherever the spirits guide me. I don't always get everything on the nose but I blame the spirits for that. You just can't get the staff these days.'

The disclaimer Richard had mentioned wrapped up in a joke. Excellent touch.

'Talking of staff, I have three helpers out there with microphones who will find you if my message is aimed at you. Talking of which, I feel myself being pulled to the centre. Blimey, they're not hanging around tonight.'

She walked to the front of the stage.

'Here somewhere. I'm getting the name Derek.'

Three hands shot up.

She pointed to the first. 'Passed?'

The woman shook her head.

Victoria motioned no and moved to the next.

'Passed?'

The woman nodded, and the microphone was thrust into her hands by one of the helpers.

'He's an older male figure. I'm gonna say father.'

'Yes, yes,' the woman said eagerly. 'He's my dad.'

Victoria's hand went to her chest. 'I'm sensing breathing problems.'

'Lung cancer,' the woman offered.

'He's a cheeky chappie, isn't he?'

The woman nodded as tears began to roll over her cheeks.

'He's not in pain now. He said to tell you he's free of all that and when you hear those noises in the house, that's him. He's always around you.'

'I knew it,' she said with a mixture of triumph and relief.

'Thank you for coming,' Victoria said, moving away.

The microphone was removed as the crowd offered a round of appreciative applause, but Kim's attention was on the woman who'd received the reading. She turned to her friend with a happy, relieved, almost joyful expression on her face. She looked as though a great weight had been lifted from her shoulders. She was satisfied. She'd come here full of hope and she'd been rewarded. She would not go home and poke holes in the reading. She would not look for reasons to doubt the authenticity. She would take comfort from what she'd been told.

There was nothing factual that Victoria had offered, but that wouldn't matter. By the time she got home, her memory would have embellished the event so that she would feel that Victoria had known everything about her father, instead of it being a couple of well-educated guesses.

In her mind there was definitely deceit, but a nagging voice wondered where was the harm? The woman had not lost anything. She had gained eternal reassurance and comfort for the price of a ticket.

She was so caught up in her own thoughts she'd missed the second reading. The crowd was applauding again.

Victoria moved slowly to the left of the stage, coming their way.

'I'm being pushed over here. Goodness, there's a lot of emotion coming at me right now.' She was getting closer. 'It's a name beginning with H. Helen... no, Hattie... no, wait, I'm getting the name Hilda.'

Kim felt Tiff freeze beside her before her hand shot up.

Victoria focussed on her and moved so she was directly in front of them. Someone reached across Kim and put a microphone in Tiff's hand as she stood up.

'I'm getting an older woman. I'm going to say grandmother and boy is she a feisty one.'

Tiff nodded as Victoria touched the back of her own head. 'There was some kind of injury.'

'She fell,' Tiff offered in a small voice.

Kim realised it had to have been the guy at the bar. He must have approached Tiff after she had joined the crowd.

'Ah, that makes sense.' Victoria frowned. 'I'm sorry but I'm conflicted. I'm sensing the two of you were very close but there's a negative feeling too: anger?'

Kim wasn't surprised that the crowd was enraptured by the

reading. Emotional investment was high.

Tiff nodded and swallowed.

'Did the two of you argue before she passed?'

Again, Tiff nodded and then seemed to remember the microphone in her hand.

'Y-Yes,' she croaked.

'I'm feeling regret over here and guilt over there.'

She paused as though listening to something. Her thumb was rubbing her forefinger in an unconscious gesture as she waited.

'Your grandmother is saying to let it go. You were both as stubborn as each other and that last week of not talking doesn't take anything away from all the years of wonderful memories you made together.'

Jesus, even Kim could feel a lump forming in her throat.

'She said she's got all the salty crisps she can eat now and that she's very proud of you.'

Kim heard a small sob as Tiff nodded and handed the microphone back.

A wave of emotion was sweeping the theatre.

Victoria started to move away but then stopped and turned.

'Sorry, looks like Hilda isn't done with me yet,' Victoria said, raising an eyebrow.

The crowd laughed.

'She's saying that there's something you want to do but you're holding yourself back. She says be brave and do it.'

Victoria finally moved away as Tiff gave another gentle sob.

To better understand her killer, Kim had come here looking to see the effects of the power of suggestion from a person claiming to have divine knowledge. She'd wanted to see the depth of emotional investment and level of trust given by the client to the psychic.

She didn't have to look far. The answer was sitting right beside her.

FORTY

It was almost 10 p.m. by the time Stacey put the key in the door to the flat. Her Uber driver had been pleasant and polite, and she would make sure she gave him a good rating.

Tuesday was her weekly night for visiting her mother, and she always chose to play safe and avoid public transport at this time of night.

Devon knew not to expect her any earlier, having been present many times when her mother had launched into a full friends and family update, which was more like a military briefing but filled with information that she didn't need.

Somehow her mother had become the nexus of the wider family since Stacey had moved out. Cousins Stacey didn't even remember now visited her mum for a cuppa and a catch-up, thereby giving her the scoop on all the family gossip.

There was something comforting in sitting in her old child-hood home, doing nothing but listen as the family shenanigans were relayed to her. The whole process washed away the day at work, and brought her home cleansed and revitalised. And much as she loved that time with her mum, there was nothing like letting herself into her own home where her own wife was waiting for her.

A smile plastered itself to her face as she removed her jacket. The haunting sounds of Enigma could be heard from the kitchen, where the only light in the flat burned brightly. An array of aromas greeted her, making it impossible to guess what Devon had been cooking. One scent that she could detect was the Yankee festive Christmas candle Devon had received as a gift; with 150 hours' burning time, it was still going strong in March. Devon cared nothing for the fact that the season was long gone. She liked the smell of berries and birch and eucalyptus that filled the flat every time she lit it.

'Hey, babe,' Stacey said, stepping into the kitchen. Every surface was covered with plastic containers, mainly recycled after Chinese takeaways. The roll of stickers and a marker pen lay on the kitchen table ready for the labelling process.

'See anything you fancy?' Devon asked with a wicked smile.

'Yep, but it isn't in any of those containers,' Stacey responded as Devon moved towards her.

They shared a long kiss before Stacey turned her attention back to the filled food containers.

Unlike her, Devon loved to cook. Her job as an immigration officer didn't afford her lots of time to indulge, but on certain days off she would spend hours batch cooking some of their favourite meals, portioning and labelling them for the freezer.

'Over here is lasagne, and that is chicken korma, pasta bake, beef casserole and lastly jollof rice.'

'Really?' Stacey asked, taking a closer look. Devon rarely attempted the cuisine of their heritage. Her two visits to Nigeria had barely prepared her to tackle it.

'I got the recipe from your mum,' she said with a shrug and a cheeky wink.

Oh that would have earned her brownie points, Stacey

thought, taking a fork from the drawer. She dug into one of the containers for a taste.

'Not bad at all,' she said, nodding appreciatively.

'Not bad?' Devon laughed, swiping her with the tea towel.

'Okay,' Stacey said, defending herself. 'It's the best I've ever tasted.'

'Something we definitely won't be sharing with your mum,' Devon said putting the fabric weapon down. 'And what would be your choice tonight?'

'Hmm...' Stacey said, surveying the choices. Even though it was late, they tried to eat together whenever they could. Their shifts and long hours didn't always allow it. 'You know I'm gonna have to go with the lasagne.'

Knowing how much she loved it, Devon didn't skimp on the béchamel sauce that oozed over the mince and pasta.

'Wow, what a surprise,' Devon said, heading for the freezer. 'Go take a shower and I'll warm some bread and pour the wine.'

Stacey paused and observed the scene from the door, wondering if this really was her life. A job that challenged and stimulated her and a home life that filled her with contentment and warmth. She was already anticipating good food and chilled wine and a couple of episodes of *Downton Abbey*. They were late to that particular party, having not watched it while it had been current, but were now bingeing their way through it.

If only they could see us now, Stacey thought as she headed to the bedroom. Their colleagues were a mixture of hardened police and immigration officers, all of them used to dealing with the worst the Black Country had to offer, and here were the two of them spending their evenings watching period dramas. Yeah, that could stay within these four walls.

She removed her shoes at the bedroom door, ready to slip on the next morning, and padded across to the window. Although the bedroom was at the rear of the flat, there was still an alleyway that separated the building from the houses behind.

Devon loved reminding her that the pathway was gated at both ends, but as a child, Stacey's bedroom had been on the front of the house and old habits died hard.

She reached up to pull the curtain across when something caught her eye; a slight movement.

A frown formed on her face as she focussed, trying to pierce the dense darkness. The house opposite had a motion sensor light that sometimes lit up their bedroom, and it had a wide enough beam to give decent illumination to the whole area. Great – when she wanted the bloody thing on, it was dormant.

She narrowed her eyes at the spot where she thought she'd seen movement. The branches of the trees that lined the rear of the property were bare, but she still struggled to see through them in the darkness. She could just about work out what looked like a solid mass behind the middle tree, but by now she wasn't sure if it had always been there.

Probably a cat teetering along the fence, she reasoned as she pulled the first curtain across.

The spotlight illuminated, lighting up the whole area in a ten-metre arc.

Her gaze went straight to that middle tree. Her breath caught in her throat as her brain struggled to process what she saw.

A solid figure, a man, dressed in black, looking right up at her.

She let out a small cry as she realised that the person staring up at her bedroom window was Terence Birch.

FORTY-ONE

At the end of the show, Tiff elected to return to the car while Kim completed the second part of her mission.

Now the show was over, there was no need for them to pretend to be strangers, and Tiff had acted as if she needed some air.

Kim was waiting for the manager to return to see if her request had been accepted.

The show had continued in much the same vein, and if the audience noticed some very definite misses, they certainly didn't show it. The chatter as the crowds had filed out had been positive and appreciative, with Kim hearing many promises that they'd be back to see her again.

Kim had learned about the sequencing of the act. If you started strong, the audience was already with you and would forgive you anything. How something began imprinted the mind-set pretty much for the whole show. After her reading of Tiff, the audience had been putty in Victoria's hands. She probably could have had a whole string of misses and the crowd would still have been on her side.

Kim spotted the manager heading her way as the last few stragglers left the foyer.

'Victoria has a couple of minutes,' she said, beckoning Kim through a double set of 'Staff Only' doors.

'It's just down here,' she said, barrelling down a well-lit corridor. After one left turn she knocked on a door.

'Just head back to the foyer once you're done and someone will let you out.'

'Come in,' Kim heard as she nodded her understanding to the manager.

Kim took a breath and entered.

She was surprised to see Victoria had already changed into a powder-pink tracksuit.

'Saves time when I get home,' she said, folding the clothes she'd been wearing on stage.

'The manager told you who I was?' Kim checked.

'Yes. It's the only reason I'm still here. I like to get straight home for a restorative gin and tonic as soon as I'm done.'

'Well, thank you for assisting a police officer,' Kim said.

'Oh, I'm not talking about you being a police officer. I'm talking about your insistence on getting tickets. The manager told me you were going to watch my show tonight even if you had to sit on stage to do it.'

'I wanted to see you in action,' Kim said honestly as Victoria folded the oversize white shirt carefully and placed it at the top of the case.

'Why?'

'Because I needed to understand the level of influence you exert over your audience members.'

'You don't care if I'm genuine or not?' Victoria asked, taking a seat and indicating for Kim to do the same.

'It's actually not relevant to my investigation. Only if clients believe you're the real deal.'

'But you watched the show?'

'Of course,' Kim answered, wondering what kind of validation she wanted.

'And what's your view now?'

'I remain unconvinced.'

Victoria started to laugh. 'There are few people who would be quite so candid, so I appreciate your honesty. How can I help?'

'Monty Dunhill,' Kim said.

'Oh, what's the vicious old bitch done now?'

'You know him well?'

She shook her head. 'Not well but we've met a couple of times.'

'And?'

'And what? I called him an elitist, superior, snobby, privileged knob, and he called me a nouveau, tacky, tawdry low-class fraud. We've always been very honest with each other. It's how it works within such a competitive industry.'

'Competitive enough that he wrote a scathing hit piece where he had a lot to say about you.'

'Yes, I was flattered that he felt I was such a threat.'

'And are you?'

'Absolutely not. Monty likes the sterile intimacy of one-on-ones. He likes the feeling of exclusivity, as though he's some kind of secret weapon to the rich and famous. I don't do many private readings as I prefer the energy of a crowd. I like to feed off their emotion and anticipation. It's heady stuff.'

'And did the article bother you?'

'For about ten minutes while I wondered how it was going to affect my livelihood, and then the phone began to ring.'

Kim nodded for her to continue.

'No one north of Stoke had heard of me and suddenly my name was out there. The day the article came out I was booked for a show in Edinburgh and one in Liverpool, both venues I have now visited repeatedly. The article did me a favour. I now get to pick and choose the shows I want to do. And, I might add, they're always sold out.'

Well, that had been a definite miss on Monty's part, Kim thought.

'It didn't really do Monty any good either, if you want the truth,' Victoria offered.

'How so?'

'It was intended as an exposé of us, but many of his own clients relied on him being totally out of the limelight. The article mentions his rich, influential clients and, though he doesn't name names, many of them dropped him because of his sudden media visibility. I'm sure you've seen his house. It's not cheap to run.'

'You think he's broke?' Kim asked. Did Monty somehow blame other psychics because he'd lost money exposing them? Twisted but possible, given the size of his ego.

Victoria shrugged. 'I don't know, but it's fair to say he had a lot less disposable income after the article, and I've heard his current client list includes a couple of Z-list reality stars and a WAG or two.'

'Ouch,' Kim said, not finding it hard to imagine Monty's feelings about that.

Victoria cringed. 'Needs must, I suppose.'

'I'm sure you'll remember that Sandra Deakin was featured in that same article, and you obviously know that she was murdered on Sunday night.' The name of the victim had been officially released by the press liaison team earlier that day.

'Of course, yes, but I had completely forgotten that she was ripped to shreds in it. He loathed her. He has little nicknames for us all. He calls me Show Pony for obvious reasons, but he called Sandy Fish Course.'

Kim shook her head.

'Because he said it was the course at a dinner party that no one wanted. He called her bland, vanilla, forgettable and many other cruel names.'

And yet she'd still been trying to meet with him just days before her death.

'And then of course he had one name that was meaner than anything.'

'Which was?'

'Germ.'

'For who?' she asked, although she could take a pretty good guess.

'Phone psychics. Much of his venom was reserved for them. Hated them with a passion.'

Kim bristled. The nineteen-year-old boy lying in a pool of his own blood had been anything but a germ.

'They're not germs. They're just folks doing a job,' Kim said, surprising herself.

'Tell that to the precious purist. He's lobbying for a governing body.'

Kim wasn't all that surprised. But her thoughts turned from Monty Dunhill to the foremost reason for wanting a chat.

'We've got a second victim,' she offered.

'Linked to Sandy?' Victoria asked, frowning.

'Linked to the community,' Kim said and allowed a few seconds for that to sink in.

'Jesus.'

'Have you noticed anything strange?' Kim asked. 'Weird phone calls, same face turning up close to home, particularly unhappy customers?'

Victoria shook her head. 'Absolutely nothing. Can you tell me who the second victim is?'

'A phone psychic. I don't think you'd know him.'

'You are kidding me?'

Kim shook her head.

'Bloody hell.'

'I think you need to take precautions.'

'You think I might be in danger?' she asked as her eyes widened.

'Someone is attacking your community and you were named in that article.'

'You can't think Monty had anything to do with it?'

'We don't think anything. My sole intention here is to warn you to take precautions. Make sure you're not alone. Tell people where you're going. Check in with family members throughout the day.'

'I'll be fine,' she said dismissively. 'I'm psychic. Surely if anyone was coming after me, I'd be the first to know.'

Kim was unsure if she was joking, but again she was reminded that the most dangerous psychics were the ones who thought they were real.

She stood. 'Okay, thanks for your time and stay safe.'

Victoria nodded, and Kim headed for the door.

'Officer, there's something I'm tussling over whether to share with you or not.'

Kim turned but didn't take her hand off the door handle.

'That sentence dictates you've already made that decision.'

'It's probably nothing. It's just something Monty Dunhill said at a party a couple of months ago.'

'Go on.'

'He was roaring drunk but he had quite the audience. He started spouting off about frauds and fakes and charlatans. Got himself quite hot under the collar, and it was entertaining to watch until the end when he kind of peaked.'

'What did he say?'

'He said he'd wipe them all off the face of the earth if he could.'

FORTY-TWO

It was almost eleven when Terence let himself back into the house. The heavens had opened during his walk back and he was soaked through, his hair plastered to his head, but it didn't matter. His heart was soaring.

A quick walk around the outside of Stacey's property had told him that her bedroom lay at the rear of the flat, and it hadn't been hard to scale the gate to access the alley that ran behind the house.

He had stared up, willing her to come to the window so he could get a glance at her. The moment that she'd peeked out before drawing the curtains had been intimate and special. A moment between the two of them, when the security light had illuminated him and she'd realised that he was there. Just for her.

She may have thought that he couldn't see her, but she hadn't turned off the hallway light, which gave him not only a perfect view of her but a view of the hallway, enabling him to work out a rough floor plan of the flat.

He knew she had seen him. Now she knew that he would protect her.

If he'd had any doubts about her feelings, they had been squashed when she had repeatedly appeared at the window for the next two hours. Every visit had gladdened his heart further and reaffirmed that she felt the exact same way. She had been looking for him. She had been willing him to be waiting in the shadows, watching her, protecting her. That same spark that had electrified him during their first meeting had been there for her too.

He felt just a frisson of concern as he removed his coat. Whatever he'd done for Charlotte hadn't been enough. However he'd tried to prove his love, she'd wanted more. He'd taken it slowly and it hadn't worked.

He didn't want to make the same mistake with Stacey. He knew what he had to do. He had to try harder, work quicker to show her just how special she was to him. That he would love and treasure her like no one else ever could. He would show her that she had settled for the wrong person but it was okay.

He was here to rescue her now.

FORTY-THREE

After a restless night where sleep had remained just outside her clutches, Kim parked the bike outside the small house in Dudley, aware that the events of the night before were still on her mind.

The journey back from Wolverhampton had been silent. Tiff had travelled off into her own world and had been uncharacteristically quiet. Kim had dropped her home with the request that she attend the morning briefing. She'd changed the time to 8 a.m., to give Richard a chance to get in, and it also offered her an opportunity to make this early house call. Her mind was unsettled and there was only one person who could help her restore order. She knew this meeting wasn't going to help her solve the case, but it might help her settle her own mind.

The door was opened by a woman who showed no surprise to see her despite the years that had passed. And somehow Kim didn't think she had changed one bit, even though she was hovering around her mid-seventies.

'How lovely to see you again. Come in, Kim,' she said, stepping to the side.

Eloise Hunter had come into her life a few years back, when she'd been investigating the abduction of two young girls. Eloise had tried to insert herself into the case, claiming to have divine knowledge. It was the same case on which she'd first met Symes. Eloise herself had been placed in danger, and had survived only because she and Bryant had found her in time.

'To what do I owe this pleasure?' the woman asked, guiding her to the kitchen.

A second mug was sitting beside the kettle.

'You knew I was coming?'

Eloise chuckled. 'No, dear, I saw you pull up and it's just gone seven, so why wouldn't you want a cup of coffee?' The kettle boiled and Eloise poured the hot water into the mug. 'Although, it's progress on your part that you even asked that question.'

Kim said nothing as she followed Eloise to a small conservatory that was catching the lightening sky of the sunrise. The garden was an overgrown wilderness of small trees and thick shrubs. She counted three stocked bird feeders around the small space.

'What troubles you, my dear?' Eloise asked, placing Kim's mug beside her own on a wicker table that stood between two chairs. She closed her book and folded her reading glasses neatly on top.

'A case I'm working on. I have two dead psychics.'

'Gifted or not?' Eloise asked.

'One definitely not and the other I'm not sure about, but I don't really know what gifted is or if it truly exists.'

'Ah, that's why you're here. You have questions.'

Kim nodded.

'Ask away and I promise I won't be offended.'

'Are you a fraud? Do you take people's money and tell them what they want to hear?'

Eloise laughed. 'Enough small talk, Kim – just get to the point.'

Kim smiled and took a sip of her coffee.

Eloise continued. 'I'm going to start at the very beginning. I heard and felt nothing until I was eight years old. I was an only child and my parents and I were holidaying in North Wales. I was swimming in a lake.

'Just a couple of minutes was all it took. Some kind of weed wrapped itself around my ankle. I was being pulled under. I struggled to release it; the panic made my breathing worse. I was terrified and I kept trying to pull myself free. It just kept tightening. And then through all the noise in my head I heard one single, calm voice telling me to stop struggling, to just let go. That's what I did and lost consciousness. Apparently the weed unattached itself and my parents pulled me out.'

'So your gift came to you that day?' Kim asked.

Eloise shrugged. 'I don't know if it had always been there, but that was the first time I heard the voice inside my head.'

'And after that?'

Eloise smiled. 'The next time I frightened the life out of my mum, who was baking while I was colouring at the kitchen table. She muttered to herself, "Where's that eight-inch cake tin?" and straight away I said, "Bottom cupboard, top shelf." I don't know where the words came from but they just came out of my mouth. That happened more and more over the next couple of years. I just found that I knew stuff. Knowledge was in my head and I hadn't put it there.'

'Were you scared?' Kim asked.

'No, the first experience I had with the voice, it saved my life. I never saw it as anything other than a friend.'

'Were your parents worried?'

Eloise shook her head. 'They accepted that I knew things but my dad advised me it was best not to tell anyone else, that not everyone could do what I could.'

'Did it progress?' Kim asked.

'It changed over time. I remember once at the end of a school day, my teacher was packing away everything on her desk. I had the urge to tell her that she didn't need to do that, and as I left the classroom, I was besieged by this overwhelming sadness. I just wanted to cry. I said nothing but I wasn't as shocked as others to learn the next morning that she'd been killed in a car accident. Obviously I was distraught. I felt like it was my fault, that I'd been given a message and that I should have warned her.'

'Of what?' Kim asked.

'That's what my parents said. I didn't know exactly what was going to happen; I only felt that something was going to happen.

'That kind of thing happened for many years. One time, in high school, my best friend finally started going steady with the boy she'd fantasised over for months. It got to the time they were talking about sex. I broke my own rule and told her he was going to leave her as soon as he got what he wanted. She called me jealous, we fell out and he did exactly what I said he'd do. She hated me even more after that, and I learned a valuable lesson.'

'Which was?'

'Don't offer the truth to someone who isn't ready to receive it.'

'How does that work with readings?'

'I do very few now, and only for people who are desperate for my help, and if I can't help, I tell them that.'

'How can you not help everyone?' Kim asked, trying to understand.

'Because it doesn't work that way. I don't know everything about everyone, and I can't dial in to the voices as and when I choose. Anyone that can do that has a different kind of gift to me. To explain, yesterday I went shopping at Asda. I passed a man picking some tomatoes. I knew that his debit card was going to be declined. When I got to the checkout, I knew the girl that served me was going to get a call to confirm she'd been accepted at Aston University, but I passed dozens of other people with no premonitions at all.'

Eloise regarded her silently for a minute. 'I can see the doubt in your face, and I'm not going to do any party tricks to convince you. Like I said, I occasionally offer my gift, free of charge, to people who want to receive it or who really need it.'

'Who really needs it?' Kim asked.

'I visit a hospice in Netherton every Tuesday and Thursday. I offer comfort.'

'But you just said that sometimes you don't feel anything.'

'And if I don't feel anything, I don't say anything. I'm just an old lady, spending a few hours keeping some very poorly people company. If I can offer comfort, I do.'

'Okay, but what about people with less integrity? What about fraudsters?' Kim asked.

'What about them?' Eloise asked. 'Every profession has them.'

'But how do you feel about them? I went to a stage show last night and I have no idea whether the psychic was genuinely gifted or not. My natural scepticism tells me not, but I struggle to see the harm if she's a fraud. She gave many people comfort.'

'And she probably did very well out of it.'

'You're saying I'm wrong to feel that way?' Kim asked.

'I'm saying it's up to you how you feel about it. Let me use this example. People love designer handbags – not sure why, I don't get it myself, but horses for courses. If someone unknowingly buys a fake one and never finds out because it is such a good copy, does it affect their enjoyment of the product?'

'You're saying that fakes do no harm?'

'I'm not saying it's right or wrong for people to do what they do. I'm saying that the indignation is only an issue if the fakery is discovered.'

Kim opened her mouth but Eloise held up her hand. 'You're not going to stop until I give you a straight answer so here it is; no, I don't approve of people using clever techniques to read people. It's not something I would ever do. For me the truth is the truth and that's the end of it.'

Kim said nothing. She was not getting the answers she'd hoped for.

'I can see that you're still conflicted but I can't reach a resolution for you. Your indecision tells me that you're not yet ready to receive your gift.'

'You have one for me?' Kim asked, surprised.

'I've always had one for you. To be passed on at the right time, which is not now.'

Kim couldn't help the curiosity that had been piqued, and yet she knew Eloise was right. She wasn't ready for the suspension of disbelief.

'So, in the meantime, I'll send a gift via you. There's someone linked to you that needs to be told to check the pocket of a camel coat.'

Kim raised an eyebrow, and Eloise opened her hands.

'That's it.'

Kim thanked her for her time and let herself out the front door. She had hoped to leave this meeting with a firm opinion one way or another, but as she straddled the bike, she was no longer sure what she believed.

FORTY-FOUR

'Great, everyone's here,' Kim said, stepping out of the Bowl.

Tiff had pulled up a chair next to Stacey, and Richard was back with his laptop and books at the spare desk.

'A quick debrief about last night and then Tink can get back to work,' Kim said, looking towards Richard. 'It all happened like clockwork. Tink was approached and questioned. Everything she told the stooge was repeated back to her by the psychic. Totally got everything you said about emotional investment and willingness to see past the misses. We may have been the only two non-believers in the audience,' she said, looking at Tink, who coloured slightly but smiled and nodded.

'I spoke to Victoria afterwards, to try and warn her. She didn't seem too bothered and I doubt she'll take my advice. She did, however, reveal that Monty Dunhill's hatred of frauds went beyond the limits of professional disapproval. He even made some kind of drunken threat about wiping them all off the planet. Most likely nothing but he stays on our radar.'

They all nodded their agreement.

She turned to the constable. 'Tink, you wanna share your experience last night?' Kim asked, folding her arms.

'Err... yeah... I... umm... decided on a story that was pretty much true about me and my gran. I told Neil all about our argument and her fall. I told him how close we were.' She swallowed. 'And the psychic got it all. She told me that my gran forgave me and was with me every day.'

'Don't forget that small detail about the crisps,' Kim said.

'I didn't tell him about the crisps,' Tiff said.

'You must have done,' Kim said.

'I didn't,' she insisted. 'I didn't tell him that she ate a bag of salty crisps every night before she went to bed. I didn't tell him!'

Kim opened her mouth to say something, but Richard stepped in.

'She probably didn't.'

'Huh?' Kim said.

'Still no mystery, I'm afraid. We go back to trivia and percentages. Crisps in one form or another are the most popular snack in the country. Safe bet. People of a certain age prefer plain crisps because there wasn't much choice when they were children. So it wasn't beyond the realms of possibility that a woman of your gran's age would have liked a bag of plain crisps.'

Despite the time she'd spent with Eloise earlier, Kim had to admit that Richard made a compelling argument.

But it wasn't one that Tiff needed to hear, Kim realised. Regardless of her own beliefs on the subject, the girl had received something positive from the fact-finding mission that did her no harm in believing to be true.

'Okay, Tink, thanks again for helping us out last night. You're an absolute star, but we'd best let you get back to your sergeant.'

'Okay, boss, thanks for taking me,' she said, standing. 'And always happy to help.'

They all called their 'see ya laters' as she left the office, but Kim had an unexplainable void in the pit of her stomach.

'She believes it, doesn't she?' Stacey asked, once Tiff was out of sight.

Kim nodded. 'She barely spoke in the car.'

'But even after the proof of hearing her own words to the stooge repeated back to her, she still—'

'Did you believe in Father Christmas?' Richard interrupted Stacey to ask.

'She still does,' Bryant said, with a mischievous smile.

'Of course,' Stacey answered.

'Do you remember how you found out that he wasn't real?'

'Yeah, I saw my mom carrying my presents down the stairs.'

'And what did you tell yourself?'

'That she was Santa's helper.'

'Anything else?'

Stacey thought for a minute. 'Actually, yes. I told myself that Santa had to drop some presents off early, so he could get them all done.'

'So even when presented with the evidence, you found a way to continue the belief?'

Stacey nodded.

'Because you wanted to. You didn't want to lose that belief that represented magic and wonder. The wish to continue believing in something despite evidence to the contrary is very powerful.'

'It's true,' Stacey said. 'I was still looking for reasons to believe until somewhere in my mid-teens.'

They all laughed but Kim could completely see Richard's point.

'Okay, so Azim's phone will be dropped off later this morning,' Kim said, bringing their focus back to the growing to-do list. 'Stace, I want you to see if you can find any threats similar to the ones sent to Sandy.'

'Okay, boss.'

'And dig a bit deeper on Father George. I don't like the fact he put his hands on Sandy when she wouldn't listen to him. Is it something he's done before? And find out who I speak to about his conduct. Who is his boss? First person to mention the man upstairs is buying the coffee for a month.'

Bryant lowered his hand.

'Penn, can you work with Stace once you've put the other thing to bed and tucked it in?'

'Hey, boss,' Stacey said. 'I got an address for the kid who was with Bradley Foster on the day he disappeared. Josh Adams lives on Hollytree.'

'Which bit?'

Stacey pulled a face, indicating it was the worst bit. One of the three tower blocks that rose up from the centre.

'Text it to Bryant.'

She saw the brief look of disapproval that passed over his face, but it was worth a ten-minute chat with the guy. They had nothing to lose, and if there was anything they could do to ease Rose's loss then they would.

And while they were on the subject of nothing to lose.

'Hey guys. If anyone has a camel coat, it's worth checking the pockets.'

She was aware of the looks from her team as she headed into the Bowl to grab her coat.

They were wondering if she'd lost her mind, and she was half wondering if they were right.

FORTY-FIVE

Stacey let out a sigh of relief as the office emptied around her after the briefing. Richard didn't know her well enough to recognise the tension she'd been holding and the supreme effort it had taken to appear her normal self.

She didn't do well on little sleep at the best of times but last night she'd been unable to get the image of Terence Birch out of her mind.

When standing at the window, she'd blinked and he'd gone, leaving her to wonder if she had really seen him there at all.

Her logical, sensible brain had told her that she'd been seeing things. That there was no reason for the man to be outside staring up at her window. It was a view she'd enforced to herself while taking a shower.

She'd been about to call Devon and then realised how ridiculous it would sound that she thought she'd seen a man she'd interviewed recently, standing in a restricted area, staring up at their bedroom window.

No, she must have been mistaken, she told herself repeatedly.

She had dried herself, dressed and continued their evening

as though nothing had happened. She'd pushed the food around her plate until it looked like she'd eaten something and pretended to watch *Downton*. She had no clue what had happened in the episode, and hadn't even realised what she was doing until Devon asked her if she had a dodgy stomach.

'No, why?' she answered, feeling the heat flood her face as she retook her seat on the sofa.

'That's the third time you've been to the loo. You sure you're okay?'

'Yeah, yeah, I'm fine,' she'd reassured Devon with a squeeze of the hand.

She hadn't been to the loo once. She'd repeatedly visited the bedroom window to take another look outside, either to see if he was still there or to talk herself out of what she thought she'd seen in the first place.

At around 11.30 p.m., she'd feigned a headache and headed off to bed, where she had lain in the darkness playing the event over and over in her mind. She'd felt Devon get into bed an hour later and had been lying in the darkness long after. She guessed she'd dropped off somewhere around 3 a.m., only to wake a couple of hours later to immediately check the window again.

Her conscious mind was trying to find all kinds of loopholes for what she'd seen, including trying to convince her that she hadn't really seen it at all. With every hour that passed, the more convinced she became that the vision had been nothing more than a trick of the light.

Focus, focus, focus, she told herself over and over while looking at the rough notes of tasks from the boss.

Given what they'd learned about Father George's hands-on approach to certain members of his congregation, she decided to start there.

She looked down the list of the placements and found herself gravitating towards the shortest stays. Gloucestershire was barely a year and wasn't too far away. Although she knew that no criminal charges had ever been filed against him, she knew that complaints didn't always result in a charge. Due to the time that had elapsed, Stacey knew trying to track down anyone from the church might be a problem, but she had a long shot she was willing to try. Just because Father George had never been charged didn't mean he wasn't known.

Gloucestershire Constabulary served 1,024 square miles and 637,000 people with approximately twelve hundred full-time police officers. She didn't want the headquarters of the force. They probably wouldn't know anything, but the neighbourhood station might. She searched for the details of his placement and saw that he'd been just on the outskirts of Tewkesbury. Tewkesbury had its own station.

She rang the number, not exactly sure what she was going to say. It was only when the line was answered that it came to her.

'Hi, may I speak with one of your sergeants, preferably one that's been there for over fifteen years?'

'Excuse me?' the female voice answered.

Yeah, she was going to need to give a better explanation than that. She introduced herself and continued.

'It's about an active murder investigation and a name has come up from your area. It's a long shot but I just need to talk to someone about him.'

Stacey wore the silence while the woman chose between telling her to naff off or actually trying to be helpful.

'One sec,' she said, before chamber music entered her ear.

After about three minutes of repeat a gruff voice came on to the line. 'Sergeant Brownhill.'

'Sergeant, thank you for sparing the time to talk to me,' Stacey offered. 'I explained to the—'

'Name?' he growled.

'My name is—'

'Not yours. I've been told that already. Your person of interest?' he asked irritably.

'George Markinson. That's Father George Markinson. He was vicar at St Matthew's in Tewkesbury from 2006 to 2007.'

'I was a beat officer back then,' he answered.

'Do you recall any kind of complaint made against the man?' she asked, holding her breath.

'You checked the records?'

'Yes,' she said, fighting the deflation. 'No criminal charges, but that doesn't necessarily mean there was no chatter.'

'As you say, there were no criminal charges and it was a long time ago.'

'It was, but thanks for talking to me anyway.'

'No probs. This your mobile number?' he asked.

'Yes, why?'

'No reason. Just in case I remember anything of interest, like when I'm on a break or something.'

Stacey felt a rush of hope. All calls were recorded. He couldn't be talking to her about rumours and hearsay on an official police line. From his own phone to hers was a different story.

'Again, thanks for your time, Sergeant Brownhill.'

Stacey ended the call and, like a word association game, thoughts of Father George inevitably led to the face of Terence Birch appearing in her mind.

A rock plummeted to the pit of her stomach every time she thought of him. No matter how many times she told herself she'd been mistaken, the feeling of dread wasn't leaving her stomach.

She had a sudden idea.

'I'll just be a minute,' Stacey said, stepping out of the office, unsure why she was explaining her actions to Richard, whose attention was very firmly fixed on his laptop. She key-carded herself out of the building and finally stopped moving about twenty feet away from the station entrance.

Her gaze did a quick sweep of the area but she was being stupid. Her mind was just playing tricks on her after seeing his aggression and knowing what he'd done to Charlotte.

Even so, she decided to reassure herself by calling someone who could put her mind at rest.

She leaned against the wall and scrolled to the contact in her list.

'Hey, buddy,' Alison said as she answered the phone.

'Got a minute?' Stacey asked.

'For my bestie, always. Wassup?'

She'd worked with psychological profiler Alison Lowe on numerous occasions. Outside of that working relationship, the two of them had struck up an unlikely but very firm friendship.

'Wanna talk to you about stalking.'

'Oh, come on. I thought we weren't gonna bring that up,' Alison joked.

Normally, Stacey would have laughed at that but not today.

Intuitive enough to know her humour hadn't landed, Alison launched straight into helpful mode. 'What do you need?'

'Just tell me what you know,' Stacey said, moving further away from the building.

'Okay, the majority of stalkers are male. Women stalkers are rarer and tend to target other women. What are we talking about?'

'Men stalking women.'

'Us psychologists group stalkers as either psychotic or non-psychotic. The majority are non-psychotic and their pursuit of victims is angry, vindictive, focussed, obsessive depending on the type they are.'

'There are types?' Stacey asked. Surely if she knew what Birch was, she'd have a better chance of understanding how to deal with him.

'You've got five types of stalker. Rejected stalkers follow their victims in order to reverse or avenge a rejection. Resentful stalkers start a vendetta cos of a sense of grievance against the victim, motivated mainly by the desire to frighten and distress. Intimacy seekers are trying to establish a relationship with their victim. This type believes the victim is a long-sought-after soulmate and that they were meant to be together. Incompetent suitors are the type that have poor social skills and develop a fixation, a sense of entitlement, about those who have attracted their interest. And then you have predatory stalkers who spy on the victim in order to prepare and plan an attack which is often sexual.'

The third one, intimacy seeker, sounded like Birch's fixation on Charlotte, but the last description Alison had offered had chilled her to the bone.

'Can there be a crossover?' Stacey asked, crossing her fingers.

'I wouldn't rule it out. I'm not sure every stalker stays the same, but I don't have any data to back that up.'

'Do they go for a certain victim?' Stacey asked.

'Victims are normally prior intimates for the rejected stalker but otherwise victims can be casual acquaintances, friends, neighbours, professional contacts, colleagues, strangers and sometimes famous people. Has the victim contacted the National Stalking Hotline?'

'No... I mean... I don't think so.'

'They should,' Alison advised. 'They should also keep in close contact with their local police force. I know that's not CID but I'm just saying. Since the law changed in 1997, the Protection from Harassment Act makes reporting incidents to the authorities much easier than it used to be before stalking was an actual crime. It's now a criminal offence, punishable by up to six months in prison, to make a course of conduct which amounts to harassment on two or more occasions. The court can issue a restraining order which carries a maximum punishment of five years if breached.'

Stacey allowed her friend to keep talking as though she wasn't on the line with a police officer, while all the time thinking that none of this improved protection had helped Charlotte.

'You are treating her seriously, aren't you?'

'Of course,' Stacey said.

'Good. I'm not sure anyone who hasn't experienced it can properly appreciate the devastation being stalked can have on the victim's life.'

Charlotte had moved thousands of miles away, so she was starting to get a good idea.

'It's not referred to as psychological rape for no reason,' Alison continued.

'Go on,' Stacey said.

'It affects everything. Stalking is a form of mental assault in which the perpetrator repeatedly breaks into the life-world of the victim. The separate acts that make up the intrusion can't by themselves cause mental abuse but do when taken together.'

'What do you mean?' Stacey asked. Surely any unwanted attention was mental abuse.

'Try telling people that you're being distressed by some nut job sending you a bouquet of flowers every day. Tell them that you're seeing a man outside your home repeatedly. Tell them that you're getting barraged with text messages on a daily basis. Singularly it appears dismissible, but put it together and you're provoking real fear and it's the fear that changes your life.'

'You mentioned the help available to protect the victim, but what if that doesn't work? What if he doesn't get the message?' Stacey asked.

Nothing had worked to dampen Birch's fixation on Charlotte.

'Resentful stalkers demonstrate an almost pure culture of

persecution. There is little punishment that will deter them. They will take the court appearances; they'll even take the prison time; but none of these actions will prevent them continuing once they're back on the streets. I mean, obviously don't tell your victim that, but this type of stalker can't be reasoned with or punished. They thrive on the chaos they cause.'

'Go on,' Stacey urged, still waiting for the 'this could never happen to me' moment.

'They love the effects on the victim. They know that being stalked affects every part of a victim's life – their psyche, their health, work and social life. Victims suffer stress and anxiety, depression and symptoms associated with PTSD. They can become fearful of leaving the house. They suffer denial, confusion, self-doubt, guilt, embarrassment, self-blame, terror of being alone. They feel isolated and helpless to stop it. They're unable to sleep because of nightmares and rumination. They become hyper vigilant, which in itself is exhausting, and all this can lead to suicidal thoughts.

'Physically, victims suffer from fatigue, stress headaches, gastrointestinal problems, weight loss, ulcers, psoriasis, dizziness, heart palpitations and sweating. Many lose their jobs due to either deteriorating performance or increased sick leave. Social lives suffer through avoidance of usual activities, trying to protect others and changing phone numbers, name, appearance, everything really. If you give me a couple of specifics, I might be able to help more.'

Stacey took a breath. 'He has form. He stalked another woman for years, believed they were meant to be together. She did everything she could. He served time and it made no difference. She left her family and friends and moved halfway around the world to escape him.'

Silence. 'Alison, you still there?'

'Yeah, digesting what you just said.'

'And?'

'How do you stop a man that sees a prison term as nothing more than an interruption? The system is improved but it won't send someone away indefinitely.'

'So how does it end?' Stacey asked.

'It doesn't. Sounds like your man has transferred his affection to another victim and all I can say is bloody good luck to her. She's gonna need it.'

'Thanks, Alison,' Stacey said, needing to get off the phone before she gave herself away.

'Okay, should I bill you direct or send it to the station?' Alison joked.

'Put it on my tab,' Stacey said, before ending the call.

She'd learned a lot but she hadn't got what she'd hoped for: reassurance.

In fact, Alison hadn't put her mind at rest at all.

FORTY-SIX

After a good walk around Stourbridge looking for Jericho, Penn found himself back at the food bank as a woman in her thirties was opening the door.

'Hi, I'm looking for Jericho,' he said, showing his ID.

'Jericho who?' she asked, looking away.

'He's done nothing wrong,' Penn assured her.

'I didn't think he had but I still don't know him.'

Penn frowned.

'Look, just leave him alone. He doesn't want to be saved. He's not an addict, he's not an alcoholic, he's not violent and he's all right as he is.'

'I just want to give him an update on Barry Sharpe.'

'Who?'

'Dan,' he said, using the man's nickname.

'Oh, yeah I heard about that. He died in the underpass?'

Penn nodded. 'Jericho was helpful in getting him identified and the man's family were informed of his passing.'

Penn saw the indecision on her face. 'I don't want to harm him.'

'He'll probably be over at the Tesco Superstore. It's where a lot of them go in the morning just to clean up a bit in the toilets.'

'Okay, thanks.'

'You sure you don't want to save him?' she asked.

'Absolutely not.'

'If you hang about for ten minutes, he'll be here.'

Penn was confused. As far as he knew they didn't offer breakfast.

'We get our delivery from the food bank around nine thirty. He helps us unload if he's around. He gets a bacon sarnie and Kizzy gets a tin of Chappie.'

'Thanks,' Penn said, following her inside. It was good to know that both the dog and the man were guaranteed one meal a day.

'You said when he's around,' Penn noted, following her through to the kitchen that although dated with prehistoric appliances, appeared spotlessly clean and functional.

'He's not one of our permanents. He appears a couple of times a year around the same time for a few days and then disappears again. Doesn't give us a minute's trouble and is always polite and well-mannered.'

So why the hell was he on the streets? Penn wondered.

'I can see that look on your face. I've already warned you. Don't be trying to save him.'

'I won't. I'm just curious.'

'Well, here he comes now,' she said as a Luton van pulled up out front.

Jericho walked in with Kizzy walking faithfully beside him.

'Hey there,' he said pleasantly.

'Hi, I just wanted a minute to update you on Dan.'

'Okay, but you gotta unload at the same time,' he said, nodding towards the van. The roller door on the back was already being raised. The woman had already fussed the dog and was opening a tin of dog food.

Penn followed Jericho to the back of the truck.

'That batch there, mate,' the driver said, pointing to a pile of goods on the left.

Jericho grabbed the first sack of potatoes and made the carrying look effortless. Penn tried to do the same, but Jericho was already behind the counter as Penn made it through the front door. Best save the talking until they were done unloading, he reasoned to himself and made a mental note to rejoin the gym.

Second trip in and Penn could smell the bacon cooking. He'd had breakfast but his stomach still grumbled in appreciation.

Four more trips each and the van had been unburdened of potatoes, fresh veg, countless tins, pasta, rice and bread.

Jericho hit the back of the van to tell the driver it was all done.

Penn followed him back inside.

Two plates of bacon sandwiches were waiting on the counter.

'You help, you get fed,' the woman said.

He smiled his thanks as he pushed his plate towards Jericho.

'So, that guy. His name was Barry Sharpe and he leaves behind an ex-wife and teenage daughter.'

'Ah, man,' Jericho said, wiping a dollop of brown sauce from around his mouth. 'Poor kid.'

'You were right about the gambling. His problem was extreme. He gambled the family home on a local football game and he lost, leaving the family homeless. Out of shame, he disappeared and took to the streets.' Penn shook his head, still unable to believe it himself.

'Ah, that explains it,' Jericho said, taking a sandwich from Penn's plate.

'Explains what?'

'He often mumbled something about a goal. Can't remember exactly but he muttered about it often.'

'Well, I just thought you'd like to know.'

'Cheers, buddy,' he said.

'So how did you end up here?' Penn asked.

The woman offered him a warning glance but he couldn't help being intrigued.

'It's where life took me, man.'

'But you seem. I dunno...'

'Circumstances aren't always by force. Sometimes by design.'

'Sorry, I don't get you.'

'Some folks don't belong in your world, bud. Some folks choose to check out, live differently. They make their bed and then they've gotta lie in it. That's all.'

Penn could see that was the end of the conversation, but he'd liked to have learned more about the note of regret that had crept into his tone.

'Okay, well thanks for your help and take care,' he said, moving away from the counter.

'No probs. Oh, hang on,' Jericho said, chewing the last bite of sandwich.

Penn waited.

'The other word that Dan kept saying about that goal.'

'Oh yeah,' Penn said.

'Dodgy. He kept saying dodgy.'

FORTY-SEVEN

Trips to Hollytree never filled Kim with a warm feeling. The estate had been her home for the first six years of her life. It was also the place where her twin had died of starvation in her arms. His killer was now deceased herself, but nothing would ever lessen the overwhelming pain of loss whenever she came near the place. Thankfully they weren't going into Chaucer House this time.

Bryant followed her gaze and finally let go of the disapproving look he'd been wearing since they'd got in the car. He knew exactly what had happened to her on this estate.

She'd looked over the notes of Bradley's disappearance ten years earlier and, like Stacey, could see little wrong with the investigation. But sometimes time and distance offered the opportunity to look back on an incident and recall only the facts without the emotion.

They knocked the door on the eighth floor of the tower block.

It was answered by a red-haired freckled male in his mid-twenties. From the notes she'd read the night before, she knew they were looking at Josh Adams.

He nodded when she said his name.

His face went into panic mode when they both showed their IDs.

She had the urge to tell him he'd done nothing wrong but something stopped her. She hadn't stepped inside yet and this was Hollytree. There were innocents and good people but not very many of them. Hollytree had the distinguished reputation of housing the area's worst dregs so that other council estates in the area could breathe more easily.

'May we come in?' she asked.

He looked behind him. 'It's not really a good time.'

'We'll only take a minute,' she said, appraising him. The dirty toenails protruding from the grubby jogging bottoms said he was barefoot, and the grease-stained T-shirt indicated he wasn't going anywhere in a hurry.

He pointed to the living room at the end of the hallway. She didn't need telling. It was the same layout as the other two blocks. The long windows that offered a view of the small playing ground below were drowning beneath heavy brown curtains that were both too wide and too long.

He rushed to clear the sofa and two armchairs.

'Sorry, flatmate's a pig.'

Kim said nothing as she took a seat. Her eagle eye had spotted nothing untoward except for a can of beer that could easily have been from the night before.

Josh disabused her of that notion when he lifted it to his mouth and finished it off.

Not illegal. Just early.

'Josh, can we just ask you about that day ten years ago when Bradley was abducted?'

He swallowed. 'Yeah, sure,' he said, reaching for the can that he'd already emptied.

'Can you take us through it once more?'

'Yeah, yeah, but why?'

'We want to offer his mother closure if we can.'

'Oh, okay, well, yeah, I mean we set off for school; Brad said to race through the woods. He took off and I got a puncture. By the time I got to the end of the woods, I saw a van closing its back door and driving off at speed. I didn't know Brad hadn't carried on to school until I got there. Then I told the teacher what had happened.'

The same story he'd told the police at the time. Almost.

'Could you tell us again but in more detail?' Kim asked.

'There ain't no more detail. We were going to school, we raced, I got a puncture and my mate got grabbed by some sort of pervert who killed him and hid the body in Cannock.'

'Was there any particular reason he wanted to race?'

'Nah, we did it all the time.'

'Did he normally win?'

'About fifty-fifty.'

'Sometimes you won?' Kim asked.

'Oh yeah.'

'But not that day?'

'I got a puncture,' he repeated.

'Yes, you said,' Kim offered, slowing down the questions. 'Had you ever seen a van like that on your way to school before?'

He shrugged. 'Probably wouldn't have noticed if I had.'

'And what colour was it?'

'White.'

'Young or old.'

'Oldish I think.'

'What makes you think that?' Kim asked. He hadn't been able to say either way when questioned ten years ago.

'Err... I dunno... I think cos when I see it in my mind now there's some rust around the back doors.'

'Any letters at all in the registration plate?'

He shook his head.

'Company name?'

'No.'

'Dents or marks?'

'No.'

'Bumper stickers?'

'No. Look, I was a kid. I didn't even know that the van mattered until I got to school.'

'Okay, and how did you fix your puncture?'

'Oh, err... I just blew up the tyre with my pump.'

'And you remember doing that clearly?'

'Of course,' he said, looking anything but sure.

'Okay, Josh, thanks for your time,' she said, standing. 'We may need to speak to you again.'

'There's nothing more I can tell you. There's no point in you coming back.'

'We'll be the judge of that,' Kim said, once they were at the front door.

He closed the door behind them, and Bryant let out a long breath.

'Jesus, I need a lie-down after that.'

'The questioning?' she asked.

'No, the tension. It was coming off him in waves. He really doesn't like to talk about it, does he?'

'Not at all and I can now understand why. He can't keep his story straight.'

'Guv, he offered no story at all.'

'Yeah, but what he did offer has changed. Ten years ago, he was delayed in the woods because his chain came off. Today, he specifically said he got a puncture and he remembered stopping to pump it up.'

'His very demeanour says he's lying, guv.'

'Absolutely, Bryant, but about what?'

FORTY-EIGHT

'Fuck, fuck, fuck,' Josh shouted, throwing the empty can against the wall. He'd messed up and he knew it.

No one had taken too much notice of the lack of detail and nervousness of a fifteen-year-old boy, given what they thought he'd been through. But his inability to lie successfully was a different story now he was an adult.

He slumped down on a chair in the kitchen, reliving the events of that godforsaken day after the police had been called. He'd talked to them for what seemed like hours, telling them the same story over and over again. Of course he'd said the chain had come off. He'd known there was no way anyone could disprove that. He'd even wiped his fingers over the oily gears for good measure, congratulating himself on his creativity. No one had questioned him further. His story had been watertight, until now.

He'd weathered the police officers back then; he'd battled through the media storm and the attention it had brought to his family, and his story hadn't changed once. Until now.

'Damn,' he cursed, running his hands through his hair. That detective had sussed something. As soon as he'd forgotten his original story, the nerves had kicked in and he felt as though the events of that day had been playing like a video across his forehead. His heart was still beating out of his chest.

After talking to the police, he'd joined the search party. Of course he had. He was Bradley's best friend, the last person to see him before he was abducted. Where else would he have been?

His own parents, who had loved Brad, had searched every minute they could. They'd comforted Brad's mum, who had bravely tried to carry on while fighting back tears.

He had watched her closely, battling away the guilt of lying to her. She had cooked him many meals, had him over for sleepovers, given him lunch money when his mum forgot. Once or twice she'd even helped him with his homework. She was a nice lady, and she hadn't deserved what she was having to endure.

The guilt for what he'd done to her had started then and it had never gone away.

He had the answers to all her questions but he couldn't share them. She would hate him. They all would.

No. He could never tell the truth. But he had to do something. He had to find a way to stop the police sniffing around. There was only one thing he could think of and that meant coming face to face with the person that haunted his dreams. Just the thought of it sent his stomach churning. He had to remember not to panic. If he did, he could give himself away and bring the whole house of cards tumbling down. He needed to think.

It was time to do what he always did when the remorse threatened to overwhelm him.

He opened the fridge and grabbed another can of beer.

FORTY-NINE

Stacey put Azim's phone to the side as Richard approached the coffee machine and raised his cup in her direction. He sure could rival the boss on caffeine intake.

'I'm good thanks,' she said, pointing to her can of Diet Coke, dreading the moment the boss rang.

She had found the grand sum of zero threats on Azim's phone. She had found plenty of memes and messages to friends. His email communication wasn't extensive, which was pretty normal for a nineteen-year-old, and there was no sign of any negativity. His search history was focussed on hotels in different parts of India and train routes. He'd mentioned nothing strange to friends in his messages, thereby giving them no link to Sandra's murder, other than their profession and manner of death. The boss was not going to be pleased.

Immersing herself in her work had put some distance between now and her conversation with Alison, and it had given her a clearer perspective. She was getting worked up about nothing. None of what Alison said applied to her. She still wasn't even sure she'd seen Terence Birch in the shadows the night before. It could be her imagination playing tricks on her, following the hostile encounter with him on Monday. And even if it was him, he was just trying to scare her because she'd challenged his ego and his fantasies about Charlotte. She had resolved in her mind that he'd consider his job done; he'd given her a bit of a fright and she would never hear from him again.

'So, how's the book going?' Stacey asked Richard as he headed back to his seat. More content in her thoughts, she could afford to take a breather before starting the next task, and hopefully Penn would be back soon to pick up a shovel and do some digging of his own.

'Oh, I'm trudging through the soggy middle at the minute,' Richard said, putting on his glasses.

'The soggy what?'

'I often know how I'm going to start and end a book and the middle tends to take care of itself, except that it's taking its time at the minute. I feel like this whole chapter is repeating an area I covered in the previous book.'

'Maybe you should consider a section where you question your own beliefs and convictions.'

Richard threw back his head and laughed. 'Oh, I can see why you gave Santa so many excuses. You really don't like to adapt your belief system, do you?'

Stacey chuckled with him. She knew she was giving him a hard time.

'I still don't see how you can answer every psychic's hits with your analysis,' Stacey said. 'Can you not even consider that some of it may be real?'

'I'm not here to try and alter your convictions. I believe wholeheartedly that psychics don't exist.'

'My mum used to watch an American talk show, Montel something, and there was this one woman...'

'Likely Sylvia Browne,' Richard advised. 'Who happens to have quite a lengthy chapter in my new book which focusses on celebrity psychics.'

'She just seemed so on the money,' Stacey said.

'Sylvia Browne told the mother of kidnapping victim Amanda Berry that she was dead. She was found alive in 2013. Incidentally, her mother had stopped looking and had died by the time her child was found.

'In 2002 she told the family of Shawn Hornbeck that the eleven-year-old was dead. He was found alive four years later. She told a family that six-year-old Opal Jo Jennings had been forced into slavery in Japan. An autopsy showed she'd died within hours of abduction. To name but a few.'

'Did no one call her out as a fraud?' Stacey asked.

'James Randi tried to. He was a Canadian-American stage magician and scientific sceptic who offered a one-million-dollar bounty to anyone able to prove to him that they were psychic. Sylvia Browne, amongst others, was invited by Randi to take up the challenge. The prize remains unclaimed.'

'Okay, but there are some psychics or mediums that have helped on police cases, yes?' Stacey asked.

'Not according to a group named UK Sceptics that called every police force in the country. Every force but one said no and the Met offered no further details.'

'Sorry,' Stacey said as her phone started to ring. She could have listened to the man all day, but she did appreciate that they'd offered him a quiet workspace in exchange for his expertise.

'Hey, boss,' she said. 'The answer is no. There are no threats on Azim's phone. Our killer didn't make contact with him from what I can see.'

'Damn it,' the boss growled. 'If he was an opportunist victim based purely on his place of work, we're stuffed.'

Silence for a minute.

'Okay, double the efforts on the threats on Sandy's computer. At least we have a connection there.'

'Okay, boss.'

'Before you go, can you grab a file from my desk? Top one with statements taken on the day of Bradley's disappearance.'

'One sec,' she said, putting down the phone to go look. She hadn't realised that the boss was going to spend so long on the Bradley Foster case. It had looked quite well run and thorough.

'Got it, boss,' she said, picking up the phone.

'There was a note in there of a woman in her mid-sixties who gave a conflicting account. Got a name?'

'Nancy Houseman. Lives at twenty-six Baker Street. One minute she said there was a van, then said there wasn't.'

'Okay, thanks, Stace,' the boss said, ending the call as a bouquet of roses appeared at the door.

'DC Wood?' asked the constable carrying them.

'Y... yes, that's me,' she said as he started walking towards her.

He laid them on her desk, and she thanked him as a spear of panic surged through her. What occasion had she forgotten? It wasn't their anniversary.

'Hmm... nice,' Richard said, raising his glasses and then returning his attention to the screen.

Stacey plucked the card from the centre of the flowers and opened the envelope. Her blood froze in her veins.

Forever.

She threw the card on the desk and pushed the flowers away from her. There was no doubt in her mind that they were from Terence Birch. She stared in horror at the bouquet until she became aware of Richard watching her.

She grabbed them. 'I'll just go and put these in some water,' she said, rushing from the room. She stormed into the small kitchen used by the control-room staff and threw the flowers into the sink, eager to get them out of her hands, as though they could contaminate her. That card. Just that one word had chilled her to the bone.

She took a good few breaths and realised that she couldn't lie to herself any more. She needed to just get through the rest of the day so she could be alone to think. Make a plan. Work out how she was going to handle it.

She composed herself and strode back to the office. For now, she would focus on the tasks at hand. She had a job to do.

She grabbed Sandra's computer and decided to have a closer look at the email threats sent to her.

They were from a Hotmail account and Stacey instantly pressed the view button, then scrolled to message and headers, which gave her a page of code. Her gaze instantly picked out the IP address.

Normally, once she had the IP address, she could approach the virtual private network and try to force them to give up the information by court order, but on this occasion she didn't need to.

She checked her findings again.

Well, that didn't make any sense.

FIFTY

Penn made a quick call to Stacey to say he'd been delayed and then headed into Stourbridge library. He could do what he wanted to do on his phone, but unlike his brother, he couldn't negotiate a mobile keyboard as quickly or effectively as a real one.

He took the end computer in a row of three and typed in the month that Barry Sharpe had gone missing, and then he added Halesowen Town FC fixtures. Two videos came up. The first match was against Kidderminster Harriers and it had been a draw at one all. The second was a match against the Wordsley Wasps, and Halesowen had lost by one goal. The stats told him the goal had been scored in the seventy-seventh minute by Trevor Rollins against goalie Peter Matheson.

Penn dragged the cursor to the seventy-sixth minute and watched as Rollins worked his way around two defenders and then shot the ball into the net.

Penn sat back in the chair wondering what the hell he was thinking. He was sitting here watching a home-made video of two local football teams, while trying to make something out of nothing.

He shook his head before watching it again. No matter what his logical mind said, his gut was telling him he was on to something.

The second time he watched it, he didn't feel it looked as natural as his first viewing. There was a pause, a stutter.

He watched it once again with the speed slowed down, only this time he wasn't watching the guy with the ball; he was watching the one in the goal. Peter Matheson's eyes never left the ball as it worked its way towards him. Both defenders were defeated and then it was just the striker and the goalkeeper.

Rollins paused.

Matheson paused.

But the slowed-down footage revealed that they didn't reanimate at the same time. Rollins was just one second ahead of the goalie, who dived for the ball that swept past his fingers into the back of the net.

Penn kept the tab open and did a second search on Halesowen Town FC and the goalie's name.

He watched the goal attempts in the four games previous and not once had the goalie hesitated for even a millisecond before committing himself to a save. He was on the floor, in the air, using every inch of his body to protect the goalmouth.

He returned to the footage of that one fateful game, and after watching the previous saves, Penn was more certain of one fact than he was of his own name.

Peter Matheson had thrown that match.

FIFTY-ONE

It took them a good ten minutes to walk from the home of Nancy Houseman in Baker Street to the edge of the woods where Bradley Foster had been abducted.

'They said I'd go quicker if I had this new hip,' Nancy said, putting all her weight on the walking stick. 'They said it'd loosen up but it's still stiff. Damn liars.'

Kim had offered to bring her in the car but she'd refused, saying she hadn't yet completed her step count.

'It was around here, wasn't it?' Kim asked as she stopped walking.

'A bit further. I'd just come out of Jean's, which is number eleven.'

Four houses down from where Kim had been standing.

'And you first of all said that you'd seen a van?' Kim clarified, already feeling this was a waste of time.

'Well, no, I think I was asked about the van before I said I'd seen one. I saw the boy come thundering out of the woods on his bike, cos me and Jean were stood here talking for a few minutes. The police officer told me there had been a van over on the layby, so I nodded, but I didn't remember seeing it. I knew she'd got the wrong end of the stick and it mithered me, so I went back to the police station to put her right. I'm not saying it wasn't there, only that I can't remember seeing it.'

Kim was no wiser now, but she had a sudden thought.

'Was Jean interviewed?'

Nancy shrugged. 'I don't know. The officer never asked me where I'd been. Lovely young lady, she was. Had very pretty nails.' Nancy looked around her. 'Ask Jean yourself – she's at home.'

Kim nodded and started walking up the path.

She knocked, and a woman around ten years younger than Nancy answered the door.

Her face lit up as though any interruption was a welcome distraction from whatever she was doing.

She looked from one to the other.

Kim and Bryant held up their identifications.

'May we ask you about the teenager that went missing approximately ten years ago?'

'Of course. We still remember it, don't we, Nancy?' she called out to the woman making her way up the path. 'We were stood here, gassing. Saw the boy come tearing out of the woods and carried on riding up the hill.'

'You didn't see a van over the road in the layby?'

Jean shook her head emphatically. 'There was no van. Not while we were out here. I'm a woman alone, Officer – have been for fifteen years. You think I don't take notice of strange vehicles parked up opposite my house?'

Kim was finding it hard to doubt her word.

'You saw the boy come out on the bike? No pausing, no hesitation, he just carried on riding?'

'Yes, that's exactly it.'

'Okay, thanks for your time,' Kim said.

'You coming in for a cuppa, Nance?' Jean asked.

'Don't mind if I do, if they've finished with me,' she said.

'Thank you for your time,' Kim said, relieved that the walk back to the car would be a little bit quicker.

The door closed and Kim was about to say something when her phone rang.

'Go ahead, Stace.'

'Boss, I'm gonna need you to go somewhere if you're free.'

'Two minutes. We're just heading back to the car.'

Kim took a final look back at the woods. There was a distance of twenty metres or so from the edge of the woods and the place Josh said the van had been pulling away from. That twenty-metre gap was right opposite where the two women had been standing.

They hadn't seen Bradley exit on his bike and they hadn't seen any white van, which begged the question.

What if he'd never left the woods at all?

FIFTY-TWO

Will Deakin had lost the deer-in-the-headlights look that she'd seen on his face when first informed of his wife's murder. Now he greeted them with empty, tired eyes.

'Officer, you must be psychic,' he said, offering a weak attempt at humour. 'I was just about to call you.'

'Is your daughter home?' Kim asked, stepping into the house.

He nodded towards the stairs.

'Yeah, got her music going, but there's something I want to show you,' he said, heading towards the kitchen.

She followed as he continued to talk.

'I was going through the mail holder. We would always put envelopes here. Things we didn't need to deal with immediately: credit-card statements and stuff. I forgot that Sandy used to keep her receipts here to balance with her bank statements. I started going through them and found this.'

Kim took the receipt. It was dated the Thursday before Sandy's death. It was for two people at the Harvester in Stourbridge, and it was stamped right around the time she was supposed to have been meeting Monty Dunhill.

'May I take these?' Kim asked, pointing to the pile of receipts.

'Of course, Officer, anything that will help,' he said as Nicola breezed into the room.

'Oh, hello again,' she said putting a dirty plate and cup into the dishwasher.

Kim nodded in her direction.

'We're here about another matter,' Kim said slowly.

'You've found him?' Will asked.

'Not yet but we will,' Kim answered. 'We're here about the email threats Sandy was receiving. We know where they originated from.'

'Really?' they said together, in surprise.

One exclamation was more genuine than the other. And it gave her the answer she'd come here for.

'But you knew that already, didn't you, Will?' Kim asked, turning towards the man.

For a split-second, Kim thought he was going to try and deny it, but he slumped further into his chair.

His eyes filled with tears. 'I just wanted her to stop doing it.'

'Dad?' Nicola said, horrified.

'You didn't even like her,' he said.

'I wouldn't have tried to frighten her though, that's... that's just...' She stopped speaking while shaking her head, as though she couldn't believe what she was hearing.

'Would you like to share your reasons?' Kim asked.

'Nothing that's going to seem even remotely excusable now that she's gone.'

'But still?'

'I loved my wife, Inspector,' he said with an honesty that Kim didn't doubt.

Even Nicola sat down to listen.

'I know you hate the way we met, Nic, but that's one of the reasons I fell in love with her. She took me on knowing full well

I was still in love with your mother. She let me talk for hours about her, comforting me and helping me through the grief and loss. She knew how much I was suffering but she hung on in there and just waited until the fog lifted. And when it did, there she was and I was happy to see her.'

Kim saw Nicola's eyes soften and then harden again.

'So why do it?' she asked, saving Kim the trouble of urging him along.

'A lot of reasons, Nic. You were getting shit at school. I knew you were being teased over it.'

'Blimey, Dad. It wasn't anything I couldn't handle,' Nic protested.

Kim was growing to like the girl more and more.

Will nodded his acknowledgement and continued. 'My colleagues and some of my students were having a pop. Even my mates wouldn't let me hear the end of it.'

Kim tried not to show her reaction. He was right about what she'd think. Scaring his own wife for such reasons was pathetic.

'From day one my mates wouldn't leave it alone. At work, down the pub. It was relentless. "Ask your missus for the lottery numbers." "Who's gonna win the match on Saturday?" I thought it'd grow old but it never did; in fact it got worse cos sometimes they insulted her.'

His right hand curled around his left fist. 'Lost more than one friendship over it.'

And not just through words, she thought, realising from his unconscious body language that he had defended her physically on occasion.

'I just thought we'd all be happier if she stopped doing it. I asked her to give it up and do something else, but she refused.'

Kim would have liked to point out that it was her career that had brought them together in the first place.

For a moment Kim considered the fact that Sandra had been a psychic before they'd met, and yet she'd been asked to give it up because it was causing him embarrassment with his buddies and his daughter some teasing at school.

'I thought if I scared her a bit she'd stop doing it. I knew she wasn't in danger.'

Kim chose not to mention that Sandy was dead and that she'd been in danger from someone.

'She never even mentioned the messages,' he said, shaking his head.

'She wouldn't have. It would only have given you more ammunition,' Kim offered.

That realisation seemed to help him not one bit.

Nicola's face was a picture of mixed emotions. Clearly, she adored her father but the disappointment in her eyes was clear.

'Okay,' Kim said, standing. 'We'll be in touch when we have anything further.'

They saw themselves out and Kim was about to speak when her phone rang. Her blood ran cold.

'Don't say it, Keats,' she said, answering the call.

'Not saying it isn't going to make it any less real, but while you've got your fingers in your ears, you might want to start heading towards Lanesfield.'

Damn it. His summons only ever meant one thing.

FIFTY-THREE

'What business could you possibly have back here?' Janice Sharpe asked, opening the door of her Hollytree home.

'May I come in?'

She hesitated and then stepped aside.

Despite the fact she'd made the home as comfortable as possible, Penn still felt the same injustice he'd felt the day before. This woman had lost her real home through no fault of her own. It wasn't even as if she'd been widowed and she'd been given the chance to maintain it on her own. It had literally been gifted to someone else without her agreement.

'I'm sorry to intrude again but do you still have the paper-work?' Penn asked.

'Paperwork?' she asked, moving into the kitchen.

Penn realised he'd made his usual mistake of thinking the person with him was up to date on the thoughts in his head.

'Sorry, the agreement that your husband signed.'

'I have no idea where—'

'I know where it is,' Tanya said from the doorway, startling him. He hadn't heard her approach.

She disappeared from view. Penn wanted to offer the

woman something, anything that might give her a little peace, but after what she'd divulged the day before, he knew the pain was still raw.

He stood silent until Tanya reappeared and put a document in his hand.

'Why do you want it?' Janice asked, finally showing some curiosity.

'Mrs Sharpe, I'm not convinced your husband lost the bet. It may be nothing so I don't want to raise your hopes.'

He had to be careful to manage expectations. He had to take a good look at the document in his hand.

'You think Dad didn't lose the bet?' Tanya asked.

Penn shook his head. 'I don't think it's as clear cut as this document suggests. I hope you take some comfort from that,' he said, looking to the girl's mother.

She shook her head. 'Not at all, Officer. I know that you mean well and I thank you for your concern, but whether he lost the house or not makes little difference. The fact he was prepared to is the betrayal.'

Penn nodded and left. There was nothing he could say to that.

FIFTY-FOUR

Lanesfield was a district in the Spring Vale ward of Wolverhampton but lying within the ancient manor of Sedgley. Like many villages in the Black Country, it had grown around the area's industries. Many houses had been built in the nineteenth century as the coal mines began to appear.

The name originated from the Lane family who had once owned the land, and which was now mainly a residential area.

The postcode texted to Bryant seemed to be taking them towards Goldthorn Hill, where some of the pricier properties of the area lay.

Sure enough, a road cordon greeted them at the bottom of the hill.

Bryant slowed as she lowered her window and showed her ID.

The officer lifted the tape high enough for the car to pass underneath.

Bryant pulled to the left and parked.

No matter how many crime scenes they attended, her colleague never parked behind the ambulance. Given that their attendance ensured the vehicle was never going to leave at speed, it was an unconscious act.

As they walked around the other vehicles, she assessed the property they were entering. The driveway came in straight off the road despite some of the neighbouring houses having gates.

The property appeared to be side on to the road so that the front of the house was facing the neighbour on the right. The gable end had enormous glass windows across its width. Even from the end of the driveway Kim could see some detail of the room beyond, and that it was a dining kitchen.

On a dark night with the lights on, Kim was sure she'd be able to make out what the occupants were having to eat.

With Bryant beside her, she headed up the drive and turned to the front of the house.

She stopped dead.

'Hell no,' she said as her eyes rested on a flash of material. She would know that pink tracksuit anywhere.

'Let me see,' she said, pushing her way through.

'Damn it,' she growled as her gaze took in the brutality of the attack on Victoria Sykes.

Only last night the two of them had stood in the woman's dressing room. Except then the tracksuit had been pristine, not covered with deep red stains.

'You know her?' Keats asked, always attuned to her reaction.

Kim nodded as she continued to survey the scene. The body was just two feet away from the open doorway to her home. Pools of blood had formed to the left of her body, and the slash across the mouth was no less horrific on the third occasion.

When she said nothing, Keats continued, 'We're not sure if she was going out or coming back or what time it was at this stage.'

Kim lowered herself to the ground carefully. She placed her face close to the woman's gaping mouth.

'Err... Inspector, just how well did you know her?' Keats asked as the crowd silenced around her.

Kim stood, ignoring the curious glances, including a questioning frown from her own colleague.

'She was coming home and her time of death was around 11 p.m.'

'Excuse me?' Keats said, more interested than affronted.

'She's a psychic. I attended her show last night. I spoke with her after the show. Warned her to stay safe.'

Kim realised Victoria had barely had time to act upon the warning.

'I don't think she even got inside,' she said.

Keats waited.

'Gin and tonic,' Kim explained. 'First thing she does when she gets home.'

'Ah,' Keats said, understanding her actions.

There was no smell of alcohol around her mouth.

'How was she found?' Kim asked. It was almost 3 p.m. and she'd been lying here since last night.

'Delivery guy, over there – package needed signing for.'

Bryant didn't need further instruction. He took out his notebook and headed over. Kim guessed he was going to get little. She'd already been lying there for hours by the time she'd been discovered.

Her gaze was drawn back to the woman's face, and she was reminded of Monty Dunhill's nickname for her. She certainly didn't look like a show pony now.

Only last night this woman had held an entire theatre full of people in her thrall. Her energy and vitality had energised both the audience and the room. And that had all been extinguished by one person.

Right now, Kim didn't care whether she was a genuine psychic or not. She cared only about catching the bastard that had done this.

Bryant headed back towards her, shaking his head.

As she'd thought. And her initial assessment of the property had not revealed any CCTV, not even a Ring camera at the door.

'He's got nothing, guv, except that the rest of his twenty-nine deliveries are going back to the depot.'

'Helpful, Bryant,' she said, moving back towards Victoria.

She looked towards the group of techies between her and the open door.

'Sorry, guys,' she said, taking a step around Victoria's feet. She sighed heavily. Victoria's flesh had been butchered, and she looked to have sustained more wounds than the other two. No scratches were visible through the fabric of the tracksuit, but a bloody handprint was evident on the door frame.

The techies moved aside for her to enter the house and immediately Kim got the sense that this was Victoria's domain. For a minute she'd wondered if there was a husband, wife, kids off somewhere, explaining the delay in the body being found, but right away she knew that wasn't the case. Just a couple of pairs of shoes were placed to the right of the door. One winter coat and a couple of lightweight summer jackets hung from the hooks.

As she moved further into the house she saw that the decor was soft and feminine throughout. Warm colours with flashes of pink everywhere against modern, minimalist furniture. A small TV on the fireplace wall was flanked by a floor-to-ceiling book-case on either side.

She looked closer and saw books on self-defence, gardening, fixing plumbing problems. Her novels ranged from cosy romances to crime novels, with a bit of dystopian literature thrown in.

As Kim looked around, she didn't get the sense that Victoria lived a lonely life. Her home spoke of contentment, peace and a woman who was happy in her own skin and her own company.

She pushed away the feeling that she'd somehow let Victoria down, but it resurfaced. She'd been with the woman the night before. Was there anything more she could have said or done to protect her, to have avoided this? She knew second-guessing their meeting would achieve nothing so she shoved the thoughts to the back of her mind.

Within ten minutes Kim had confirmed that there was no one else in the house and no one was expected back. It was also clear that the killer hadn't made it inside the property.

'You reckon he was lying in wait somewhere for her return, guv?' Bryant said as they headed back to the car.

She shrugged. It was hard to tell. The fact that Victoria had barely got in the door meant he had either been waiting for her when she got back or that he'd followed her home, meaning the killer had been at the theatre at the exact same time as her.

FIFTY-FIVE

'Are you sure?' Richard asked, slumping back in his seat.

Stacey nodded, having just given him the news that Victoria Sykes was dead.

Stacey turned back to her computer. The boss had said to inform him but hold back on the detail. Although he was assisting them in a consultation capacity, he was still a civilian they didn't know all that well.

'How do you do that?' he asked, not unkindly.

'Sorry?'

'Accept the information and move on so quickly?'

'We have to,' Stacey said, understanding how cold it might appear to casual onlookers.

'It's not easy – it takes time. For my first two years, I'd go home and cry for every victim, but self-preservation kicks in. You can't stay in that state or it'll eat you alive. We have to stay focussed on finding the person responsible.'

He shook his head, nonplussed. 'I just don't get... I mean, surely a minute...'

Stacey stopped what she was doing to see that all colour had dropped from his face.

'You knew her?' Stacey asked.

'I've seen her show and I've written two chapters on her, so I suppose I feel like I knew her better than I actually did.'

Stacey had to remind herself again that he wasn't a police officer. He wasn't even a police consultant. He was a man they'd harangued into assisting them.

'Tell me about her,' Stacey said, killing two birds with one stone. The boss would want background, and he needed to overcome his shock. She could get onto the receipts in a minute.

'I know she was born in Newcastle in the early eighties and was orphaned by the time she was fourteen. Only living relative was an uncle who lived in Tettenhall. I don't think the next couple of years were happy for her. She moved out when she was sixteen and they didn't try to stop her. The next fifteen years she spent working at numerous basic office jobs. There was a marriage, a divorce and her first stage show in 2010. It wasn't a large audience, just at some village town hall where she warmed up for the weekly bingo game.'

'From that to selling out the Alexandra Theatre,' Stacey noted.

'She had that something that drew you in. She had chemistry, believability, a magnetism that reached out into the audience. She honed her craft. She studied people and other psychics. She was good at what she did, and it's just not sinking in that...'

'That what?' Penn asked, sliding into his seat.

'Oh, the wanderer returns,' Stacey said, tipping her head, waiting for an explanation of his absence.

'Victoria Sykes is dead,' Richard offered.

Penn looked from the author to her.

'May I just go to the kitchen for a drink of water?' Richard asked.

'Of course,' Stacey answered.

'Serious?' Penn asked as Richard headed out the door.

Stacey nodded. 'Right outside her front door, which you'd have known if you'd been here helping me like the boss said,' she said, only half-joking.

He opened his mouth to speak, but she held up her hand as her mobile started to ring. It wasn't a number she recognised, which was exactly what she'd been hoping for.

'Stacey Wood,' she answered.

'Hey, it's Ronny Brownhill. We spoke...'

'Of course. Thanks so much for calling back.'

She'd been hoping she'd read the sergeant's signs right and that he would call her back once he was on a break.

'Yeah, I hope you understand.'

'I do,' Stacey assured him.

'Also I wanted to check with one of my buddies. He's retired now but just wanted to make sure I'd got the right person.'

So unofficially there was something, she thought, allowing her hope to grow.

'If I remember rightly, he wasn't a very likeable chap. Had a high expectation of police responsibilities in relation to his church. For the most part we just appeased him, but there was one time when we had cause to speak to him. A woman came in and made a complaint of assault. He'd pushed her and shoved her out of the church and on to the pavement, so hard she'd fallen and banged up her knee.'

'How did this not result in a formal...?'

'Complainant withdrew all charges. An hour after speaking to us she had a brick thrown through her shop window. She reckoned it was him. She was scared and withdrew any complaint. Changed her story to tripping and falling. Nothing we could do.'

There was no way Stacey would put intimidation beyond Father George's many charms, but something else occurred to her.

'You say shop window?'

'Yeah, she's gone now but she had one of those hippy shops in the High Street. It was all candles and crystals and stuff.'

'She was a spiritualist?' Stacey asked.

'Not sure what you'd call her, but the tourists loved her.'

'Anything else?'

'That's your lot. Not sure if it helps or not.'

'It does, Sergeant. It really does. Thanks for taking the time to call me back.'

Stacey ended the call and immediately sent the boss a text message. When she'd finished, she looked up to see Penn staring at her.

'Really sorry I've not been here to help, Stace. This thing kicked up a gear.'

'I didn't even know this thing was still a thing. I thought you were just updating the homeless guy on the man's identity.'

'I was, but...'

'There's always a but with you, Penn,' she said with a wry smile. 'But go on, I'll humour you, and if your "but" is interesting enough, I won't tell the boss you've been missing in action all day.'

'He didn't lose the bet,' Penn said, retrieving some paperwork from his man bag.

Stacey found herself taking a couple of steps backwards to refresh in her own mind what Penn was talking about.

Richard reappeared, carrying the roses delivered earlier. The sight of them brought bile to the back of her throat.

'I found a pint glass in the cupboard,' he said of his impromptu arrangement. 'Someone had thrown them in the sink.'

'Just put them over there,' she said, pointing to a space next to the printer.

'Ooooh, special day?' Penn asked.

'Yeah, something like that,' she said, sure her colleague

could sense her increased heart rate. For a while she'd forgotten all about them and all about Terence Birch, but now he was front and centre again.

No, she wasn't having this. He was not going to paralyse her thoughts so that she couldn't do her job. She pushed him to the back of her mind and picked up on her conversation with Penn.

'So this guy really did bet his house?'

Penn nodded.

'He wasn't coerced or threatened or...?'

'It doesn't work like that. Seriously, Stace, you wouldn't believe some of the stuff I've read. Poker legend Johnny Moss made a bet he could beat a man who had never lost a fight in his life. From his hospital bed Moss explained that he just couldn't turn down odds of fifteen to one. Then there's this guy named Brian Zembic, famous for bizarre wagers, who accepted a one-hundred-thousand-dollar bet that he wouldn't get breast implants and keep them for a year.'

'Okay, now I know you're taking the piss.'

Penn shook his head. 'He liked them so much he kept them for years.'

'That's just plain weird. And it's one thing to make a bet that affects you alone, but to bet the house his wife and child lived in?'

'Similar thing happened in Uganda. A guy placed a bet with his neighbour on an Arsenal versus Man United game. The Arsenal man lost and was evicted from his home along with his three wives and five children. It's like some kind of fever.'

'So, now you're saying that your John Doe, who died of natural causes, bet his home on a football match and lost, made his family homeless and deserted them in shame, but he didn't actually lose?'

'Exactly.'

'And you know this how?'

'The goalie threw the game.'

Stacey waited.

Penn said nothing.

'Your proof?' she prompted.

'I watched the game.'

Stacey sat back in her chair. 'You'd best get ready to have your ass kicked when the boss gets back from Worcester.'

'What's in Worcester?'

'Father George's boss, but don't try and distract me. What part of being a police officer did you actually remember today?' she asked.

He wasn't even listening as he messed with something on his phone.

He slid it across to her. 'Take a look.'

She watched the clip and then looked at him.

'Penn, how into football are you?'

'Prefer rugby but...'

'So just how qualified are you to judge?' she asked, ready to slide the phone back. Looked to her like he'd been on a fool's errand for most of the day.

'Watch it again and slow it down,' he insisted.

'Jeez, are you determined to waste my time as well as your own?'

'If I'm wrong I'll go see what Betty's giving away in the canteen.'

She said nothing. For once she had no interest in Betty's end-of-day bargains, but if she told Penn that, he'd know immediately that there was something wrong.

'Oh,' she said, watching the slowed-down version, which revealed an awkwardness, a delay, a loss of fluidity in the rhythm of the game.

'I see your point. But this isn't proof. It's a stutter, without doubt,' she said, returning his phone. 'But he could have just choked. And I'm sure that's what he'd claim.'

'Yeah, that's where I'm at,' he said miserably.

'What's his background?' she asked, feeling the burn of a potential injustice.

He shrugged. 'Not sure. Thought I'd best get back before I got in trouble.'

Stacey chuckled. As a sergeant, he was her senior and she couldn't tell him what to do if she wanted to, but never had he made any kind of distinction between their ranks.

'What's his name?'

'Peter Matheson.'

'You googled him?' she asked.

Penn shook his head.

Stacey shook her head. 'Have you learned nothing from me? Google everyone.'

Stacey tapped a few keys, read a couple of articles and learned that although only thirty-four, he'd now retired from club football and focussed only on his full-time job as a planning officer for Dudley Council.

She started searching electoral records in a radius of ten miles from the council buildings.

'Gotcha... ooh,' she said. 'Was the house in question on Orchard Lane in Pedmore?'

Penn nodded.

'Oooh, this is smelling worse than a week-old fish pie.'

'What?' he asked, standing.

'Your man lives there.'

'What?' he repeated, coming to her side of the desk.

She put the postcode into Google Maps and found the property. Without looking closely, she could see a couple of outbuildings and an acre or two.

'On a planner's salary?' she questioned.

'Bloody hell, Stace,' he said, heading for the door.

'Where are you going now?'

'To buy whatever Betty's got left in her cabinet – like, all of it.'

'No time for that now. Sit yourself down. We need to sort this out. We need a plan.'

'We?' he questioned with a smile.

'Too bloody right "we". We need to work out how the hell we can put this right.'

FIFTY-SIX

'Okay, you don't really think Father George is our killer, do you?' Bryant asked as they neared the outskirts of Worcester.

The postcode she'd given him was for the Halas Team Ministry for Worcester Diocese which covered the Halesowen area.

'I'd be interested to know if his bosses know he has these incidents of violence.'

'You think he'd still be Father George and not just plain old George if he had?'

'Sure, Bryant, cos it's not like the Church has ever covered anything up before, is it?' she asked.

He sighed. 'You know, sometimes I wish I could have the last word on something.'

'Keep trying, partner. It's very entertaining,' she said as he slowed the car down in the Lowesmoor Wharf car park. The area was a collection of nondescript two-storey office buildings which was not what Kim had been expecting.

A woman in her early thirties with a blunt fringe smiled as they approached the reception desk.

They both held up their IDs. 'May we speak to someone about one of your clergymen?'

'I'm sorry but we'd normally ask to see any complaint in writing before arranging a face-to-face meeting. If you go to our website you can—'

'We're police officers and we're here right now. We're in a bit of a rush.'

'I understand that but we still have protocols to follow. Any complaint has to be submitted in writing. There's an online form you can complete that gives us all the details we need.'

Kim kept her temper in check.

'So it has to be in writing with certain details?' she asked, opening her hand.

Like a well-trained nurse assisting a surgeon, Bryant slapped his pocket notebook into her palm.

'It's all on the—'

'What details?' Kim insisted.

'We need to know the location, the clergyman's name, particulars of the incident that occurred and a date and time.'

'That it?' she asked, scribbling away.

Bryant looked over her shoulder.

She ripped the page out and placed it on the reception desk. 'There you go. In writing.'

The woman read her hastily scribbled note.

Dear Sirs,

Father George Markinson of St John's, Halesowen is a dangerous, intolerant knob. Every day and all the time.

Yours faithfully,

The Police.

'I'm sorry, but I can't accept this as a written complaint.'

'Then we're just gonna wait over here until you throw us out,' Kim said, taking a seat on one of the chairs by the window.

It was after four so Kim was sure it wouldn't be all that long.

The woman glanced at them a few times.

Kim took out her phone and sent a text message.

Bryant took out his phone and read the message, which instructed him to look at his phone. He replied:

Are you joking?

We'll look like we're settled for a while if we're on our phones.

This is ridiculous. Is it still insubordination if I tell you you've lost your mind by text?

Yes. Check the Strictly results or something.

Absurd!!!!

It's working. She's on the phone.

I'm putting my phone away now.

Kim didn't reply as he slid his phone back into his pocket.

The woman offered them a look as she hung up, leaving Kim in no doubt the call had been about their refusal to leave.

She wasn't surprised when a portly man with thinning brown hair appeared at the foot of the stairs.

'Inspector,' he said, offering his hand.

Bryant shook it while she introduced them both properly.

'Bishop Harry Wilson. I understand you have some concerns,' he said, guiding them into a small room, furnished only with a round table and six chairs. He closed the door and indicated for them to sit.

'Yes, we're here about Father George at St John's in Halesowen.'

The man steepled his fingers and rested them below his chin. His manner wasn't cool but guarded.

'A woman was murdered in the graveyard on Sunday night.'

'We've been briefed,' he said. 'But you can't possibly think Father George was involved?'

The reassurance did not come to her lips as quickly as he would have liked, and a frown rested on his face.

'We understand the victim had been barred from the church.'

'On what grounds?' he asked, demonstrating that small fact hadn't made the briefing. 'I was led to believe she was vaguely known to the man that found her,' he continued, looking from her to Bryant.

'She was banned from attending the church by Father George because she was a psychic. More worrying is that he felt the need to physically remove her from the premises, and we understand this isn't the first or only time that Father George has put his hands on a member of his congregation.'

There was only a second of hesitation before understanding settled on the bishop's face.

'Father George is umm...'

'Intolerant, misguided, archaic, ruthless and potentially violent,' she offered for him.

'I was going to say conservative.'

'So you were going to lie?' she said before she could stop herself. Yes, he was a man of the cloth but he was giving her the runaround.

'Now, just a—'

'Avoid the truth is what my colleague meant to say,' Bryant interjected.

'He has no place being a clergyman,' Kim continued. 'We didn't come here unprepared. We did our homework. We know where he's been and the poor judgement he's displayed in his counsel. He's been passed around quicker than a cream cake at a Weight Watchers meeting.'

The knuckles of the steeple holding up his chin were whitening.

'I think you're exaggerating.'

'And I think you're in denial. Father George was quite honest with us about making decisions that conflict with the views of the Church. The man thinks he has a one-way link to God. His views are outdated and, quite frankly, dangerous. You expressed surprise that he could be involved, but if he feels he alone hears God's instructions, is it really that much of a stretch?' The more she spoke, the more she saw the bishop's face harden, and she realised she was doing this all wrong.

She sighed heavily.

'You know, it's not beyond the realms of possibility to assume that the Church might automatically adopt a position of defence and deny all knowledge of unacceptable behaviour.'

She didn't need to state the cases of sexual abuse that had been uncovered in recent years.

'So talk to us not as a bishop representing the Church of England but as a boss with an uncontrollable employee who can't keep his hands to himself.'

'Between us?' he asked as the tension left the room.

Kim nodded.

'He's a liability; to his parish, to the diocese, to the Church. He doesn't listen. He's been spoken to on numerous occasions but he treats each church like his own personal kingdom.'

'He's had many kingdoms,' Bryant observed.

'He has and that's because no one knows what to do with him.'

'Is there not some kind of disciplinary system? Like three strikes and you're out?' Kim asked.

'It doesn't quite work that way. The actual formal complaints over the years don't number all that many. And none were about violence. All were investigated, and on each occasion, he apologised for his conduct and requested a transfer, to continue improving himself.'

'He's dodged the bullet every time?' Kim asked.

'Truthfully, yes. But if we're confident that he understands what he's done wrong and demonstrates a willingness to improve, we have to have faith in his word.'

'And how's that working out for you so far?' she asked as a sudden thought occurred to her. 'He requests the transfers?'

The bishop nodded.

'The misdeeds aren't carried across to the next diocese?'

He shook his head.

'So he knows when he's getting close and moves elsewhere to clear the slate.'

'Most likely,' the bishop agreed. 'But our hands are tied. Formal complaints are not criminal charges. Obviously that's a whole different subject and classed as intolerable by the Church and—'

'Hang on,' Kim said, with her thoughts still hanging on what he'd previously said. 'If the records aren't carried forward to the next placement, we'd have to check every one if we were looking for something in particular?'

'I suppose so,' Bishop Wilson said.

Given the number of placements and the time needed to visit the appropriate bishop, they were looking at a couple of weeks.

Time they didn't have. Their killer was showing no signs of slowing down.

'Bishop Wilson, in your dealings with Father George, have you ever known him to do more than a bit of pushing and shoving?'

The clergyman considered it. 'No, I haven't.'

'Why the hesitation?' she asked, pushing back her chair.

'Because, quite honestly, I wouldn't rule it out.'

FIFTY-SEVEN

Kim continued to stare at the board long after sending the rest of the team home.

The vision of Victoria was still vivid in her mind's eye, along with the realisation that she was one of the last people to see the psychic alive.

It wasn't the first time someone Kim knew had been brutally killed, but it ensured the images stayed with her much longer. She wanted justice for every victim but having spent any time with one of them made it personal. She didn't have to imagine their demeanour or the animation with which they spoke. She didn't have to imagine the life behind the eyes. She'd known exactly what Victoria had looked like and the energy she'd exuded.

'What are we not seeing?' she said, approaching the whiteboards.

She felt they were missing something.

Her eyes roamed over the names and photos, following the lines that linked victims to witnesses. Every time her gaze passed over the name of Monty Dunhill, her stomach gave an involuntary squeeze. That could be due to her intense dislike of him, because she had a similar physical reaction to Father George.

There was an urge in her to start rubbing out lines and drawing new ones just to see where it took her thinking. She looked towards the kitchen roll as her phone rang. Probably a good thing, she thought as she took it out of her pocket.

The relief was instant that it wasn't Keats's name staring back at her.

'Stone,' she answered.

'You still here?' Jack asked from the desk downstairs.

'No, Jack, I crawled past you on all fours for my own amusement.'

'I've got a lady here by the name of Rose Foster. She wants a word and she's not very happy, so I ask again, are you here or not?'

She smiled. Jack was a good man but she was sure he knew better than to ask.

'On my way,' she said, before ending the call.

FIFTY-EIGHT

Rose Foster didn't speak until Kim closed the door of interview room one behind her.

She stood on the other side of the table and thrust her hands into her pockets.

'What have you said to Josh?' she asked as Kim sat down.

'Rose, please take a seat.'

'I'm not staying. I just want to know why you've upset him. He's a good boy and he's done nothing wrong.'

'If you sit down, I'll explain.'

Rose sat reluctantly.

'I'm not sure why he's upset. I only asked him to recount his story of what happened between him and Bradley ten years ago.'

'Brad – please call him Brad. He hated his full name. Josh would call him that to wind him up.'

'Why did Josh call you?' Kim asked.

'He'd been drinking. I could tell. I've known that boy since he was five years old. He was upset that he'd been questioned again. He swore that he'd already told the police everything and that he was sorry.'

'For what?' Kim asked.

'Not doing more. He's always felt guilty that he wasn't able to stop it from happening. He's sorry that he stopped to mend his bike. He's sorry he wasn't right behind that white van when it took Brad. He's sorry he didn't even realise Brad had been taken until he got to school. He's just sorry the whole thing happened. It wasn't an easy thing for him to come to terms with, you know. I've read about it. There's a name for why he calls me every so often.'

'He does?' Kim asked. The wind was fading from Rose's sails. Kim was far more interested in discovering why Josh had kept in contact with his former best friend's mum. What hadn't he been able to let go of?

'It's survivor's guilt,' Rose said, placing her elbows on the table. 'He feels bad that it was Brad that died and not him.'

Kim agreed that it might be guilt of some kind, she just wasn't sure which one.

'Tell me about their friendship,' she said.

'Inseparable since the first day of school. Best buddies but so different. Josh was such a quiet, studious boy. Brad was outgoing, full of life, rebellious. They balanced each other out. Brad never thought things through; he acted impulsively most of the time. He rarely saw consequences to his actions.

'Don't get me wrong, he wasn't a bad child, quite the opposite, but he didn't follow convention; he didn't like rules. I remember when he was maybe twelve and he was in a biology lesson. The teacher wanted them all to cut worms in half to show the difference between cutting off the head end or the tail end.

'Brad refused, asking to see the consent form signed by the worm. The teacher threatened him with detention, suspension, but he wouldn't budge. Most of the class followed his example so there was little the teacher could do. He was his own person and could not be swayed.'

'Not even by you?'

Rose shook her head. 'I like to think we were close, but I suppose I always felt like I loved him more, if that makes sense.'

Kim said nothing and waited for her to continue.

'It's hard to explain but I'll do my best. Punishing Brad was hard to do even from a very early age. There was nothing he was attached to enough for it to matter. I remember once telling him to clean his room. I threatened him with grounding, game console ban, the lot. It made no difference – he wouldn't do it because he didn't care enough about the things I was threatening to take away. Other times I'd get back from work and he'd be building a hedgehog refuge in the back garden. He was a good kid; intelligent but headstrong.'

'You don't feel he was attached to you?'

Rose thought before answering. 'He loved me, I know that, but he didn't need me. I often felt that he didn't need anyone. It was the same with Josh. They were definitely best friends, but it was more for the effort that Josh put in. Brad always went out with Josh when Josh came, but it was always Josh coming if you know what I mean.'

'And what if he hadn't?' Kim asked, beginning to understand their dynamic a little more.

'I've thought about that a lot and I honestly don't know. Most of me thinks Brad would have been perfectly content in his own company.'

'Was Josh ever resentful?'

'Of what?'

'Brad not being as forthcoming as he was. Surely friendship is a two-way thing?'

'I don't think so. I never thought about it. Josh was a good lad – kind, thoughtful and well-mannered. He was like a second son to me but he was also very loyal to Brad. I remember one time Brad forgot my birthday. Josh came for tea and saw my cards on the fireplace. Next day there was a small bunch of flowers with an apology note signed from Brad, except that it was Josh's handwriting. He denied it emphatically, insisting they were from Brad. He did that a lot, covered for his best friend. Even the morning Brad was abducted he was making excuses for him.'

'What happened?' Kim asked.

Rose's expression saddened. 'We were having a row, about his chemistry exam of all things. It was the first of his mock tests in a few days and he hadn't done even an hour of study. He hated tests or exams of any kind even though he normally did well. He insisted that he didn't need to study and we had words, harsh words. We were shouting at each other when Josh knocked the door. Brad stormed upstairs, and Josh put his arm round me and told me Brad didn't mean it and that he'd be fine later.'

A small sob escaped from the woman. 'But of course there was no later. My last words to my son were shouted in anger and that's something I've had to learn to live with.' She swallowed. 'But Josh is a good boy, and I know Brad thought a lot of him too, in his own way.'

Kim couldn't imagine the pain of knowing she could never take those harsh words back; but her love for her son appeared to have been transferred to deep affection for his best friend.

'Clearly you're fond of him, and I didn't mean to upset him. We're just trying to iron out a couple of inconsistent details about the day Brad was abducted.'

'Like what?' she asked.

'Nothing major that affects the loss of your son. We'll try not to bother Josh again.'

'I appreciate it,' Rose said, standing.

'How are the other ladies?' Kim asked, opening the door back into the corridor.

'No idea. Yoga class is on a break and Catherine shut down

the WhatsApp group. I saw her at Sainsbury's a few days ago and she walked straight past me.'

Kim wondered if Catherine had so many friends that she could afford to offload them all so easily.

Kim walked the woman to the door and bid her goodnight.

If Rose's visit had been intended to quell her interest in Josh and his friendship with Brad, it had actually had the opposite effect.

FIFTY-NINE

'Okay, genius, what now?' Stacey asked as they took a table to the left of the bar. She had taken a good look around the pub as soon as she'd entered. She'd breathed a sigh of relief and then chastised herself that Terence Birch couldn't possibly have known she was going to be visiting a pub she'd never frequented before, with a colleague that she very rarely drank with. She realised she was giving him far too much power in her head.

'Err... I hadn't really thought that far,' Penn admitted, taking a sip of his drink.

'You thought we were just gonna rock up, accuse him of fixing the football match, that he'd admit it and we'd throw him out of the house.'

'Something like that,' he said, watching Peter Matheson order his second round of drinks at the bar.

Not a great plan, Stacey thought, now grateful that they'd been diverted by the taxi waiting outside his house.

'Follow that cab,' she'd said, ticking an item off her bucket list and earning herself a derisive snort from her colleague at the same time.

The taxi had deposited him outside The Swan in Nether-ton, where they now sat, nursing soft drinks and trying to watch him inconspicuously.

'What's the plan, brains?' she asked again.

'Patience,' he instructed.

'You mean you have no plan?'

He ignored her and she followed his gaze. The man was clearly sociable and before long he was amongst a group of four who were moving towards the dartboard.

'You definitely taking me home after this?' she asked, taking out her phone.

'Of course,' Penn said, not taking his eyes from the target.

She sent a message to Devon. She'd been happy to help her colleague, but she wasn't sure how long she was prepared to sit in a pub watching a grown man drink and play darts.

Devon's reply was immediate with lots of emojis and hearts.

She smiled as she put her phone away. She was lucky. She had a job she enjoyed and a home to go back to with the woman she loved. Janice Sharpe had had every ounce of security taken away from her by a gambling husband. She wasn't going to allow Terence Birch to take her happiness away from her.

It hadn't taken long for Stacey to find out that the person who had made the bet with Barry Sharpe had been Peter Math-eson's brother-in-law. Matheson's wife was a part-time doctor's receptionist and there was no way they could afford what would have been over two thousand a month in rent. She got the scam. This house had cost Matheson's brother-in-law nothing. He'd won it. It was now his asset to sell and he was receiving nominal rent from Matheson and his wife until the housing market kicked back in. For his part, Matheson was paying very little to live in a very nice house well beyond his pay packet.

Win-win for everyone except Janice Sharpe and her daughter.

Penn nudged her back to the present and she followed his gaze.

'Fucking hell, Pete, you left your throwing arm at home?' one of the men asked.

Stacey analysed the scene quickly.

The four players had split into two teams, and the guy in the check shirt who had just spoken was clearly Peter Matheson's teammate. Matheson had just thrown a single twenty, a five and a one to give them a grand score of twenty-six.

Although the words had been jokey, the tone had said otherwise.

'Just warming up, mate,' Matheson said, although a muscle was jumping in his cheek.

Looking at the scores, the other team were miles ahead.

She and Penn watched silently as it worked back to Matheson's turn.

After a couple of bad throws from the other side and a good round for his teammate, Matheson was left with only forty to get. He got a twenty. Aimed for double ten, got a single ten, aimed for double five and missed.

The other team cheered. His teammate shook his head.

'Mate, you'd better get yourself off to Specsavers.'

Whether through alcohol or embarrassment, Matheson was starting to colour, and his jaw was firmly set.

As expected, the other team cleaned up with the next three darts.

'Next match I want a partner who's got his eyes open,' said Check Shirt.

'Leave it, Jake,' Matheson said.

'Come on, mate. That was shite.'

'I said lay off,' Matheson warned, more forcefully.

Check Shirt nudged him good-naturedly, but Matheson stormed off to the gents. The other team rolled their eyes knowingly. Seems they already knew what she and Penn were now learning.

Peter Matheson didn't like to be belittled and he didn't like to lose.

Stacey glanced at her colleague, who smiled in return.

'On it, Stace. Now here's what I need you to do.'

SIXTY

Stacey took her place, nestled at the bar.

Peter Matheson exited the toilets and headed back to his buddies. Penn stepped out from the side of the fruit machine and ploughed straight into him.

'Oh, sorry, mate,' Penn said, reaching out to steady the man.

'It's okay, never m—'

'Hey, you're that guy, ain't yer?' Penn said, peering closer and wobbling slightly on his feet.

Before he could respond, Penn grabbed his hand and started pumping it enthusiastically.

'Followed you, man,' Penn gushed loudly. 'Go HTFC,' he called out, punching the air. 'Can't believe you didn't get snapped up for the big leagues like a couple of your buddies. You guys never get the glory you deserve like the strikers.'

Matheson was trying to keep a polite smile on his face while attempting to edge away from him.

'Yeah, some of them guys got the big houses and the flash cars, but not the goalie, eh, mate?'

The jaw was tightening.

'Although you guys just stand still for most of the game,

don't you? It's the others that run their knackers off for ninety minutes. I bet you're on your phones most of the time,' Penn said, laughing obnoxiously.

Peter Matheson was not looking happy. Who knew Penn could be so annoying?

'All right, fella, that's enough.'

'Nah, I'm on your side, mate. It's shit you got dumped, but I suppose you was starting to lose your edge a bit.'

The rage was starting to stain Matheson's cheeks.

Stacey had been concerned that his mates would step in, but they seemed to be enjoying the show as much as she was.

She leaned towards a guy in his early twenties on her right.

'Looks like that ex-footballer's gonna kick off in a second,' she said.

She moved away but not before she saw him reaching for his phone.

Matheson folded his arms.

'I mean, that match against Kidderminster. No way I thought that goal was going in.'

'You're an expert?' Matheson asked between gritted teeth.

'Nah. But watching that guy,' Penn said, doing a little shuffle with his feet, which brought out a few more phones. 'I mean he wasn't exactly Ronaldo, was he?'

'Are you trying...?'

'How old was he, late forties?'

'He was thir—'

'Early fifties. I mean he was getting on a bit.'

'Time for you to fuck—'

'I mean, the defence was shit for letting him through, but I was sure you'd get it.'

'I've heard enough of—'

'But he just sailed it past yer, didn't, he? The old guy was too quick for yer, wasn't he?'

'Hang on.'

'Were you napping?'

'For fuck's—'

'Were you texting?'

'I'm warning you to—'

'Or was the old guy a better player?'

'Shut the—'

'Oh, mate, you lost to a pensioner. You were done.'

'Step away.'

'Granddad nailed yer. You just couldn't keep up. You couldn't stop him putting it in the back of the net.'

'I coulda fucking stopped him. I let it pass,' Matheson shouted, stepping right into Penn's face.

Penn remained still.

'Did you not hear me, thicko? I said, I didn't lose. I let it pass.'

Stacey looked around the bar that was now silent.

By her reckoning, his admission had been heard by around thirty people and captured on a dozen phones.

Penn stepped away. 'Well, Mr Matheson, thank you so much for clearing that up.'

SIXTY-ONE

'Oh shit,' Stacey said, reading the message that had just dinged to her phone.

'Wassup?' Penn said, glancing her way in the darkness of the car.

'Devon's been called out.'

'Is that unusual?' Penn asked, knowing full well it wasn't.

'Nah, just inconvenient,' she said, recovering. 'Had a night planned is all.'

'Maybe tomorrow,' Penn suggested, focussing back on the road.

He was now just under a mile away from her empty flat. A place she didn't relish being right at this minute.

She could text Devon back and ask her to come home. She could ask Penn if he wanted to come in for coffee. But both of these actions would invite curiosity and questions. Devon knew Stacey didn't mind being home alone, and Penn had never been invited in for a coffee no matter how many times he'd dropped her off at the door.

Stacey couldn't help her gaze darting all over the place as they approached her home.

Nothing.

She breathed a sigh of relief and forced herself to act as naturally as possible.

'Thanks for the white-knuckle ride, Penn, as well as the entertaining night out. We must do it again some time.'

'Thanks for helping, Stace,' he said as she got out of the car.

She closed the passenger door and took one more look around before unlocking the door. She waited for the door to close and lock behind her before mounting the stairs up to the first floor.

She breathed a sigh of relief as she locked the front door behind her, not realising just how frightened she'd been of seeing Terence Birch hanging around somewhere.

Before putting on any lights, she padded to the bedroom and took a look out of the window.

The security light had activated and there were no dark shadows.

If she'd had a cat, she knew she would have been talking to it right now. She would have been reassuring it that there was nothing to worry about and that she'd been getting herself in a state over nothing.

She worked her way around the house closing all the curtains and putting on the lights. She put the television on to the news channel just to have some voices in the room.

As she stepped out of her work clothes, her phone dinged, startling her. She hoped it was Devon, saying it was a false alarm at work and she was on her way home. Her heart sank to see it was Alison, sending her some useful links following their earlier conversation.

She sat on the bed and clicked into the first article. It detailed the 2017 murder of thirty-two-year-old Kerri McAuley by her former boyfriend, having first been plagued with texts and calls.

Reading the article did nothing to help her feel more at ease, but she was compelled to open the next link.

The second article detailed the case of Stewart Taylor, aged thirty-three, who had been killed by his wife's stalker. His wife had survived the attack but had been left with permanent injuries.

'Jesus, thanks, Alison,' Stacey said, choosing not to read any more. Her friend had no clue that the person she'd been concerned about was herself and that these articles were not particularly helpful.

She reached for a pair of jogging bottoms and a sweatshirt, resolving to have a shower later. Right now all she wanted to do was grab a blanket and a glass of wine, curl up on the sofa and wait for Devon to come home.

Her phone sounded another notification and Stacey reached for it. If that was her so-called best friend sending her more reading matter, she could bloody well keep it to herself and Stacey would find a way to tell her so.

She was surprised to see it wasn't a text message but a notification from Facebook. She hit on the Messenger button and let out a cry. A message from Facebook User was staring at her. The person had set up a Facebook account to message her and had then deleted the account, making the post anonymous.

She couldn't stop herself from clicking into it.

Hope you're not lonely tonight!!!

She dropped the phone as though it might bite her. Perspiration suddenly broke out all over her body. Every time she thought she was in the clear, he did something to throw her world back into disarray. He was telling her that he wasn't going away.

It took another second to realise that he knew she was at home and, more importantly, that she was alone.

She switched off the light and ran to the bedroom window, her heart hammering in her chest. She opened the curtain just an inch or two and scoured the area. Nothing. Her breathing eased slightly, and she managed to take one deep breath before heading into the living room. She repeated the process.

And there he was, leaning against the wall opposite, staring up at the window.

A cry escaped her lips as she pulled the curtain back together tightly, as though that would make him physically disappear.

She had the urge to burst into tears. How the hell had Charlotte put up with this for years without losing her mind?

Think, think, think, she told herself as she tried to regulate her breathing.

She weighed her options. She could call for a squad car. She could ring Devon and tell her the truth. She could ring any one of her colleagues, who would be over like a shot. But every one of those actions labelled her a victim – weak, reliant, diminished – and it gave all the power to him.

At this point he'd done nothing physical. She suspected he'd jumped out of a bush at the side of her building. She couldn't be sure. She suspected he'd been in the rear alley the night before. She couldn't be sure. She suspected he'd sent her flowers. She couldn't be sure. She suspected he'd sent her a Facebook message. She couldn't be sure.

'Okay, you bastard,' she said, raising herself to her full height. It was time for this to stop. She was not a victim and he wasn't going to intimidate her.

She grabbed her keys and phone and headed out of the door and down the stairs. The fear was crystalizing into rage with every step she took.

She slammed the front door behind her, bringing his gaze down from her window. The look of surprise was quickly hidden beneath a sneer.

'What the hell are you doing, Birch?' she asked, crossing the road.

He shrugged. 'It's a free country. I can go where I like.'

'Not really – there are laws against what you're doing,' she shouted.

'Out for a walk, needed to stop and rest,' he said, shrugging again. 'What's the law against that?'

So that was his first line of defence.

'The same law that prevents you being in the alleyway behind my flat last night.'

He shook his head. 'Nah, not me. Home all night.' He peered at her closely. 'You seeing things, sweetheart?'

'Don't you dare call me that,' Stacey spat, feeling a rush of revulsion at the endearment on his lips. 'The flowers went in the bin but not before they were seen by my colleagues.'

'What flowers?'

His constant denial was taking the rage out of her sails. She knew it was all him but proving it was another matter.

'Leave me alone, Birch. I'm not Charlotte. I won't put up with this shit for years.'

'I'm over Charlotte,' he said. 'I've met someone else.'

Her stomach turned but she held her nerve. 'Don't you even care that I'm a police officer?'

He shook his head.

'I could arrest you, have you charged.'

He looked up and down the street. 'I don't hear no sirens, which tells me everything I need to know,' he said as a Cheshire Cat grin shaped his face. 'You feel exactly the same way as I do.'

'I don't,' Stacey protested. 'I'm married. I love my wife.'

'I forgive you that mistake. We hadn't met but you'll see eventually that we're meant to be together.'

'You disgust me and if this doesn't stop, you're gonna find yourself back in prison.'

'That's fine. You're worth it.'

'I mean it, Birch. You will not win this time. You will not destroy my life.'

She turned and headed back across the road, using every ounce of determination she had to hide the trembling in her knees. His presence here tonight had wiped away every doubt that she'd put in her own way. Once or twice she'd been tempted to share her suspicions with Devon and the boss, but what would she have told them? She had no proof that he'd been outside her home or that it was him who'd sent the flowers or even that he'd messaged her ten minutes ago. He'd done nothing that she could prove. Until now. But now that she'd faced him, no one else needed to know. She'd stood up to him and she had been clear, direct and strong.

She just hoped and prayed it was enough.

SIXTY-TWO

'You don't think you've already got enough to do, Stone?'
Woody asked over the top of his glasses. She could always be
sure to catch him in the office before the early morning briefing.

'No, sir.'

'Do you want to enlighten me as to how you came across the
case?'

'The mother of Brad Foster was one of the guests at Psychic
Sandy's last engagement.'

'And what exactly is your problem with the investigation of
ten years ago?'

'Nothing. The investigation was spot on.'

'Are you messing with me?'

She shook her head. 'The SIO did everything by the book
based on the recollection of the only witness. A fifteen-year-old
boy.'

'Okay.'

'Except there was another witness who saw no white van.'

'The presence of the white van supports the story of the
eyewitness and the later developments?'

'Absolutely, sir.'

'Why do I feel that you're not really agreeing with me?'

'Because his story has changed. Ten years ago, Josh stopped in the woods to put his bike chain back on. Yesterday he told me he stopped to mend a puncture.'

'Stone, that's not enough,' Woody said dismissively.

'It's the detail, sir. When we spoke to him, he remembered actually repairing the puncture on his tyre. But back then, he remembered the oil on his hands from putting the chain back on. He's twenty-five and this happened ten years ago. No reason for such a memory lapse. He remembers everything else perfectly fine.'

'What are you suggesting?'

'I want him to walk the woods with me. Tell me exactly where everything happened, see what reaction I get.'

Woody sat back in his chair. 'And then what?'

'Send in a team with the GPR kit,' she said simply. Using radio waves, the equipment would easily detect any anomalies beneath the surface.

'The area is a mile square,' Woody said.

'I know, but right now I'm just not sure Brad ever left those woods.'

Kim didn't add that her conversation with Rose had sharpened the teeth gnawing in her stomach. The friendship between the boys had been dysfunctional at best. Such knowledge would not sway her boss one way or another.

He thought for a moment. 'I'm not committing any resources until you've got something more.'

'Understood,' she answered, heading for the door.

'Oh, and, Stone, there's talk of some video involving Penn on TikTok. Anything I need to know?'

He didn't see the smile that tugged at her lips. 'No, sir, probably a good idea for you to leave that one well alone.'

SIXTY-THREE

'Just to be clear, if we were still awarding a good-job plant, it would be sitting on Penn's desk right now,' Kim said, entering the squad room.

A smattering of applause filled the room as she poured herself a coffee from the machine.

Penn had called her the night before to brief her on the incident prior to it hitting social media.

She appreciated his creativity and had laughed out loud ten minutes later when she'd watched the video.

He'd known there was something not right with the situation and he hadn't stopped digging until he'd got to the bottom of it.

'And who knew Penn could be quite so obnoxious?' she asked.

'Me,' Stacey said, shooting her hand into the air.

'How did Mrs Sharpe take the news?' Kim asked. She knew that had been his next call after her the night before.

'Not sure, cos she couldn't stop crying after she'd watched the video. She'll be meeting with her solicitor today, and I'm pretty sure her days on Hollytree are numbered.'

'Good work,' she said and meant it. Penn had done an incredible job, but it wasn't the first thing she'd thought of when she'd rolled out of bed this morning. Before she'd even opened her eyes, the photos of the victims were firmly planted in her mind.

'Right, whatever you take for optimum energy levels, take double. I want renewed effort on everything.'

She stepped over to the printer and took off two sheets of paper. Using a biro, she put a ring around one of the subjects on the first photo.

'Stace, I want you to focus on CCTV at the theatre and keep an eye out for this woman here.'

Kim wafted the group photo under her nose before taping the page to the whiteboard.

'This is our lovely yoga group and that's Catherine Taylor. According to everyone else there on the night Sandy read for them, it was Catherine who really didn't like the answers she was given.'

'On it, boss,' Stacey said.

'Before you start looking for Catherine, I want you to check the footage of Tink with the suspected stooge. We all suspect he was working with Victoria, but I want proof. And then I want you to find him.'

The techies at the house had not uncovered details of any family members, so in the absence of nearest and dearest, they would have to make do with what they thought was a colleague. Perversely, for the sake of the investigation and being able to question someone about Victoria, she hoped he was on the psychic's payroll. For the sake of Tiff's comfort and reassurance, she hoped he wasn't.

'Penn, I want you working on those receipts we got from Sandy's. I want to know who she met with on Thursday lunchtime at the Harvester.' She paused. 'And even though no one has asked about him, Richard isn't in today cos he's given the builders the day off.'

She suspected the news of Victoria Sykes had hit him hard.

She taped the second photo to the other board.

'This is Bradley Foster and this photo was taken ten days before he was abducted. Although not directly linked to our case, we have found some inconsistencies in what happened the day Bradley disappeared.'

She retook her place. 'Bryant and I will be taking a look while you two get cracking and give us something to work on.' She looked to her colleague. 'Ready?'

'Err... boss, just one thing,' Penn said, looking uncomfortable.

'Yeah?'

'The camel coat.'

'The what now?' Her mind was already out of the building and in the car.

'You asked us all about a camel coat. Well, me and Jasper had kept a few of Mum's things. Including a camel coat. I checked the pocket. There was a rip in the lining. Found the spare key I'd been looking for to give to Lynne.'

Kim wasn't exactly sure of the appropriate response.

'Okay, well, glad you found it,' she said, grabbing her jacket.

Bryant waited until they were heading down the stairs. 'Well, that was a bit weird.'

'Coincidence,' she offered.

'Ain't nothing Richard has told us that would explain away that. And you don't believe in coincidences.'

'Always an exception that proves the rule, and that's all I'm gonna say.'

She chose not to mention the unease that had crawled into her stomach.

SIXTY-FOUR

'Oh, bless her,' Stacey said, spying Tiff standing in the corner of the theatre lobby.

'You do realise that she's a fully grown woman just a few years younger than you?' Penn replied.

'She just looks so lost and vulnerable.'

'Which was exactly how she was supposed to look. She's a police officer.'

Stacey turned her screen and showed him.

'Okay, yeah, you've got a point. She looks about fourteen.'

'Ah, here he comes,' Stacey said, turning the screen back as the guy at the bar approached Tiff.

She paused the CCTV for a second and stood to reach for a Diet Coke beside the coffee machine. She'd placed them there so that each new can would give her the opportunity to look out the window, which gave her a good view of the car park and the main road.

It was barely 9 a.m. and this was her second can. So far, nothing.

She was holding out real hope that her courage in confronting Terence Birch had done the trick. How she'd reached the other side of the road without her legs buckling she'd never know, but when she'd turned before entering the building, Birch had gone.

She'd returned to the sofa, downed half a bottle of wine and sat in silence, listening for any alien sound, until Devon had returned just after midnight.

She had woken with a fresh hope that it was all behind her and that Birch would have seen the error of his ways.

The flowers had been removed from her sight and placed in the bin in the ladies locker room.

And with that she was prepared to consider it a blot on the landscape of her happiness, keep it to herself and never think about it again.

She opened the can of Diet Coke and depressed the pause button on the footage. She knew exactly what Tiff's conversation had been about so she focussed on the crowd. She wasn't sure how she might pick out the blonde woman circled on the photo.

The camera angle was high and the people closest to the camera were only showing the tops of their heads. She could only see Tiff so easily because she was on the opposite side of the room.

Her gaze kept returning to the conversation over in the far corner. There was a subtle change in Tiff's body language while talking to the guy. It was as though the tension had eased out of her and she was relaxing into the conversation. She credited Tiff on being a decent actress but she wasn't that good. Her micro expressions were very revealing. She'd been telling the guy the truth about her grandmother and had opened herself up to all kinds of emotions; regret, sadness but above all else hope.

By the end of the conversation she was no longer the police officer tasked to do a job. She was the hopeful granddaughter hoping to connect with someone she loved. Now Stacey understood why Tiff had argued against the boss and Richard when they'd explained the techniques. Tiff had probably been hoping that the guy wasn't the stooge. For Tiff's piece of mind, Stacey wished she could give her that gift.

She watched as they parted company. Tiff headed towards the doors into the theatre with a tremulous look on her face.

The man approached the door to the gents and raised his hand.

Go in, go in, go in, she silently begged. It would be some confirmation that he wasn't the stooge.

He looked behind to where Tiff had gone out of sight.

He lowered his hand and disappeared through the door to his left. The one that led backstage.

'Bastard,' she muttered under her breath.

SIXTY-FIVE

Kim and Bryant knocked on the door of Josh Adams's flat for the second time in two days.

A man that was not Josh Adams threw open the door.

'For fuck's sake, it's still the middle of the bloody—'

Her ID in front of his face shut him up.

'Not quite, sunshine. I've already had two meetings, four coffees and I'm starting to consider what I'd like for lunch.' She paused. 'Is your flatmate in?' she asked, looking around him.

He shrugged and ruffled his dishevelled hair. 'Dunno, only got in a couple of hours ago,' he said, taking a step away from the door. 'Err... do I have to invite you in?'

'Because you think there's a legal penalty for leaving us standing out here or because you think we're vampires?' Kim asked.

'Umm... I just... Come in,' he said, opening a door on his left.

'Mate, you've got... Josh, buddy, are you up, mate?'

Silence met their ears.

The guy leaned in and switched on the light.

'Oh, sorry, he's not here.'

'Can we just take a quick look?' Bryant asked.

'I ain't lying,' he said, pushing the door open.

Kim stood beside him. The room was neat and tidy with very little evidence of a recent occupant.

'What's that?' Kim asked, taking a step towards the room.

'Hang on. No, I ain't that stupid. You ain't going messing in his room without a search warrant.'

He was right of course, which didn't improve her mood.

Before she asked him to do so, he entered the room and retrieved the single piece of paper lying on the pillow.

'Ah, it's a note, to me,' he said, starting to read it.

'Care to share?' Kim asked, making sure she didn't cross the threshold into the room.

'It says, "To Jacko," that's me,' he offered unnecessarily.

Kim nodded that she got that.

'"Gotta get away for a bit",' Jacko continued. '"Some past shit coming back to haunt me so just need to clear my head. Rent for the next three weeks is in the tin. I'll let you know after that."'

'He's gone,' Jacko offered, as though he hadn't just read the letter out loud.

'Any idea what he's talking about?' Kim asked, matching Jacko for playing it dumb.

'Dunno, but probably whatever you're here about,' Jacko answered, calling her bluff.

'I know some stuff happened when he was a kid, with that other kid getting killed and stuff, but he never talked about it to me. I've only known him a couple of years.'

'And how did you meet?' Bryant asked.

'I put a card in the newsagent's window for a flatmate after my last one got hitched. Josh answered the ad. Looked decent enough.'

Just another thing like walking home alone that guys didn't really have to consider too deeply. Women seeking housemates didn't have the luxury of assuming someone looked okay.

'Did he ever strike you as strange?' Kim asked.

'We don't vibe like that. We ain't mates. We share a flat cos we can't afford the rent on our own. We might meet in the kitchen sometimes and pass the time of day for a few minutes, but that's about it.'

'You said he didn't like to talk about the past, but you knew him well enough to ask.'

'Nah, not me. I couldn't care less as long as he coughs up his rent money. It was an old girlfriend of mine. She was at school with him, remembered them both. She asked him about it.' He paused. 'Actually, he did get a bit huffy about it.'

'Oh yeah, why's that?' Bryant asked.

'Cos, Tilly – that's my ex-girlfriend,' he explained, even though it wasn't a hard story to follow, 'she started going on about the fact they were always together and that Josh used to follow the other one around a bit. Called him a lap dog or something. Asked just how close they were.'

So far, Tilly sounded like an annoying piece of work.

'He took the huff and went to his room.'

Yeah, she'd probably have done the same.

She turned away from the bedroom. She had no cause to enter. Josh Adams wasn't a suspect in any active investigation or considered to be in danger. He had simply taken off, and she wasn't allowed to invade his privacy just because she thought he was lying.

Convinced there was nothing else of any use coming from the flatmate, she offered her card and headed out the door.

'Okay, I'm in,' Bryant said as they made their way down the stairs.

'In what?'

'Following up on this. Definitely something weird with this Josh kid, and Brad's mother deserves answers.'

'Even though she doesn't want us asking him difficult questions,' Kim observed. 'So what now, Bryant? We have nothing to offer Woody. He's not gonna commit a team to the woods because Josh Adams has taken himself on a mini break. We needed more than that,' she said as they reached the car.

'Well, let's quit waiting around for something to find us and let's go take a look at those woods for ourselves.'

She smiled as she got in the car.

She did enjoy it when Bryant finally came round to her way of thinking.

SIXTY-SIX

'Gotta hand it to her, she is pretty damn good,' Bryant acknowledged as he drove towards Tettenhall. They had been on the way to the woods when they'd received a call from the detective constable.

He was right. It had taken Stacey less than an hour to find out the stooge's name was Neil Dobson. He was twenty-two and lived two miles out of Wolverhampton.

Due to him accessing the rear corridors at the theatre, Stacey had known he would have needed ID, and the manager had confirmed that she had seen his driving licence as proof of identification. Although the manager had been unable to offer his address due to data protection, she'd given hints that he didn't live very far away. With Stacey's almost intimate knowledge of the electoral register, she'd pinned him down to an address within fifteen minutes.

'Looking a bit tired, I thought,' Kim said, recalling the constable's slightly bloodshot eyes.

'Newly married, honeymoon phase. Probably up all night...'

'Okay, Bryant. More info than I needed,' she said, shaking her head in despair.

'Hey, have you ever heard of Tettenhall Dick?'

'Oh, Jesus,' she groaned.

'It's a pear.'

'Pair of what?' she asked, knowing she was going to find out whether she asked or not.

'Pear as in fruit. It's a variety originally found in Perton and dates back to before the eighteenth century. They're small and dry and used for making perry.'

'Okay, marginally better than talking about Stacey's love life but still not scintillating conversation.'

He shrugged as though he had nothing better to offer and took a left turn behind a small park.

'That one,' Kim said, pointing to a semi-detached red brick house with a small Citroën on the drive.

'Still living with parents?' Bryant asked, parking the car.

'Unless he makes more from deceiving people than we thought,' she said, getting out the car.

Bryant grunted his agreement as they headed up the path.

The door was opened on the first knock by the male Kim had seen talking to Tiff. He was barefoot, wearing jeans and a band T-shirt.

'Neil Dobson?' she asked, showing her ID.

He nodded and opened the door. 'This is about Victoria, isn't it?'

The news had hit the media an hour earlier.

'We just have a couple of questions,' she said, following him into a lounge that was a study in the oatmeal colour palette.

'Please sit down,' he said, waiting to see where they landed before taking a seat himself. 'Can I get you anything?'

Despite what he did to earn a few quid, she couldn't fault his manners.

'No, we just need to ask about your relationship with Victoria.'

'Of course,' he said, pulling out a foot stool and placing it in front of the television. 'I mean, I can't quite believe she's gone.'

'Were you close?' Kim asked, hoping to gauge the level of their relationship.

'I wouldn't say close. We had a laugh now and again.'

Kim wanted to ask if they laughed together about the people they duped in her show. The image of the two of them chuckling conspiratorially behind Tink's back warmed her blood by a couple of degrees, but she held it in check.

'We both like the old Carry On films,' he said, clarifying, when Kim remained silent. 'Inappropriate, I know, but we used to laugh about them.'

'You worked for her?' Kim asked, moving along.

'Kind of,' he said cagily.

'You provided a service and received money?' she rephrased.

He nodded.

'Mr Dobson, there's little point hiding exactly what you did for Victoria. We already know that you pumped audience members for personal information and then fed it back to Victoria for her to use in her show.'

His surprise at the depth of her knowledge was evident. He made no effort to deny it.

'Can you tell us how that started?'

'My mum got tickets for her and my dad to go to a show about three years ago. They both got the flu and couldn't make it. I had nothing to do so thought I'd go along.'

From what Tiff had told her, it sounded as though he stuck pretty close to the truth while deceiving people.

He continued. 'I was actually gonna ask the theatre if they had any part-time jobs available, but Victoria approached and asked if I'd help her out when she toured.'

'You travelled the country with her?' Bryant asked.

He shook his head. 'Just when she was doing the Midlands. Anything over thirty miles or so and it wasn't worth it.'

'And what was the arrangement?' Kim asked.

He looked mildly uncomfortable. 'Just to talk to a member of the audience, get a few facts, pass them on.'

'Just one?' Kim asked doubtfully.

He nodded. 'Oh yeah, never more than one. I think it was her backup in case the spirits were quiet.'

'Hang on,' Kim said. 'Are you saying that you only deceived one victim each show and any other readings were completely genuine?'

She saw a bit of fire in his eyes at her choice of words, but he skated over it and answered the question.

'Only ever one and I absolutely believe that she was genuine. If you'd seen her in action—'

'I did,' Kim said. 'I was at the show on Tuesday night. Your victim was one of my officers.'

His mouth fell open. 'No fucking way.'

She waited.

'She was a police officer?'

Kim nodded.

'Bloody hell, she should have been an actress. She got me good,' he said, shaking his head.

'I think you got her good too,' Kim said, recalling Tiff's sombre mood in the car. She heard the stiffness in her tone.

'I don't feel bad,' he offered. 'It's not like I went out and hurt people. I passed along a few details and it was up to Victoria to do the rest.'

Engaging in another debate about the rights and wrongs of fraudulent readings was a waste of her time. It wasn't going to help them find Victoria's killer.

'Was she acting strange at all?'

'No.'

'Did she mention anything about weird phone calls or perhaps being followed?'

'Definitely not. I would have remembered something like that. Victoria wasn't much of a sharer. Other than the Carry On films, I know nothing about what she liked or disliked. She'd text me when she wanted me to work. I'd turn up. We'd pass the time of day and then I'd get to work. As soon as she came offstage, she'd pay me and I'd leave. We didn't have long conversations or anything like that.'

'Did she ever talk about family?'

He shook his head.

'Did you get the impression that there was any family?'

'I honestly couldn't say. I suppose I subconsciously thought there was a husband or partner somewhere that just chose not to be involved in her work.'

Kim was curious. 'Why would you think that?'

He frowned. 'I suppose it was because she never seemed lonely. She was always pretty upbeat, cheery. I just assumed there was someone waiting at home.'

Again, Kim was reminded that Victoria had seemed to be perfectly happy with her own company.

It was now clear to Kim that the closest person to Victoria they could find wasn't actually close to her at all.

Kim was about to thank him for his time when he frowned.

'There was one strange thing she said, come to think of it. She was a few minutes late and I was in the dressing room waiting for her.'

'Was that unusual?'

He nodded.

'And what did she say?'

'She said something about being pleased she didn't do private readings any more.'

'Go on,' Kim said.

'That's it really. Just said that she remembered how draining they were.'

Kim had to wonder why she'd said such a thing. What would have made her remember how draining they were? It could only mean that she'd recently done one and that it had reminded her. With no more detail that that, her theory that she'd met privately with their killer was dead in the water.

Now she stood. 'Thank you for your time. If we need anything further, we'll be in touch.'

She headed for the door and then turned. 'Just out of interest, after talking to our officer, you told Victoria about the salty crisps, right?'

'The what?'

'You told Victoria that the officer's gran liked to eat salty crisps?'

He shook his head. He had no clue what she was talking about.

Kim frowned. 'Okay. Again, thanks for your time.'

SIXTY-SEVEN

It was after 10 a.m. by the time they pulled up at the western edge of the woods, and Kim realised it must look pretty similar to how it would have appeared on that day almost ten years ago.

This side of the woods was lined with cherry blossom trees – the early risers, her foster mom had called them; flowering early before turning to leaf. The dense blossoms would have made seeing into the wooded area impossible.

'So they'd have entered here,' she said, following a well-worn path that wound through the trees and bushes. There was no straight route where you could see ahead, which must have made it great fun riding a bike through every morning.

She was around fifty metres into the woods and about to urge Bryant to keep up when she heard a rustling up ahead.

She turned to her colleague with a finger to her lips and then held out the palm of her hand, telling him to stay still.

He nodded his understanding as she looked to the ground to take care where she stepped.

Her movements reminded her of a time when she was eleven years old. Her foster mother, Erica, had baked a choco-late sponge filled with fresh strawberries and whipped cream.

She had stubbornly refused to take a bite, still rejecting all efforts to make her feel at home. She'd woken during the night and the only thoughts in her mind had been of that cake. She had sneaked downstairs, avoiding all creaky floorboards by stepping on them as lightly as possible. The cake had been everything she'd imagined and more. She had crept back up to bed and pretended it never happened. And she was mirroring those movements right now.

The path continued to wind through budding trees, but a movement of something blue up ahead caught her eye.

Five metres further, she stepped into a clearing. A fallen log blocked a path leading out of the woods away from the main road.

Sitting on the log was Josh Adams.

They regarded each other silently.

It was as if they both knew they were going to meet there.

Kim took a seat beside him.

'Oh, Josh, we know you're lying to us. Whatever you're not saying is eating you alive. You ready to get it off your chest yet?'

'I don't think I can hold it in much longer.'

She stood. 'I think this is a chat we'd be better off having at the station.'

SIXTY-EIGHT

'It's making me hungry watching this,' Penn said as he witnessed another brunch plate being brought to one of the tables.

The CCTV sent over by the Harvester restaurant in Stourbridge was made up of three different camera angles, and he had a two-hour slot before the time of the bill being paid.

'Finally,' he said as Sandra Deakin came into view.

He paused for a second and glanced at his colleague.

'Hey, you're not telling me off for talking to myself out loud. What's wrong?'

'Did you say something?' she asked without taking her eyes from the screen.

'You got something at the theatre?' he asked.

'Not sure, I'll tell you in a minute.'

Penn returned to his own task and continued to watch the recording.

Sandra Deakin ordered a coffee and some kind of fruit pastry. She was halfway through it when her companion arrived. The person who sat at the table opposite her was none other than Monty Dunhill, the man who had lied about meeting her.

Penn was about to share this information with his colleague when he saw she was giving her screen a hard, pensive stare. It could wait.

He turned back to the screen and watched the interaction between Sandra and Monty.

Monty took a seat but sat side saddle with his legs crossed so that he was side on to the table. There was something nonchalant, distracted about his demeanour, as though he wasn't giving her his full attention.

A waiter placed a small cup before him which Penn assumed to be an espresso. He neither acknowledged nor thanked the waiter.

Sandra pushed away her half-eaten pastry and leaned forward, resting her elbows on the table and her chin on her hands. The difference in posture was striking, and even without hearing the conversation, it was clear where the power lay.

Sandra appeared to be doing all the talking with an occasional shrug from Monty as the response. At times Monty was looking around the restaurant while Sandy was speaking, showing her the ultimate level of disrespect.

Sandy's posture became more animated. She was shifting in her seat, using her hands as she spoke. Monty recrossed his legs and calmly sipped his drink.

Penn wanted to reach into the screen and slap some manners into him.

There was no doubt she was asking for something that he wasn't prepared to give.

After what looked like a final plea, Monty drained his cup, shook his head and stood.

As he passed, he leaned down and whispered something in her ear, after which Sandra dropped her head into her hands.

Two minutes later, she paid the bill and left the building.

Penn sat back in his chair. Stacey did the same.

'I got him,' he said, now he had her attention. 'I got Monty on CCTV.'

'Yeah, you and me both,' Stacey said as the boss and Bryant walked in the room.

SIXTY-NINE

Kim headed back down the stairs with an excitement building in her stomach. She was on the cusp of solving two mysteries and one or both included murder. She had updated Woody and advised him to keep the ground-penetrating radar team on standby. She was hoping to have something imminently.

Penn was now on his way to bring Monty Dunhill in for questioning, and she'd given Josh a drink, a sandwich and some time to think of what he wanted to say. He wasn't under arrest. He could leave at any time. Right now, all she had on him was lying, so she had to play this right.

And that was why she was questioning him alone.

'Everything okay?' she asked, closing the door behind her.

The sandwich was gone and the cup was half empty.

'Where exactly were you going?' she asked, nodding towards the holdall at his feet.

He shrugged. 'I dunno. I just didn't want to be there when you came back.'

'You were sure I would?'

'Oh yeah, your face said you weren't done with me.'

'Did that make you nervous?'

He thought before nodding. 'I suppose I've been waiting for someone like you for the last ten years.'

'Is that why you've not really moved on with your life? No steady job? No girlfriend?'

'Maybe. I mean I'm not proud of lying, but I didn't know what else to do.'

His first admission that he'd actually lied.

'Did you have an argument?' she asked.

His face changed. The worried frown hardened. 'Is that what you think?'

'Could have happened.'

His brain seemed to be working overtime and she could see regret in his face, either for his actions ten years ago or for agreeing to talk to her, but she couldn't be sure which.

'I think I want a lawyer,' he said, nodding in affirmation to both her and himself.

'Why the change?' she asked, confused.

'I need to know how much trouble I'm in before I tell you anything.'

'I thought you wanted to come clean, unburden yourself?'

'I do, but once I say the words, I can't take 'em back. I need legal advice.'

'Josh, did you hurt Brad?' she asked.

'No comment.'

She wasn't bound by procedure because he wasn't under arrest. Once cautioned, she would be unable to ask anything once he requested legal services, but right now she could ask him whatever she wanted. He was free to give her the finger and leave.

'Did you make a pass at him?'

'No comment.'

'Were you in love with Brad?'

'No comment.'

'Did you really see a white van?'

'No comment.'

'Did Brad ever leave those woods?'

A hesitation.

A lick of the lips.

'I've already said, no comment.'

SEVENTY

'Damn it,' Kim said, heading back into the squad room.

It had been so close. She'd almost had the answers. For all she knew, a lawyer might just advise him to keep his mouth shut, but she couldn't prise the information out of him.

She replayed the conversation in her mind to work out exactly where she'd lost him. It was almost as if the first question that had left her mouth had brought back the enormity of what he was confessing to and that he was speaking to a police officer. Her hopes of being able to go back to Rose with some closure and a body to bury were dwindling by the minute.

Even though Josh wasn't under arrest, he was calling a lawyer from the interview room. She hoped that in allowing him to do so, he might suddenly change his mind and admit what he'd done.

She had no choice but to wait until he was ready to talk, and she didn't do waiting well, she acknowledged as she poured herself a cuppa.

Penn burst into the room.

'You got him?' Kim asked.

'Oh yeah, arrested, cautioned, waiting and not too happy

about it either. Apparently this is a really bad day for us to have chosen to bother him.'

'He actually used the word bother?' Kim asked.

Penn nodded.

Damn but this man was truly insufferable. He'd been arrested on suspicion of murder and he was acting as though they were no more than an irritant, a wasp buzzing round his food on a sunny day.

Kim banged her mug down on the desk, causing some of the liquid to splosh over the sides. It was time for Mr Dunhill to realise she was done playing games.

She nodded towards Bryant. 'You ready?'

This was going to be a whole different interview.

SEVENTY-ONE

'What's your gut say?' Stacey asked Penn.

'That the man is a first-rate, top-of-the-line knobchops.'

'I don't actually know what that is but I'm guessing it's not good.'

'He actually told me it wasn't a convenient time to be arrested, that he had important things on today and could I come back tomorrow.'

'No way,' Stacey said. 'Cheeky beggar.'

'There's no doubt that the world revolves around Monty Dunhill. He is superior, arrogant, condescending, dismissive and, well, just not a nice person,' Penn said, after running out of adjectives.

'But is he a murderer?' Stacey asked.

'Let's hope the boss is about to find out,' he said, collecting together the receipts. He caught her studious expression. 'You still working on the theatre footage?'

'Yep, I got a camera on the door that gives a good shot of people leaving once the show's over. Just wanna see it through to the end,' she said, glancing at the photo of the group where the boss had circled the face of Catherine Taylor.

He put the receipts into date order. The one he'd checked and verified was the last but one. The final receipt was from a small café in Quinton dated Saturday. The boss hadn't mentioned it because it was only for a few pounds. They'd assumed she was there alone. But what if she did meet someone but only paid for her own coffee?

A quick Google search gave him the phone number for the café.

He called the number, which rang out for what seemed like forever. It was eventually answered by a deep male voice that almost shouted the name of the café and not in a welcoming tone.

Damn, he'd caught the lunchtime rush.

Penn quickly introduced himself.

'Good for you, mate, but unless you got a massive takeout order for your whole station, I got customers to serve.'

And I've got a murderer to catch, Penn almost retorted but realised that wasn't his best approach.

'I'll be quick. You got CCTV?'

'You having a laugh? I make thirteen pence on a cup of coffee.'

Penn considered asking about a customer he'd served on a busy Saturday but guessed what the response would be.

'Gotta go, fella, but the gym across the road's got a camera that catches a couple of my outdoor tables, if that helps at all.'

With that the line went dead in his ear.

Penn wondered if he was wasting his time following up on this lead.

He considered his colleague, who was still checking the theatre even though their prime suspect was now downstairs.

He typed a new search into Google. It wasn't over until it was over.

SEVENTY-TWO

With the formalities over and the tape switched on, Kim leaned her elbows on the table.

'Mr Dunhill, may I clarify for the record your willingness to proceed without the presence of a legal representative?'

'Why would I pay someone to tell you I've done nothing wrong when I'm perfectly capable of telling you that myself?'

Oh no, he wasn't doing that. An obscure answer and any doubt about police protocols being followed was a defence lawyer's dream.

'If you can't afford a lawyer one will be provided at—'

'Ha, that's laughable. No thank you, I'm fine,' he said, changing his position and sitting to the side, much as he'd done on the footage Penn had shown her. It gave her a good indication of the derision he was feeling about his arrest.

'I'll have far more use for a lawyer when I'm suing you for false arrest.'

'You've been arrested so that we can effect a prompt and efficient investigation into your involvement in the murders of Sandra Deakin, Azim Mahmood and Victoria Sykes.'

'Preposterous. Your ineptitude is truly astounding. Do you really think I look like a killer?'

'Do you think anyone actually looks like a killer?' she asked.

'You are wasting your time; you should be out finding the real killer, and you'll be very quick to realise your mistake.'

'Then you should be out of here in no time and free to continue with your day.'

'Today, of all days. I honestly don't know how I can help you.'

'You can begin by telling us why you lied about meeting Sandy last Thursday. We have the CCTV footage of you two together.'

'I don't recall actually stating that we didn't meet.'

'Oh, I think you'll find that you did. My colleague here writes down things in his pocket notebook, habit from his constable days. I'm sure we can read it back. He keeps impeccable records. You lied to us and I'd like to know why.'

He recrossed his legs. 'I think I evaded the question, but if you must know, it was for this very reason. I didn't want to get caught up in this distasteful business.'

'The distasteful business of a woman losing her life?' Kim asked.

'Yes, it's all so tawdry. I didn't want my good name anywhere near it.'

'Why did you meet her?' Kim asked. 'You didn't like her, you had a cruel nickname for her, as you did for all of your fellow psychics, so why did you agree to meet her?'

A flick of the left shoulder.

'She asked you many times. We saw the entries in her diary. Why agree this time?'

'I decided to put her out of her misery.'

'About what?'

He rolled his eyes. 'My second article.'

'You've written another hit piece?'

'I prefer to call them exposés,' he said blithely. 'The first one hit her career hard, and she wanted me to kill the second one.'

'And what did you tell her?'

'No, of course. She deserved to be exposed for the fraud that she was.'

The CCTV images flew into her mind. Sandra, literally begging him not to publish, and his uncaring manner, his cold refusal in the face of her pleas.

'What was the last thing you said to her, as you left?' Kim asked.

'I told her that her career was over.'

Kim fought hard to keep control of her emotions. There was not one ounce of regret in his tone despite the fact the woman had been brutally murdered.

'Mr Dunhill, where were you on Sunday night?'

'At home, alone.'

'Where were you in the early hours of Tuesday morning?'

'In bed asleep like most normal people.'

'Interesting. How about Tuesday night into Wednesday morning?'

'At home, alone.'

'After Victoria's stage show?' she asked.

He nodded.

'You see, you're at it again. You just chose not to mention that you were in close proximity to our third victim within hours of her murder.'

'I watched the show, got a taxi home and went to bed.'

'Obviously you'll be able to give us the name of the taxi company so we can confirm it. Why did you go and see the Show Pony if you detest her so much?'

'The publication of my article was imminent and I just wanted to ensure my observations were still correct.'

'And?'

'I'm sad to say they were. She was still the Show Pony she

always was.'

'And now she's dead,' Kim observed.

Dunhill said nothing.

'No response?'

'I don't recall hearing a question.'

Oh, his arrogance was unfailing, despite the fact he was under arrest for their murders.

'Did Victoria know about the article?' Kim asked. She hadn't mentioned it during their conversation.

'She knew and didn't care. Her career was not harmed by the first.'

Yeah, she had admitted that much.

'But what about yours, Mr Dunhill? We understand that the first article didn't exactly increase your client list?'

His eyes sparked but he covered it with a long blink that lasted almost two seconds.

'Natural wastage, Inspector. It happens in every successful business. I can assure you that I have not suffered financially and my current client list is incredibly healthy.'

'With ex-reality stars and WAGs?' Kim asked.

His jaw tensed but he remained silent.

'So what was the angle for the new article going to be? More nicknames, more insults, more victims?'

'You say that as though the article is in the past.'

'Isn't it, given that two of your subjects have been brutally murdered within days of each other?'

'Quite the contrary. Public interest is at its highest. There's no better time to publish.'

Kim was appalled at his bad taste.

'And to answer your question, yes, there is a new addition to my stable of subjects.'

'And does this one have a nickname too?'

He smiled. 'Yes, I call her Grandma.'

A chill began to steal over her.

'You're talking about Eloise Hunter?'

'Actually, yes I am. She's earned a mention.'

And everyone else mentioned in Dunhill's articles was now dead.

'When is the article being published?' she asked, dreading the answer.

'It went online this morning which is why your timing in hauling—'

Kim was no longer listening.

'Damn it,' she growled as she headed for the door.

SEVENTY-THREE

Penn received the CCTV footage from the gym just a minute after he saw the boss and Bryant run out of the building.

He'd thought he was just tidying up, crossing his Ts, and that their murderer was sitting in interview room one, but now he wasn't so sure.

From the size of the file he'd been sent, he was guessing the footage was around twenty minutes long.

He loaded it and saw that the time stamp began at 11.01. The camera faced the café and managed to pick up one and a half of the tables outside. The seating area was facing south-east and bathed in sunshine.

The prayer he was silently formulating was answered as he saw Sandy exit with a tall latte glass. She took a seat at the half table so that she was in view.

She set her drink down and took out her phone, indicating she was alone.

He was just starting to think his gut had failed him and that it was a simple cuppa on her own, when she thrust the phone back into her bag and stood.

She pointed inside but then sat back down.

So, she had met someone and that person was out of view. It appeared that Sandy had offered her companion a drink and it had been refused.

He watched for any clue as to who was sitting at the table just out of shot, but all he could see was Sandy, who held her glass, sipped and listened, offering only the occasional nod.

After a few minutes, she put the cup down and started to speak. Her hands were carrying out explanatory gestures. Penn noted the difference in Sandy's body language to when she'd been talking to Monty. Here, she wasn't tense or stiff or uncomfortable. She would take breaks from talking to sip her drink and listen.

Penn knew that this could be a perfectly innocent meeting with one of her friends except for two things: this took place the day before she was murdered, and normally if you met a friend for coffee, you both had a drink, a chat and then you went your separate ways. The person sitting across the table wasn't here for coffee, so they were here for something else.

Sandy was now opening her hands and shaking her head with an occasional shrug. Something in her demeanour said she was sad, regretful, even apologetic.

Her hand moved across the table towards the other person but then shot back, as though she had tried to offer a comforting touch and it had been thrown off.

Sandy shook her head again and looked up. The person must be standing.

After a minute, Sandy continued to sip from her cup without speaking. Her companion had gone.

It occurred to Penn that the other person had left the meeting unhappy with the result.

SEVENTY-FOUR

'So now you think he's not our guy?' Bryant asked, pulling off the car park.

'I'm not saying that. I just want to make sure she's safe.'

The fact that Eloise hadn't answered her calls was just one of the things not helping the tension in Kim's stomach.

The minute Monty had mentioned the woman's name, she'd felt a surge of danger course through her. She knew that if she had been totally convinced that Monty was their killer, the alarm bells in her body would have remained silent.

Everything they had pointed his way: he hated all the victims enough to want them gone. He was a despicable human being, but did that make him a murderer? Right now, the jury in her nerves was out on that one. It wasn't often that she had to persuade herself that they had the right person. Normally she just knew. Usually when they arrested and questioned a suspect, her gutometer was at a full one hundred, but when she pictured Monty Dunhill murdering Sandy, Azim and Victoria, the needle was sticking somewhere around eighty-five.

She took out her phone and tried Eloise again.

'Come on, come on,' she growled at her phone, willing the elderly woman to answer.

What she wanted was for Eloise to answer the phone calmly and tell her that the call had disturbed her from a really good part in the book she was reading and that she was being ridiculous. But that didn't happen and once again her phone went to voicemail.

'Hang on, hang on,' Kim said. 'Head to Netherton. It's Thursday afternoon. She goes to the hospice. She won't be answering her phone.'

'Got it,' Bryant said.

Kim just prayed that being at the hospice had kept the woman out of reach and given her the breathing space she needed.

SEVENTY-FIVE

'Jesus, Bryant, hurry up,' Kim growled as he stopped at another crossing.

'What exactly do you want me to do, run them over?' he asked, nodding to a grateful parent accompanying three children over the zebra.

Catching school throw-out time made getting anywhere a nightmare. It was bad enough to be dealing with parents trying to shoehorn SUVs into tiny spaces as close to the premises as possible, but once you escaped the chaos of one school building, you were right into another.

'Well, just do something,' she growled.

He stayed silent. He knew full well how she got when they were in a hurry. Her brain always reverted to the worst-case scenario. She was already imagining Eloise being butchered and left dead in a pool of her own blood.

Bryant had no choice but to stop for a crossing. Ahead, the traffic was at a standstill.

She removed her seat belt.

'Guv...'

'Child lock, Bryant,' she hissed.

'Don't be—'

'I'll be quicker. Catch me up.'

He shook his head as he hit the button. She jumped out of the car and threw the door shut. It was half a mile to the hospice, and the pavements were littered with parents and children, but the traffic was stationary. She stepped into the road and sprinted along the gap between the cars and the pavement.

One more set of lights and two crossings and she turned left into the car park of the hospice.

A nurse was just exiting the premises. Kim made to pass her but the woman blocked her path.

'Excuse me, I need—'

'I'm not moving,' she said. 'Until you tell me who you are.'

She nodded towards the call point, signalling that Kim wouldn't get any further even if she wasn't standing in the way.

Kim took a second to get her breath.

The nurse filled it. 'I'm sorry but I don't know you. I can't just let you in.'

'DI Stone,' she said, reaching for her ID.

The woman took a good look and waited.

'I'm not here for any of your patients or staff. I'm here to see Eloise.'

The nurse frowned.

'She comes here to talk to—'

'I'm well aware of who Eloise is. I just can't fathom why you'd want to speak to her.'

'Is she here?' Kim asked. If she was, Kim could relax and entertain this woman's security check. If not, she was running out of time.

The dread filled her stomach as the woman shook her head. At that second, Bryant pulled up behind her.

'Where is she?'

Hesitation.

'I think she's in danger,' Kim said. There was no time to play games.

'She went home. She got a call. Her neighbour said something about a break-in and...'

Kim heard no more as she turned and opened the car door.

Damn it. She'd thought she was being clever in working out where Eloise might be and she'd been wrong.

She might have just signed Eloise's death warrant herself.

SEVENTY-SIX

Stacey felt as though her eyes were bleeding after staring at the screen for what felt like hours.

She was viewing the footage from the camera above the entrance catching the audience members as they left the theatre. She stopped the video every few seconds and searched the faces for any she recognised. The theatre had a 1,200 capacity and the show had been sold out.

Penn had pointed out to her that she'd already struck gold in finding their prime suspect, Monty Dunhill, but that hadn't been her instruction. She'd been told to look for a woman named Catherine.

She looked again at the picture circled on the wall and imagined her with her hair up or without make-up. It was possible she wasn't going to look exactly how she did on the WhatsApp group photo.

She moved the cursor so the video let through another batch of people.

This group contained Tiff, who had left the theatre as the boss headed away from the throng of people.

Two frames further and both the boss and Tiff had disappeared from sight.

Stacey frowned at the screen and went back to play it again. Although she'd been distracted by the boss and Tiff, something had caught her eye.

In the top left of the shot was a figure walking with a bent head. She moved forward again to the moment where the boss had disappeared and the bowed head was raised.

Stacey looked at the board and back at the screen.

'Penn, come here,' she said.

He came to stand behind her.

'Is that who I think it is?' she asked as he too looked at the screen, and then at the board.

He started to nod while his gaze remained fixed on the wall.

His expression was of deep concentration.

She reached across him for her phone. 'I'd best let the boss—'

'Two minutes, Stace, just give me two short minutes,' he said, sprinting out of the room.

SEVENTY-SEVEN

Motive. That's what was causing her problems, Kim realised as Bryant turned the car into Eloise's street. That was why the needle on the superior psychic wasn't quite hitting the jackpot.

Yes, Monty Dunhill despised Sandra Deakin, Victoria Sykes and anyone else in the psychic community that wasn't him. But it was a professional hatred; disgust at the way they did business. The attacks this week were personal, emotional, uncontrolled, feverish. Multiple, vicious stab wounds were not the work of someone with a professional gripe. They were the actions of someone who felt a burning rage that could only come from personal pain.

Bryant parked where she pointed, and Kim's gaze scoured the property. She could already see that Eloise's car was on the drive and there was a shattered glass window to the right of the front door. The bait. The call from the neighbour to get Eloise home.

As she got out of the car, the events of the week started to play back through her mind and a picture began to form. It was sketchy. She didn't have it all, but things were starting to make sense.

'We gotta get in there quick,' Kim said. 'You guard the front door and I'll head round the back. We don't want anyone getting out.'

Hearing the urgency in her voice, her colleague turned.

'You really think the murderer is in there?' Bryant asked.

She nodded, and if she was right about their killer, they didn't have a minute to lose.

She ran around the back, praying that Eloise had opened the back door.

Her fingers were inches away from the door handle when her phone tinged a message. She took it out quickly.

It was Penn with a one-line text.

But that one line told her everything.

SEVENTY-EIGHT

Kim gave herself a count of three, rushed through the back door and stopped dead.

Eloise was in her favourite chair, her face frozen in terror. A seven-inch blade was poised above her chest.

Kim was eight feet away in the archway that connected the kitchen to the dining area.

Too far.

'Put the knife down, Rose,' she said, trying to keep her tone steady.

'Take one more step and she's dead,' Rose said, staring straight at her.

She was poised behind the chair, holding the knife with both hands. She was as far away from Kim as she could be, with Eloise and the armchair in between them. Eloise wasn't being held down, but if she tried to move, the blade would drive deep into her chest. Kim had no chance of rushing Rose without putting Eloise's life in danger. The woman had cold-bloodedly killed three people already, and Kim guessed she wouldn't hesitate in killing one more.

Eloise looked back at her with terror in her eyes. Her body

was trembling with fear and the need to remain still.

'Rose, no one else needs to die,' Kim said, raising her gaze from Eloise to the woman holding the knife.

'They all need to die. They're all liars. They all prey upon people, taking their money under false pretences. They all say they can talk to the dead. They're all fake.'

'Eloise isn't fake,' Kim said, surprising herself.

'Of course she is. She's just like all the others.'

Eloise let out a little whimper as the knife dropped lower towards her chest. Just one good plunge and it would all be over, and there was nothing she could do about it.

She had no choice but to try and keep Rose talking, keeping the attention on her. She hoped her failure to open the front door would give Bryant the nod that there was something wrong and he'd follow her in. She had to stall until Penn got there. If he did what she'd asked, he would only be minutes away.

'They couldn't give you the answers you wanted, could they?' Kim asked softly.

'Brad would try and talk to me and none of these tricksters can give me a message.'

'So you killed them?' Kim asked, hearing sirens in the distance.

Rose heard them too. The knife wobbled in her hand.

In her peripheral vision, Kim could see the fear in Eloise's face, but she couldn't turn her attention away for a second.

'Stay with me, Rose,' Kim begged. 'Explain it all to me properly and I can help you.'

Kim felt no remorse for barefaced lying to a woman wielding a seven-inch blade.

To her left, she saw Bryant approaching the back door. She shook her head to indicate that he should not enter. He could see she was safe and he could watch her from there. The tension in the room was like a tightly strung guitar string. One movement and it might break.

'Don't you see how utterly despicable they are?' Rose asked. 'They say they talk to dead people, commune with the other side. They've all earned their living from people like me; desperate, grief-stricken people who had a loved one ripped away and who want to say goodbye properly. I have to tell him I'm sorry. Don't you understand that? I shouted at him. I called him names. That's his eternal memory of me, his mother.'

By Kim's estimate the sirens were about a mile out.

Rose heard them but continued anyway. She wanted to explain why she'd taken three lives. She wanted Kim to understand.

'These tricksters give us hope that we can connect with them again, be reassured that they're not suffering, that they are at peace. I don't know what was done to my boy by whoever was in that van. I don't know how they tortured him or made him suffer. I don't know if he's at peace. I have to know that he's okay and these people promise they have the power to do this, and it's nothing but a scam, a ruse to make money.'

Her voice was filled with rage, but a tear was also forcing itself from the corner of her eye.

Half a mile.

The tip of the blade was an inch from Eloise's chest and her ragged breathing was bringing it even closer.

Kim said nothing. Her best strategy was to let Rose talk herself dry.

'None of them could contact my Brad because they're all fake. Surely you can see how cruel that is?'

'You don't know the whole story, Rose,' Kim said as the squad car pulled up outside the house.

Bryant had left his position at the back door to bring Penn and his companion to the rear of the house.

Rose frowned but she didn't move the knife.

'Just stay still, Rose,' Kim said, holding up her hand. 'Don't hurt anyone else. It's time you knew the truth.'

SEVENTY-NINE

'Wh... what's going on?' Rose asked as her mouth tightened and her eyebrows drew together.

'Just stay still, Rose,' Kim instructed as Penn entered the house.

'Who's that?'

And then she saw the person who'd walked in behind him.

'Josh... wh... what are you...? I don't understand.'

Kim was unsure who was more in shock: Rose or Josh. She was sure that Penn had explained the situation to Josh, but she guessed that seeing his friend's mum poised, ready to commit her fourth murder, was a terrifying sight.

'Josh knows why no psychic can reach Brad,' Kim said, touching Josh on the arm.

'He isn't dead, Mrs Foster. I lied. I made it all up. He told me to. He ran away.'

Rose began to shake her head and looked beyond Josh to Kim. 'I don't know what you're doing or how you're trying to trick me, but I know he's dead. These people have put you up to this. I know you, Josh.'

Josh shook his head. 'I'm sorry. I didn't want to do it, but he was my best friend. He asked me to lie, and I agreed. I felt so guilty when I helped you search for him. I was fifteen. I didn't think it through. I didn't understand the hurt it would cause.'

'No... no...' Rose protested.

'Brad planned it all. He waited for a stretch of good weather. He'd been saving his dinner money for months and doing odd jobs after school like cleaning cars and mowing lawns. I didn't think he'd actually do it. I thought he was just talking rubbish, until that morning when I turned up and you were having that argument. He ran back upstairs to grab the money he'd saved. He told me that your row was a sign that this was the day.'

That explained why he'd done no studying for his exams, Kim thought. He'd known he was never going to sit them.

Josh continued. 'He told me how long to wait and he told me to say I saw a white van speeding away, but not to raise the alarm until I got to school to allow him enough time to get away from the area. The story of the white van meant no one was looking for a kid on a bike.'

'Josh, why are you lying?' Rose begged.

'I thought he'd be back in a few days, a few weeks at most, and then his stuff was found in Cannock. I guessed he'd done that himself but it was too late. I was too scared to tell the truth.'

Kim could hear the misery and regret in his voice, but Rose was still shaking her head.

'It makes no sense.'

'Bradley staged his disappearance and later his death,' Kim reiterated.

'He wouldn't do that. He wouldn't just leave. It was just an argument. He was a child. You're lying. If he was alive, I'd know it.'

'He opted out, Rose,' Kim said, having more information on that than Josh. 'He chose another way of life. He's a vagrant that goes by the name of Jericho.'

'But Josh knew and—'

'Josh was his best friend,' Kim said, defending the man who had now gone mute as though the consequences of his silence were just starting to sink in.

Kim continued. 'Josh swore to keep his secret, and he's been living with the guilt for ten years. He knows what it's done to you and he hates himself.'

'I... d... don't... believe...'

'Yes, you do, Rose. You even told me yourself that Brad wasn't like other kids. Possessions meant nothing to him. He couldn't follow rules and he craved freedom. He wanted a life with no ties.'

'But I'm his—'

'No ties,' Kim emphasised. 'No one else has to die, Rose,' she continued gently. 'Now you know the truth.'

'I'm so sorry, Mrs Foster,' Josh said, stepping forward.

Kim reached out to stop him, but it was too late.

The hurt and disbelief in Rose's eyes had hardened into something else, and it was directed at just one person in the room.

'You lied to me. This is all your fault,' she said, moving towards him with the knife outstretched.

'I n... never meant... I'm so...'

'Rose,' Kim warned.

'They're all dead because of you,' she cried, lunging forward.

It was one of those moments when time slowed down and everything seemed to happen at once.

Everyone in the room called Rose's name.

Josh cried out in pain.

Kim, Bryant and Penn all moved forward as though a starting gun had been fired.

Bryant grabbed the weapon.

Penn bent over Josh.

Kim ran to Eloise. She could see that Bryant was cuffing and moving Rose.

Penn was trying to stem the bleeding from a gash in Josh's left arm.

In the distance she could hear someone calling for an ambulance.

Kim looked down at Eloise, whose colour had drained. Her hand went to her chest and her face contorted in pain.

'Oh no,' Kim said, grabbing the feather-light body and easing her to the ground.

'It's okay, Eloise, I've got you,' Kim said, helping her to a lying position. 'I'm right here,' she said, placing a cushion beneath her head. 'You're going to be fine. Help is coming. Stay with me, Eloise.'

'I... c... can't...'

'Yes, you can. It's not your time yet,' Kim said, even though she could feel the life draining out of her.

'It's t... time,' she said from beneath heavy, hooded eyes.

'It is not your time,' Kim said, placing her fingers on Eloise's wrist. The pulse was weak, and she had to keep the woman alive. 'Hang on for me, Eloise.'

She felt the pulse again. With every passing moment it was weakening.

'Eloise, you can't go,' Kim said, feeling the woman slipping from her grasp. 'Where's the fucking ambulance?' she cried.

Rose sat sobbing in the corner. Kim had no idea who she was crying for. Was it for her son who had chosen to simply leave his life behind? Was it for his friend who had kept the secret for all these years? Or was it for the three victims who had died horrific, brutal deaths for absolutely no reason?

Kim didn't care who she was crying for, satisfied that she was feeling pain for something.

Josh was groaning as Penn was ripping his own shirt to

make a bandage. She cared little more for him. It was a nasty flesh wound but he would live.

She cared only for the frail old woman who had been frightened into a heart attack and who was now clinging to life by the leanest of threads.

Through her fingers she could feel the pulse weakening until it was barely detectable.

Kim felt the emotion rising in her throat.

She heard sirens in the distance but her heart told her they were going to be too late. She gave it one last try. She had to keep the woman alive.

'Stay with me, Eloise. I'm finally ready,' she said. 'I'm ready to receive my gift.'

EIGHTY

It wasn't a normal occurrence for Kim to find herself in the ladies locker room at 7 a.m. on a Saturday morning but today warranted it.

The rest of her team were enjoying the start of their weekend after an exhausting week that had culminated in a full confession from Rose Foster, revealing the details of the crimes.

The catalyst appeared to have been the psychic dinner party in conjunction with the ten-year anniversary of Bradley's supposed abduction. Rose had met with Sandy a couple of days after the dinner party, to seek contact with Bradley. It was Rose that Penn had been unable to see on the CCTV from across the road. Sandy had been trying to offer comfort even when she couldn't offer assistance, and Rose had rebuffed her attempts. When Sandy had been unable to reach Bradley, Rose had become convinced that she was a fraud and was causing distress and heartbreak to grieving, vulnerable people. She had consulted with a psychic hotline, who had given her a standard reading about good things coming in her future. She had waited half an hour and called again, only to get the exact same reading. She had tracked the calls to the Waterfront offices, and although Azim had taken neither of her calls, Rose had set her sights on the first person that had left the building. As far as she'd been concerned, anyone working those phones was peddling the same lies and deserved to die.

Stacey had uncovered that Rose, not Catherine, had been at Victoria's stage show. Rose had admitted to following Victoria home and confronting her on her doorstep.

During the interview, Kim had witnessed Rose's desperation for answers, for knowledge of what had happened to her son, ten years after he'd disappeared. She had also witnessed the depth of faith that Rose had been willing to offer to someone who professed to have a psychic gift. Was that the fault of the psychic or the individual?

In a twist of irony, Kim had realised that not one psychic had actually lied to her. Whether genuine or not, none of them had pretended to pass on a message that they weren't receiving from the other side. In a further twist, lives might have been saved if someone had lied and given her what she wanted. It wouldn't have been honest and it wouldn't have been the truth, but it would have definitely saved lives.

Learning that her son was still alive and had chosen this way of life had finally unlocked Rose's remorse for the lives she'd taken.

It was Penn who had joined those dots. On seeing the footage of Rose, he had taken a good look at Brad's photo on the board and had seen a resemblance to Jericho. He had pictured him without the facial hair and the premature aging around the eyes from hard living. He had then hot-footed it down to Josh to pose the question to him.

Josh had broken down and admitted that he'd lied for his friend. He really had expected Brad to come back within a few days and straighten it all out. When the investigation turned to murder, after Brad's possessions were found on Cannock Chase, he'd known he was in too deep and had been frightened of the consequences if he revealed his own involvement in the plan, as well as the loyalty of keeping a secret for his friend.

Eventually, the CPS had confirmed there would be no charges and he'd fled from the building. He would always live with the guilt that his secrecy and loyalty had helped contribute to the murder of three innocent people. If he had found the courage to come forward, Rose would have faced a different kind of heartbreak, and Sandy, Azim and Victoria would still be alive.

Only one other person had any culpability in this situation and he was long gone.

While she and Bryant had been interviewing Rose, Penn had been out searching for Jericho. The shelter had informed Penn that there'd been no sign of him that morning and that generally meant he'd moved on again. Looking back, the dates of his visits tended to coincide with Rose's birthday and the anniversary of his disappearance.

However Kim tried to conclude things in her own head, everything came back to the selfish actions of one person.

Rose had explained that Brad had been a complex teenager who was often cold and unemotional, detached from his friends and family. She had also offered examples of his warmth and generosity. She had known that he didn't like to follow rules and convention and that he lived to the beat of his own drum. But still she couldn't help wonder at the level of detachment needed by Jericho to fake his own abduction and death instead of running away. Regardless of the argument he'd had with his mother, it seemed unnecessarily cruel to subject her to such torment. Penn had commented that during his conversations with Jericho, the man had expressed some regret at decisions made in the past, and Kim wondered if, like Josh, he had felt trapped by what he'd done.

Would he see a newspaper? Would he watch a snatch of TV news and learn of his mother's actions, and would he care?

That he felt compelled to return around important dates and risk discovery indicated an emotional connection. Leaving his mother and best friend to be eaten alive by grief and guilt did not. Penn had said that Jericho had never exhibited any signs of nervousness around him, even though he was a police officer. But was it really such a risk returning? He hadn't killed or hurt anyone. He'd left his belongings in a pile at a beauty spot and had run away. He was now an adult, and even if discovered, he would face no charges and would simply take off again. Kim doubted she would ever understand his need to opt out, but one thing was certain: if he wanted to reconnect with his mother, she wasn't going to be hard to find. She would spend the rest of her life in prison.

Kim had taken the time to make a couple of calls before the news of the arrest hit the press.

Her first call had been to Richard, to thank him for his input. His insights into the trickery and the psychology of psychics had been invaluable. She had learned during the call that Victoria's murder had affected him more than he'd let on, and that he was taking a break from the book while rethinking the content.

She had understood the difference it made being up close and personal with the murder instead of simply seeing it on the news. She had wished him well before making her second call to Betts. The woman had been stunned but had assured her that she'd pass the news along to the other members of the group.

Kim couldn't help wondering how they would all fare after that fateful dinner party. Had it helped them in any way? Was Catherine any closer to finding out if her husband was cheating on her and if, in any split, she'd be allowed to keep the kitchen? Had Lisa found a way to bring her project back on track and keep her job, reputation and lifestyle? Would she always live in fear of her violent past being discovered? Was Betts any further along in her journey to finding meaning and purpose in her life, or leaving her overbearing husband? Had Emily found comfort in accepting whatever came next? Despite their protestations that it had all been for a laugh, they had all wanted something deeper from Psychic Sandy.

The only blot on her landscape of completion had been a quick call to the Worcester Diocese to progress her complaint about Father George. She had been informed that Father George was no longer attached to St John's in Halesowen and had been replaced. Her initial euphoria had been destroyed when the bishop had revealed that the man had been transferred elsewhere.

Her protests had been silenced when he'd ended the call.

What he hadn't ended was her determination to do something about it. His brief spell of concerned supervisor had been replaced by full-on defensive bishop mode. She supposed it was easy for him to do that now that Father George was no longer his problem.

Kim had no doubt there were other poisonous apples in the Church, and that she couldn't deal with them all, but this particular one she'd met, and had experienced the level of negativity and harm he might have on vulnerable people. She would track him down and she would not rest until the man was removed from the Church. She and Father George would meet again. Of that she was sure.

But that was a battle for another day.

Right now, her priority was in righting a wrong that had occurred earlier in the week, and the subject of that had just walked into the locker room.

'Hey there, Tink,' Kim said, getting to her feet.

'Hey, boss,' the girl said, offering a bright smile.

'You know, I was thinking it must seem like we just pick you up and drop you any time we feel like it, eh?'

'No, boss,' she said, opening her locker door. 'I'm a police officer. It's what I'm here for.'

Her response, although true, hit Kim somewhere below the ribs.

'Ah, but see, that's the thing. We don't come looking for you when we need any old police officer. We come looking for you when only you will do, and as far as me and the guys upstairs are concerned, you're definitely one of the team.'

'Really?'

'Really,' Kim answered. 'And as you're part of the team, you should have a debrief. Of course you already know the case is solved and we've got our killer, but I'd like to know why visiting the psychic was unsettling for you.'

Tiff sat down and sighed. 'Because I've been plagued ever since my grandma died, and I'll just never know if she forgives me. I swear to you I never said anything to the stooge about the salty crisps, so I suppose I was desperate to believe it was real.'

'I believe you,' Kim said.

'You do?'

'We spoke to Neil. He's pretty sure you never mentioned crisps to him, and he's absolutely certain he never passed that on to Victoria.'

She shook her head. 'See, now I'm all confused again. A lot of what that Richard guy said made sense. I'd convinced myself that it was all fake.'

'I still can't tell you what's real or not,' Kim said honestly, because she had no answer for that herself. 'But I can tell you something that has never let me down: logic and common sense. Tell me why you and your gran got on so well?'

'Because we were so similar,' Tiff said with a watery smile.

'Both stubborn?'

Tiff nodded.

'Both generous?'

Tiff blushed and nodded.

'Would you have forgiven her?' Kim asked.

'Of course.'

'So why wouldn't you think she's forgiven you?'

'I dunno. I just...'

'And what about the other thing? The thing you've been wanting to do but haven't found the courage, which applies to most people by the way.'

'You'll laugh.'

'Try me.'

'Apply to CID.'

Kim said nothing.

'See what I mean.'

'I'm waiting for the funny bit,' Kim said, raising an eyebrow. 'Why would I laugh?'

'Cos this is me; Tiff, Tink, a police officer that does great with lost kids and domestic disputes. I'm chirpy and I give good directions.'

'And you've helped us solve three different murder investigations,' Kim reminded her, not liking the opinion the girl had of herself.

'Nah, I didn't do—'

'What are you scared of, Tink?' Kim interrupted.

'Failing. Not being good enough.'

'I mean in life,' Kim said.

Tiff thought for a minute and then shook her head. 'Nothing.'

'Exactly. You're pretty fearless. Ain't nothing we've thrown at you that you haven't been prepared to catch with both hands. Not sure I've ever heard you say that you can't do something. I don't know what your gran would say, but as someone who has worked with you, I'd tell you to go for it.'

'You would?' she asked with her wide cartoon-character eyes.

'I'd have you on my team any day,' Kim said and meant it.

Kim watched as Tiff's eyes grew watery. She shifted from

one foot to the other. Jeez, there was something about this kid that got to her.

'So, you all good?'

A wide, tremulous smile. 'Yeah, boss, I'm all good. And thank you.'

Kim nodded and headed out of the locker room.

She had one more place she had to go.

EIGHTY-ONE

Kim heard the soft beeping of the machines as she entered the room.

Eloise's eyes opened and lit up. 'Oh, how lovely to see you again,' she whispered.

Kim took a seat beside the woman, who was pale and shrunken against the covers.

Despite the secondary heart attack she'd suffered on the way to the hospital, Eloise was alive and almost out of the woods. Doctors had insisted on keeping her for a few nights for observation.

'Eloise, you are gonna have to give me some lifestyle tips cos clearly you ain't ready to go anywhere.'

'And you must give me some idea of how you always seem to know when I'm in trouble, as we seem to be making a habit of you turning up to save my life. Are you psychic?'

'Nothing supernatural there. I'm just following the clues.'

'I suppose I'm doing the same thing,' Eloise said with a smile.

Kim allowed the silence to settle between them. Eloise would speak when she was ready.

'Ask me anything,' she said, smiling wider. 'I can see the questions spilling out of you.'

'I'm curious,' Kim said, sitting back in the chair. 'I know you couldn't tell Rose anything about Bradley because he wasn't dead, but did you feel anything at all?'

Eloise nodded. 'I knew she was never going home again. I didn't know exactly what that meant, but I knew it beyond doubt.'

'Would you have considered lying to her for her own good?'

Eloise shook her head. 'It's not our truth to tell. I receive messages and if they're welcomed, I pass them on, but I wouldn't lie to someone. That's not what the gift is about.'

Kim nodded her understanding. Eloise's answer was important to her.

'And I heard what you said,' Eloise offered quietly.

Of course she had.

'Did you mean it? Are you ready for your gift?'

Kim took a breath. Throughout the week, she had been in conflict with her own convictions. Seven days ago, she had known exactly what she felt, but she'd heard and seen things that weren't as easily explained away as Richard would have them believe. Was she ready to suspend her original deep-rooted beliefs and give Eloise a chance?

Slowly, she nodded.

Eloise tentatively pushed herself to a sitting position, swatting away assistance from Kim.

'It's strange that you've spent your whole life looking for evidence of him when Mikey has been with you the whole time.'

'Wh... what?' Kim asked.

'He's your twin. Where else would he be?'

Kim had a realisation when she thought about Eloise's greetings.

'It's not me you're happy to see again, is it?'

Eloise shook her head. 'I'm always glad to see you but no, you're right, it's the beautiful little boy you bring with you. I saw him the first time we met, years ago, but you wouldn't have believed me.'

Kim swallowed back the emotion.

'He has the most gorgeous smile. He's free of pain, he's free of fear. He's carefree. He's happy. Tell me of a time that you remember him joyous.'

'Running,' she said without thinking.

Eloise waited.

'I used to get him to run to and from school. We'd race. Even if we'd had nothing to eat, he was like a whippet. I never let him win but as soon as I shouted "go" he'd run like the wind. Whenever I caught him up, his face would be flushed, he'd be panting, but his eyes would be alive with happiness as though he'd just managed to outrun the devil. I always did it to make him smile.'

'And that's how he looks now,' Eloise said, nodding.

Kim felt the sob rising in her throat. She desperately wanted to believe Eloise, but there was a major obstacle.

'I had an incident recently. I was—'

Eloise held up her hand to stop her speaking. 'You have questions?'

'Just one?'

Eloise's eyes crinkled at the corners as she met Kim's gaze. 'He knows and he understands. He said to tell you, he will be.'

Kim allowed the sob to escape from her lips as Eloise leaned back into the pillows with a contented smile.

Within seconds, her breathing signalled that Eloise was in a deep sleep.

Kim was in no rush to leave.

She sat back in the chair and enjoyed the feeling of warmth from the gift she'd just been given.

'I love you, Mikey,' she whispered and for once she felt sure that he'd heard.

EIGHTY-TWO

Terence Birch zipped up his jacket as he leaned back against the wall.

Although the curtains were closed, the light was on and he could see shadows moving around inside the room.

He already knew her routine from the lighting switching on and off throughout the flat.

She got home from work, removed her satchel and coat in the kitchen before heading into the bedroom to get changed. The light wasn't normally on long enough for her to be showering but he suspected she liked to have one before dressing for work. There was an eagerness in her to shed the work day, instantly revert to her home self. Once they were together, he'd make sure her favourite outfit was clean, pressed and waiting for her on the bed. Their bed.

Next, she would have a glass of wine, either with that foul woman or alone. He made a mental note to find out her favourite wine and send her a bottle. It was easy enough to file through someone's rubbish and find out pretty much everything you needed to know: what food they liked; where they did their shopping; what they bought from Amazon; the soap they liked to use; little lists of things to do; letters with appointment dates and times. Not a clean task but one he was prepared to do every day so that he could plan for their time together. Such a gesture, such effort, would just prove to her how much he already loved her. Even more so after their recent encounter.

He smiled as he remembered the spirit she'd shown. How she had pretended to be angry with him but secretly she loved the attention. She thought he didn't know but he had done this dance before. He knew the steps and he would lead because that's exactly what she wanted him to do.

The whole exchange had reminded him of his time with Charlotte. Oh, Charlotte, how he missed her, but she would understand that it was time for him to move on. She would forgive him. Destiny was not aligning their stars, and he needed another love in his life. Someone who could brighten his days just as she had.

This new love would not be as pure and gentle or comforting as it had been between him and Charlotte. He could feel that already. This attraction would be more passionate, fiery. There would be heat, flames, aggression. He felt excitement stir within him at the thought of it.

His love for Charlotte had been formed of pastel rainbows and hearts; images of moonlit walks, summer picnics, laughter and light before going home to tender caresses.

His attraction to Stacey was darker, filled with black and red explosions, pain, rage, lust, desire. He could feel the heat that would engulf them and he relished it.

He sighed, feeling the anticipation build within him.

He stared hard at the window, willing her to appear, to see him, appreciate him.

She hadn't yet looked out of it.

Eventually she would, and then she would know.

They were meant to be together.

A LETTER FROM ANGELA

First of all, I want to say a huge thank you for choosing to read *Deadly Fate,* the eighteenth instalment of the Kim Stone series, and to many of you for sticking with Kim and her team since the very beginning.

I thoroughly enjoyed writing *Deadly Fate,* and if you enjoyed it, I would be forever grateful if you'd write a review. I'd love to hear what you think, and it can also help other readers discover one of my books for the first time. Or maybe you can recommend it to your friends and family...

And if you'd like to keep up to date with all my latest releases, just sign up at the website link below. Your email address will never be shared, and you can unsubscribe at any time.

www.bookouture.com/angela-marsons

For as long as I can remember, I've been interested and intrigued by psychics, mediums, clairvoyants, spiritualists, sensitives. I've wondered if the gift is real or fake. I've questioned the emotional investment and trust of the people that use them. I've often thought about the harm they might or might not do if they're not genuine, and it was this fascination that drove me to explore the subject further.

To pose these questions to Kim Stone while attempting to answer them for myself was an interesting idea, and I'm not sure either of us came out of it with a solid answer.

Ever since writing *Lost Girls,* I've been waiting for an opportunity to bring back Eloise, the kindly psychic who tried to help. The scenes with her and Kim are some of my favourite moments in the book.

I'd love to hear from you – so please get in touch on my Facebook or Goodreads page, Twitter or through my website.

Thank you so much for your support – it is hugely appreciated.

Angela Marsons

www.angelamarsons-books.com

 facebook.com/angelamarsonsauthor
twitter.com/WriteAngie

ACKNOWLEDGEMENTS

Oh where to start on this one: with my eternal thanks to my partner in crime and life, Julie. From the very first line, this wasn't an easy book to write. It was one of those journeys that I knew where I wanted to go but often couldn't find the right bus, train or airplane. Cue Julie who, with a single conversation, had the ability to find the right mode of transport, the timetable and even helped me buy the tickets. The analogy might be poor, but it really does emphasise her essential involvement in the process. Her excitement for each new project is as passionate as it's ever been, which inspires me to write the best book I possibly can.

Thank you to my mum and dad who continued to spread the word proudly to anyone who would listen. And to my sister Lyn, her husband Clive and my nephews Matthew and Christopher for their support too.

Thank you to Amanda and Steve Nicol, who support us in so many ways, and to Kyle Nicol for book spotting my books everywhere he goes.

I would like to thank the growing team at Bookouture for their continued enthusiasm for Kim Stone and her stories.

Special thanks to my editors, Claire Bord and Ruth Tross, who both worked tirelessly to help make this book the best it could be. Both of these amazing ladies have offered more than just editorial support through a difficult, personal time for me and it has been truly appreciated.

To Kim Nash (Mama Bear), who works tirelessly to promote

our books and protect us from the world and has offered a much appreciated helping hand through this one. To Noelle Holten, who has limitless enthusiasm and passion for our work, and to Sarah Hardy and Jess Readett, who also champion our books at every opportunity.

A special thanks must go to Janette Currie who has copy-edited the Kim Stone books from the very beginning. Her knowledge of the stories has ensured a continuity for which I'm extremely grateful. Also need a special mention for Henry Steadman, who is responsible for the fabulous book covers which I absolutely love.

Thank you to the fantastic Kim Slater, who has been an incredible support and friend to me for many years now, who despite writing outstanding novels herself always finds time for a chat. Massive thanks to Emma Tallon, who keeps me going with funny stories and endless support. Also to the fabulous Renita D'Silva and Caroline Mitchell, both writers that I follow and read voraciously and without whom this journey would be impossible. Huge thanks to the growing family of Bookouture authors who continue to amuse, encourage and inspire me on a daily basis.

A special thanks to a lovely lady named Emma Jones who has very kindly offered her advice and guidance on all morgue-related queries. I think we're gonna have some fun conversations.

My eternal gratitude goes to all the wonderful bloggers and reviewers who have taken the time to get to know Kim Stone and follow her story. These wonderful people shout loudly and share generously not because it is their job but because it is their passion. I will never tire of thanking this community for their support of both myself and my books. Thank you all so much.

Massive thanks to all my fabulous readers, especially the ones that have taken time out of their busy day to visit me on my website, Facebook page, Goodreads or Twitter.

Milton Keynes UK
Ingram Content Group UK Ltd.
UKHW041934200923
429024UK00004B/91